DARKEST
HOUR

RACHEL CHURCHER

Darkest Hour (Battle Ground #3)

First published by Taller Books, 2019

Text copyright © Rachel Churcher 2019

ISBN 9781692779313

Cover design by Medina Karic:
www.fiverr.com/milandra

WWW.TALLERBOOKS.COM

Notes

Margie's name is pronounced with a hard 'g', like the 'g' in Margaret: Marg-ie, not Marj-ie.

Leominster is a town in Herefordshire, UK. It is pronounced 'Lem-ster'.

NOVEMBER

BEX

Prologue

I'm lying in the dark, hidden and silent, the gun shaking in my hand while Ketty tears the room apart, searching for me.

My knees press against the line of boxes, my body twisted and curled to keep me hidden. My hands grip the gun, finger trembling on the trigger.

She kneels down. Lifts the valance. Glances under the bed.

I won't go with her. I won't go to London.

She reaches out for the box, tucked against my knee.

She lied, and she used my family to bring me here. I'll shoot if I have to.

I aim the gun, willing my hands not to shake.

The box begins to move.

NOVEMBER

(ELEVEN DAYS EARLIER)

Dreams

Bex

We're shifting boxes again. The morning delivery is in, and Dan and I are stacking the goods in the store room. Neesh is taking the delivery – we're staying out of sight. Our pictures are all over the news again, and we can't risk anyone seeing us. We've been doing this for weeks, and we've turned it into a slick operation. No more asking where each item goes. No more stacking stuff in the wrong place. We know what to do and we put our heads down and get on with it. The sooner we're done here, the sooner we can have breakfast and figure out what else needs doing today.

Someone slams the delivery truck doors, and there's the sound of the engine starting up. The truck drives away, and Neesh walks back inside.

"All clear, you two. Thanks for making a start on this. There's a couple of pallets outside the door – can you handle the rest?"

Dan assures her that we've got it in hand, and she heads back to the shop.

I stand up and lean backwards, stretching and straightening my spine. Dan rolls his shoulders and leans against a stack of boxes.

"You OK, Bex?"

"Yeah. Just aching from the heavy lifting."

He shakes his head. "That's not what I meant."

I turn to look at him, at the look of concern on his face.

"I didn't, did I?"

"Twice. Woke us all up with the screaming, but when Charlie checked on you, you were still asleep."

I can feel the blush rising on my face. "I'm so sorry …"

"Don't be. It's not your fault. We just … we worry about you."

7

I nod. "Yeah. Thanks." I lean against the boxes, next to him.

"Was it Saunders?" He asks, gently.

I have to think for a moment. What was I dreaming about last night? Which nightmare woke everyone up this time?

"I think so. Saunders and Margie. Leaving people behind."

It's always about leaving people behind. Jake, Amy, Saunders, Margie, Dr Richards. There's always someone I can't take with me. There's always someone I can't save, and it is deeply, horribly upsetting. Sometimes it's people I know are OK, and I think I'm losing them, too. I've dreamt about Dan before, and Mum and Dad. People I could still lose. People who could still suffer from my mistakes.

Dan puts a hand on my arm.

"Come on. The truck's gone. Let's get some fresh air."

My hands are shaking as we walk back to the loading bay. Dan grabs two hoodies from the hook next to the door, and we put them on, pulling the hoods up to hide our faces. Bright lime green, with 'Morgana Wholefoods' printed across the back, the hoodies aren't subtle, but most people will be paying attention to the colour rather than the people wearing them.

We step outside. The service road is empty, so no one will notice if we're not working. The sun is just rising, and the clouds are streaked in orange and pink, with deep, purple shadows. It's beautiful, and it's wonderful to be able to stand in the open air, just for a moment.

*****

I start climbing the stairs back to the flat. Dan cracks open the back door of the shop and gives Neesh a wave, keeping his face hidden, and she waves back. The delivery is stacked. The pallets are leaning against the wall, the hoodies are back on the hook, and we've closed the shutters on the loading bay. Time for breakfast.

Charlie lets us in, toothbrush held between her teeth as she negotiates the locks on the door.

"How'd it go?"

"Good."

"You thirsty? Kettle's on." She grins, and waves a hand at the kitchen as she walks back to the bathroom. "Mine's a tea, thanks!"

I close the door and reset the locks, then follow Dan into the kitchen. He's pulling mugs and teabags from the cupboard, so I lean into the fridge and pull out the milk. The fridge shakes as I push the door closed with my knee, and the biscuit tin on top rattles.

The biscuit tin that holds two handguns and a pile of bullets. Our desperate attempt at buying ourselves a last stand, if the government tracks us down.

I take the milk to Dan.

Amy walks in, still in pyjamas, still yawning. She walks over to me and gives me a warm hug. When she pulls back, I see that her eyes are puffy and red.

"Was it Joss? The dreams?"

"Yeah." I nod, closing my eyes. Amy's the only one who knew Saunders' first name. In all the time I knew him, I never thought to ask.

She hugs me again, and this time I hug her back.

"We'll get through this, Bex," she whispers. "It's not your fault."

*****

We didn't talk about the night at the bunker. Not until we got here. Not until we felt safe again.

On our long walk north, each of us lived with what had happened alone. We walked. We split up to walk through towns, we joined up again on quiet country roads. We slept under bridges and in disused buildings. We kept ourselves out of sight, and we kept walking, putting more miles between us and the farm. Between us and Saunders, who died protecting his friends. Protecting us.

We didn't have a destination in mind. We just wanted to get away. I thought we might cross the border into Scotland, but we realised it would be too dangerous to try. The guards on our side of the border would catch us, and we'd be handcuffed and sent to London for questioning. Used to get to the people who took us in.

But someone was watching. Another resistance cell tracked our progress, and when they had the chance, they picked us up and brought us here. At first, we thought we'd been found, that the government had tracked us down. Two cars pulled up, blocking the country lane, and when we turned back, two more drove up and stopped behind us. We all reached for the guns, buried in our backpacks, but before we could get to them we were surrounded. The rebels searched our bags, and questioned us at gunpoint until they were happy with our story, then they bundled us into their cars and drove us to Newcastle. Not Scotland, but far enough away from Makepeace Farm to offer us some comfort.

Neesh's health food business is the front for their operation. The money they make subsidises their safe houses. Five of us share the top-floor flat above the shop. Neesh lives in the flat downstairs, and Jo and the others from the bunker are in other safe houses, elsewhere in the city. We work when we can, and we do what we can to help – but our faces are on the news, and on Wanted posters across the country, so we're mostly stuck in the loading bay and the flat. The hoodies are useful, but we can only use them in the service road, out of sight of the street.

So we learn to live together, in each other's pockets. We learn to do what Neesh and Caroline ask us to do. And we try to ignore the locks on the door, and the handguns in the kitchen. I don't want to think about what happens if we're traced here. I think the nightmares will seem tame if we have to fight, trapped in our tiny safe house. And I don't want to lose anyone else.

*****

"You know what we need?" Dan pushes away his empty cup, and stands up.

Amy laughs. "You think you're the king of this kitchen, don't you?"

"I am!" Dan puffs out his chest in mock offence.

We're crowded round the small table – two chairs, a kitchen stool and a couple of packing crates to sit on. Charlie's come back to drink her tea, and Jake snuck in while no one was watching.

Dan walks to the fridge and throws open the door, and looks upset when we drown out his announcement by shouting over him.

"Sandwiches!"

"Breakfast sandwiches," he corrects us. "Bacon and sausages and eggs and … what else do we have?"

He peers into the fridge, and starts pulling out packets and boxes, passing them behind him without looking. Amy and I jump up and ferry the ingredients to the worksurface, and then we're all helping. Opening, chopping, mixing, frying, while Dan stands behind us, slicing bread at the table.

I find I'm blinking back tears. I don't know what I'd do without these people. They're holding me together, after the camp and the bunker. After Ketty and Jackson and Bracken. They're reminding me that I haven't lost everyone. That I can still get up in the morning, eat sandwiches with Dan, be useful to the group, laugh, watch the sunrise.

That this didn't end with Saunders. That we're still walking.

Promotion

Ketty

Early meeting this morning, so I'm up and out of the tiny rooftop flat by seven, checking my khaki Service Uniform in the mirror by the door before I leave. After a week in the job, I still can't resist a smile at the Corporal stripes – Brigadier Lee might want to leave me as an RTS Senior Recruit, but someone else in the Home Forces wants me and Bracken in London. No argument from me – I'm out of the Recruit Training Service, I'm out of Camp Bishop, and I'm not going to waste this promotion. I just need to keep *Colonel* Bracken sober enough to do his job.

Down five flights of stairs, painkillers and the elastic support bandage on my knee controlling the limp in my stride, and out onto the street. It's a short walk to the office at the Home Forces Building, and I want to be at my desk before Bracken gets in, ready with coffee and this morning's briefing. There's a chill in the air as I walk, and the thin slice of sky between the buildings is striped with orange clouds. It takes getting used to after life at camp, this feeling of being hemmed in by buildings. No training fields and woodland here. No one to train, and no one to discipline, either. No Lead Recruit job. I'm at the bottom of the ladder in London, and so is Bracken, but if we work together we can climb our way up.

At the end of the street I wait for a bus to drive past, then cross the road to the HQ building. I flash my pass at the door, walk through the scanner, and wait while the guard checks my gun and searches my bag. The document case is hardly large enough to smuggle anything into the building, but it gives the guards something to do every morning. I push the gun back into the holster on my belt and pick up the bag.

Past the lifts and up three flights of stairs, pushing my knee and building the strength back up. I will not be limping forever, and the more I use the muscles, the stronger they get. I push the pain to the back of my mind and keep climbing, one step after another.

Bracken's outer office has space for a desk, a chair and a filing cabinet on one side, and a leather-upholstered bench on the other. There's a map hanging over the bench – strategic locations across England, Wales, and Northern Ireland; Scottish border posts; ports, roads, and rail links. Major towns are marked, and there's a grey shaded area where Leominster used to be. Behind the chair, there's a window that looks out onto a narrow light well, and a view of other office windows. Everything in here is old – the worn dark green carpet, the dark wood furniture, the vertical blinds at the window – and there's a dusty smell that never goes away.

But it's better than a hut in a field, and a flat of my own is better than the Senior Dorm and the Medical Centre. Lead Medic Webb isn't here to hand me crutches every time I stand up, and I don't need Woods' permission to talk to Bracken. I'm Bracken's assistant now, and I get to decide who comes in, and who gets sent away. It's also up to me to keep him sober, brief him with what he needs to know, and get him to meetings on time.

I drop the document case on the desk, and head out down the corridor to the coffee machine. I put two cups of coffee on a tray, and stop at the document drop on the way back to the office. The Private on duty hands me Bracken's briefing folder, and I carry everything back to my desk.

Before I check the documents, I pick up the phone and dial a number I know by heart.

"Nevill Hall Hospital, High Dependency Ward."

"Corporal Ketty Smith, calling about Liam Jackson. Do you have an update for me?"

There's a pause while the nurse rustles some papers.

Come on, Jackson. Pull out of this. Don't let the terror-ists beat you.

"Sorry Corporal – no change. He's stable, but there's no improvement."

"You'll call me if he wakes up?"

"It's on his file, Corporal. We'll let you know." She sounds impatient, like the nurses every morning.

"Thank you," I say, and hang up, as I do every morning.

*****

When Bracken arrives, the paperwork is ready and I've finished my coffee. Not long to go before his first meeting of the day, so I need to make sure he's briefed and alert. I give him a few minutes to hide his whisky bottle in the filing cabinet, then let myself in and put his coffee down in front of him.

"Thank you, Ketty. Have a seat. What's waiting for us today?"

He looks exhausted. With one elbow on the desk and his forehead resting on the fingers of his hand, he looks as if he's shading his eyes from the light in the office.

"Coffee, Sir," I say, jokingly, indicating the cup with my pen. "And then a meeting with the big boss."

Sober up, Sir. I need you to do your job.

He takes a sip of coffee and makes a face. "That's today, is it?"

I make a show of checking my watch. "In about ten minutes, Sir."

He sits upright in his chair. "Right. Right. So what do I need to know?"

"The agenda says you're talking about tracking the ter-rorists. Specifically Ellman and her friends from the bun-ker." He nods, and drinks more coffee. "And then there's the prisoners. Questioning of William Richards and some of his co-conspirators. And there's still the mystery of the women from Makepeace Farm." I look up. "Apparently they haven't responded to interrogation yet."

He raises an eyebrow. "Tough women," he says, with a note of respect in his voice.

Very.

I remember the prisoner at Camp Bishop. How she sat in silence and looked right through me, even after Jackson and I had used our fists to persuade her to talk. If her friend is anything like as tolerant of persuasion, it could be a while before we learn who they are, and what they know.

"What's the latest on the bunker group?"

"Still missing, Sir. No trace of them after we tracked them through Skipton." I flick through the papers. "Some rumoured sightings of Ellman and Pearce, but none near their last known position, and none together. Ellman's been reported in Kendal, Durham, and ..." I look again at the report. "... Margate."

"That seems unlikely. They were heading north from Makepeace."

"Yes, Sir. And there are reported sightings of Pearce in Birmingham, and from agents in Edinburgh."

Bracken shrugs. "So we haven't found them yet."

"No, Sir. But we've got units on alert all over the country. It's only a matter of time."

He drinks the last of his coffee. "Anything else I need to know?"

"It says here that the interrogation of William Richards is scheduled for this week." He nods. "Can I assume that we'll have access to the recordings?"

"I'm going to push for access to the interrogation, live. I want to see what he's hiding."

"Very good, Sir." I can't keep the smile from my face. "That would be useful to know."

Bracken pulls a notepad from his desk drawer and pushes a pen into his breast pocket. He looks up at me again.

"And Jackson?"

I shake my head. "No change, Sir. Thank you for asking."

*****

We make it to the meeting on time. Major General Franks' meeting room has a large table, and a view of the London Eye across the Thames. It's a reminder of her place at the head of the Home Forces, and ours as new arrivals. I send Bracken in with his paperwork, and take a seat in the corridor outside. As the assistant of the lowest-ranking officer present, I'm the runner for this meeting. Runner, guard, message carrier. Whatever they need.

I'm making myself comfortable when Franks marches out of the room. I jump to my feet and salute.

"Corporal Smith. At ease."

"Sir."

She holds out her hand for me to shake. Her grip is firm and confident, and she's smiling. She's an older woman, slim and athletic, with short-cropped silver hair and an air of relaxed authority.

"Welcome to London," she says. "We're very pleased to have you and the Colonel working for us. I've pushed to bring you here – I think you can offer us some unique insights into our missing terrorists. Help us track them down. I gather you knew some of them personally, at Camp Bishop?"

"Yes, Sir. I was the Lead Recruit."

She raises an eyebrow. "So you taught them everything they know?" She laughs. "I'm sure your insights will be invaluable to our investigation. You've briefed Colonel Bracken?"

I nod. "I have, Sir."

She lowers his voice to a stage whisper. "And does he need coffee this morning, Corporal?"

I keep my face neutral. "Another cup wouldn't hurt, Sir."

She smiles again, and winks at me. "Keep him on his feet for us, Corporal Smith. We're going to need you both if we're going to find your missing recruits. There's a place on the Terrorism Committee for him if he can show some progress."

And she turns and walks back into the meeting room.

So that's my job here. Keep Bracken sober, and give you profiles of the kids we lost.

Consider it done.

Learning

Bex

"Watch out!"

"Brakes! Brakes!"

I slam my foot down on what I hope is the right pedal, and the car stops dead, and stalls.

"And the clutch, Bex. Don't forget the clutch."

Neesh pulls on the handbrake as I slam my palm into the steering wheel in frustration, looking out at the empty service road, and the wooden fence panel in front of my bumper.

"I'm never going to get this, Neesh." I lean back and stretch my arms.

"Don't be so negative." Dan leans through the gap in the seats. "You learnt to run the assault course. You learnt to clip the stupid guns into the armour. You can learn to do this." He squeezes my shoulder and sits back in his seat. "Might want to think about reversing now, though. We're a bit close to that fence."

I don't need this. I take hold of the steering wheel, and grip it until my knuckles turn white. Neesh gets the message.

"Dan – why don't you go inside and wait for us. I'll give you a shout when it's your turn, yeah?"

He shrugs, pulls his hood forward to cover his face, gives my shoulder a final squeeze, and gets out of the car. He hunches his shoulders and pushes his hands into his pockets as he walks back to the loading bay.

"Ready to try again?"

I nod, and try to remember everything I need to do before I start the engine.

*****

"So? How did you do?"

"Disastrous. Again."

Charlie puts her hand on my shoulder as she crosses the kitchen to pick up a bowl of chopped vegetables from the table.

"Don't stress about it, Bex. You'll get there."

"I thought the point was for me to drive a getaway car if we need to run."

"Uh-huh."

"I've only ever driven in the service road, in the dark, and I can't even stop without stalling. We're not going to get very far if it's me in the driving seat, are we?"

"Not if we need to get away tonight." She turns to face me. "If we need to get out of here tonight, you've got me. And Neesh. And Dan, if you're feeling brave." We both laugh. Dan's driving is enthusiastic, and we've all had white knuckles, sitting in the back seat. "The point isn't to get you ready now. The point is to start training you now, so you have time to learn."

"I suppose."

"And we're not going to be here forever," she waves a hand at the kitchen. "We might move on. We might be stuck somewhere where we don't have people looking out for us. The point is for you to be ready when we need it."

"Yeah. OK. It just feels like I'll never be any good."

"So what? If you can get yourself where you need to be, and do it safely, who's judging? It's not as if you'll be taking a test – not with your face all over the news. Stop being so hard on yourself." She pours the vegetables into a saucepan and starts to stir them. "Pass me the tomatoes?" She holds out her hand, and I pass her the tins from the table, opening them as I hand them over.

She's right. I'm not learning to drive so I can have a job and visit my friends. I'm learning to drive so I can get us away from soldiers with guns. I don't need to be perfect. I need to be good enough.

"Stick with it, Bex", she says, stirring the pan. "One day you'll be glad you did."

I pull the plates from the cupboard and start laying the kitchen table for dinner.

"Six places tonight. Neesh is coming."

I pull out the extra plate, and go searching for something for her to sit on.

*****

"And then Neesh started shouting, and I couldn't work out what the problem was …"

"… until you drove into the bin bag …"

"… and the whole world turned white!"

Neesh is laughing, and Dan is waving his hands over his plate.

"The charity shop put out an old beanbag or something, out by the bins, and Dan turned it into a polystyrene snowstorm. Credit to him – he did switch on the windscreen wipers pretty quickly, but the service road's a mess."

"So we should send Dan ahead with a distraction car, driving into bins and fire hydrants and fruit stalls, while the rest of us sneak out and let Charlie drive?"

"Just like in a film!"

"That could work! Dan – how do you feel about going out in a blaze of distracting glory?"

We're all laughing, but there's an edge to the laughter. We all know how close we might be to the truth, how futile this might turn out to be.

Neesh eats the last of her meal, puts her cutlery down, and leans her elbows on the table as the laughter dies.

"So. I need to ask you all something."

No one's laughing now. Neesh looks down at table.

"Our … superiors … they'd like to know some more about you. More than you've told them already." She pauses, but nobody says anything. "Things they might be able to use to our advantage."

"Like what?" Jake says, eventually. His voice is cold, defensive.

Neesh shakes her head. "I'm not sure. Things that might be useful."

We sit in silence round the table, the laughter vanished.

Charlie looks round at us. She lays her hand on my arm. "I know that the resistance has taken us in. Undoubtedly saved our lives. And we're grateful – and we want to help. But these kids," she holds her hand out at the four of us. "These kids have been through hell. They've witnessed things that will never leave them, and don't forget that they didn't all get out alive. They've been used by the government. They've been sent out in public, to put an acceptable face on the anti-terrorism effort. They had their faces on TV while the government committed atrocities behind their backs. And with respect, they didn't get out of Camp Bishop just to be used by the other side.

"So if the resistance wants more from us, we need to have a conversation about what that means."

Neesh nods. "Fair enough." She turns to the rest of the table. "What about the rest of you? Is there anything you think they should know? Anything they could use?"

My thoughts are racing. I look at the others round the table.

"Are they looking for sob stories?" Amy sounds angry. "Real-life bravery, that sort of thing? The terrible things we've seen and survived?"

Neesh shrugs. "I'm not sure. Maybe."

"Propaganda," says Dan. "Stories from the resistance. That's what they're after?"

"Wouldn't hurt. Escaped recruits being brave and heroic. They could use stuff like that."

Amy shakes her head. "Don't they understand? Our friend died at the bunker. *Our friend*!" She's shouting, suddenly, leaning over the table, half out of her seat. "He didn't want to be there either. He didn't volunteer for camp, or for training. But he volunteered when it mattered. And he was killed for being our guard." Dan puts his hand on her arm, but she shakes him off. "That was *brave*. That was *heroic*. But you know what? That's *his* story, and *our* story. It's not a sentimental fiction. It's real and it's bloody and it hurts." She sits back on her packing crate, tears in her eyes. Her voice is quiet. "It hurts, and they can't have it."

Jake takes her hand, and she grasps it, wiping tears from her cheeks.

"Kills," says Dan, looking Neesh in the eye. "Would they like to know about who we've killed?"

Neesh looks away.

"I'll start. I killed two guards at Makepeace Farm. Shot them at point-blank range through the soft parts of their armour. I took their weapons, and I walked away. No idea who they were." He shrugs. "They might have had children. Husbands. Wives. They might have been someone's favourite auntie, or captain of their football team. Didn't stop me. I shot them to protect this lot, and get us out of the bunker alive."

Neesh shakes her head, one hand held up. "There's no need to …"

She's going to ignore Dan. She's going to ignore what Amy said. She doesn't get it.

"There is, though, Neesh," I say, trying to stay calm. "The thing is, this is who we are. You don't get to be heroic without getting your hands dirty. If they want the heroic stuff, they have to take the scary stuff, and the uncomfortable stuff, too. It's a package.

"We wouldn't be here if Dan hadn't shot those guards. We wouldn't be here if Jake hadn't fought off Ketty and her friend in the woods. That might be two kills for Jake – we don't know. We didn't stand around keeping score.

"There's no time to think that way when you're facing the barrel of a gun. You do what you need to do, and you get away. Heroism is an idea that lets other people understand our actions. Shooting someone isn't heroic. It's scary, and it's cruel, and it's messy."

Jake is nodding. Dan is looking at his plate. Amy is staring at the ceiling, blinking away tears.

"What I'm saying is that our stories, our pain and fear and violence – they're not for other people to use. They're ours, to live with, every day, forever. They're not propaganda. They're not for sale."

"Yeah," says Amy, quietly. "Not for sale."

Charlie looks round the table, and makes sure we've all finished talking before she turns to Neesh.

"You heard them. These are sixteen- and seventeen-year-olds. Ask your superiors to back off, and rethink what they want from us." She leans back. "We're happy to help, really. But not like this. We're not here to be used as pretty faces for the resistance."

*****

"Headline news on the Public Information Network again!" Dan sounds happy, as if he's beaten a record or a personal best. "They need to find some new photos, though." He squints at the TV. "I swear they looked for the worst photos they could find, just to embarrass us into giving ourselves up."

"Except Bex," says Amy. "Yours is good." She turns to me. "You look all brave and serious."

I know this is just gallows humour, keeping our minds off the reality of being wanted terrorists, but I can't answer. I feel sick. That's my face, on the news. The photo of me from the patrol in Birmingham. Armour on, helmet off, gun combat-ready in my hands. Dan's right – we've been headline news since we arrived here, but it doesn't get any easier.

The others are laughing it off, pretending that they don't care, but I can't forget that the people watching want us dead, or tortured, or shot to pieces on live TV.

Me, and my friends. The people I haven't lost yet. And that photo – the photo I was ordered to pose for. The photo I hate. Amy's right – I do look serious. I look proud, as if I believe in the uniform I'm wearing. In the people who were destroying Leominster while the photographer was pressing his button.

I shake my head and curl myself further into the corner of the sofa.

We're in the living room, watching PIN as we do every night. Dan and Jake sleep in here, on camp beds against the walls, but every evening we all crowd in and sit on the beds and on the tiny sofa, and watch the news. We need to know who's been caught. We need to know if we're still the nation's favourite fugitives.

The newsreader moves on to the next story, and we're watching another firing squad. Three prisoners in orange jumpsuits, handcuffed and standing on a platform in front of a cheering crowd. I close my eyes as the gunfire sounds, hiding my face in my hands.

"Anyone we know?" Asks Charlie. She sounds exhausted. We do this every night, and every night we're checking the faces of the prisoners, looking for the people we've lost. Looking for Will and his soldiers. Looking for Margie and Dr Richards.

"Don't think so. Not tonight." Dan sounds tired.

And I can't shake the idea that one day it'll be one of us on the screen. One of us taking a bullet for the cameras.

Profiles

Ketty

Another morning in the office, and I'm going over the files from Camp Bishop. Franks wants to know who our missing recruits are, so I need to put together profiles. See if we can figure out what they're likely to do next. Pull out the weak points in their little group, and see if there's anything we can use to catch them.

Top of the pile is Saunders. Mr Sleepy. I can't help smiling as I push his file to the far side of the desk. I can still see the look of surprise on his face as I put a bullet in his chest. The feeling of power, and the shaky, sickening knowledge that I couldn't take it back. Saunders is irrelevant to this investigation. His friends left him behind at the bunker, and they've moved on without him. He's a footnote. A distraction from the task of finding them.

Jake's file is next. Taylor. Another recruit I've stolen from Ellman. I'm smiling again, thinking about his anger – his desperation when Ellman left him behind, Bracken holding a gun to his head.

"I want to see Bex and Dan burn in hell."

Everything is personal for Taylor. Hatred for Ellman, after joining her gang on day one at camp. He couldn't forgive her betrayal. And he couldn't forgive me, either. I can't suppress a shiver as I remember dragging myself into the woods at Makepeace Farm, my knee exploding with pain, and Taylor on the path behind me, demanding the chance to kill me. There's anger here – maybe enough to pull the group apart. Maybe enough to bring us Ellman.

I turn the pages of his record. He and Amy Brown were at school together. It seems they've known each other all their lives. Even more interesting that it was Amy who held him back in the woods. Amy who saved my life, and theirs.

And Amy who stayed loyal to Ellman, even when the rest of the group drove away without her. Brown and Taylor might be friends, but they're on opposite sides of the cult of Bex.

Is Taylor alone in his hatred of Mummy Ellman? Or does anyone else hold a grudge?

I track down the report of Taylor's detention in the empty dorm. We didn't make a record of the actions that put him there, but I can see the barrel of his gun, levelled at me across the training field. The butt of his rifle smashing into another recruit's face. The smile he gave me as Jackson restrained him.

I make a note that Taylor is dangerous. Unpredictable. Someone to watch. And possibly exactly what we need.

Do something stupid, Taylor. Make my day.

Next file. Amy Brown, the try-hard good-little-girl of the group. When Ellman helped her on the assault course, she was grateful and loyal. She stuck with Ellman's followers, even when they left her at camp. She never lost faith that Ellman would come back for her, in some fantasy rescue. I don't know what she expected – unicorns? Magic carpets? What she got was the raid on the coach that put me in hospital and Jackson in the High Dependency Ward, tubes and wires keeping him alive. Brown and Taylor walked away unharmed and left Jackson bleeding in the road.

Amy never gave up on Ellman. Even when she'd been left at camp, she picked herself up, found a new set of friends, and kept her head down. She kept her anger to herself, and she convinced herself that Ellman would come back for her.

And she was right.

Amy isn't fit, or confident, or particularly bright. The school report in her file describes an average student. But she's loyal, and trusting, and she'll fight for her friends. I'd never have listed her as a problem recruit when she arrived at Camp Bishop, but in partnership with Ellman and her friends, she could be very dangerous. She's not a figurehead, like Ellman. She's not a maverick or a planner. But pushed into a corner, she'll defend the group.

I note her loyalty, and I note her devotion to Ellman. She's someone we'll need out of the way if this comes to a fight, and she's not going to have inside information for us. A smirk crosses my face as I designate her 'shoot to kill'.

Let's see where devotion to Ellman gets you when your backs are against the wall.

*****

Bracken comes back from an early meeting with Franks, two cups of coffee in his hands. He puts one down on my desk, and watches me.

"Any progress?"

"I think so, Sir." I wave a hand at my page of notes. "Some useful insights into the Ellman Inner Circle."

"Good." He nods, and sips his drink. "And Jackson?"

"No change, Sir." I keep my voice steady. Another day on life support. Another day with no improvement.

Bracken nods again.

"I'll be in my office." He turns to leave. "Oh – and Ketty? We're in on the Richards interrogation. Franks is sending us to work with Brigadier Lee on getting Richards to talk. It should be later this week."

Bracken might not be on the Terrorism Committee yet, but this is a sign that the people in charge trust him with their secrets.

"That's good news. Thank you, Sir."

*****

The next file belongs to Charlotte Mackenzie, 43. Kitchen Supervisor at Camp Bishop. I'm expecting an employment contract, maybe a CV, but I'm not expecting the police report.

A history of subversive activity. Interesting.

She was caught defacing government property. I can't work out why she's not in prison, so I flick through the report to find the details of her crime. Defacing posters, spray-painting anti-government slogans. Vandalism on government billboards. Not very clever, and it seems she took the blame when there must have been a group of people working with her. This was an organised protest, but somehow Mackenzie was the only one arrested.

Another loyal hero. Just what Ellman needs to keep the group together.

The Camp Bishop job kept her out of prison. I can't help laughing when I realise that she was a prisoner on our base, and that her sentence was cooking our meals every day. Managing the food, managing the kitchen staff, cleaning up after the recruits. I check her CV, and before her arrest, she worked at a very expensive restaurant.

And now she's on the run, with Ellman and the rest. Not for the first time, I wonder what it is about Bex Ellman that makes people follow her. Brown told me that Ellman is kind and good, and apparently that was enough for her. Maybe it's enough for the rest of them as well.

Mackenzie's a wild card. She has a history of anti-government action, and she's clearly found a kindred spirit in Ellman. But I haven't trained her. I haven't seen what she can do in a battlefield scenario. She might know more than the recruits about what's going on in the terrorist organisation, but if she took the fall for the last group she worked with, she's not likely to break ranks and give up a bunch of kids.

I think about her designation. We don't know what role she plays in the group, and we don't know what her connections are. Her record suggests that she's as idealistic as the recruits, and I'm sure she'll stick with them if it comes down to a fight. Plus the government won't want to parade her on

TV if she's already worked against them and got away with it. She has to be 'shoot to kill'.

I push her file to one side and open the next in the pile.

Dan Pearce. Posh-shabby good-looking Dan. His photo shows a harmless-looking blue-eyed private-school boy. Confident without being full of himself. A good all-round student, and a good recruit.

What are you doing, risking everything for someone like Ellman?

And I remember my conversation with Amy, after the group drove out of camp in a stolen truck. She said that Bex and Dan knew each other from school – and that they knew the prisoner we caught at Camp Bishop. There's a connection there. Are they just good friends, or is there something more going on? Could we use Dan to get to Ellman?

Everything we've seen so far suggests that Dan and Bex will be loyal to each other. But if I can split them apart? If I can use one to get to the others?

I designate Dan 'capture alive'. I think he knows what happened at Camp Bishop, before the breakout, and I think he knows what the group is planning now. It would be a shame to waste that.

Besides, I have a score to settle with Dan. He's the one who shot me, and he's the one who shot Jackson. He's the reason Jackson isn't here. And he's the reason I'm in constant pain. I'd like a few minutes alone with Dan before Lee makes him disappear into the cells.

Last file. Bex Ellman. Cult leader for this unlikely group.

Mummy Ellman, who looks after hard-luck cases. Helps other kids with the obstacle course. Rescues injured recruits. And never, ever gets the message that she's supposed to work alone. She'd be a good recruit, if she could learn to let the losers lose.

What did Amy say? *"She's kind, she's good, and she cares about us."*

I can't help rolling my eyes at the memory of that conversation. Strength, determination, and a gun will get you further than kindness and goodness when we track you down, Ellman. Can you protect your followers? Can you raise a weapon to defend them? And will they raise weapons to defend you?

I'd like to find out.

I add 'capture alive' to the end of my notes. I'd like a few minutes alone with Ellman, too.

Hostility

Bex

We're driving again. This time Amy's in the front seat, and I'm watching from the back. Charlie is instructing, and we're driving up and down the service road, as usual. Amy's managed two three-point turns in the turning circle at the end, and Charlie's trying to make sure she knows the width of the car. Each time we drive up and down, she's nudging Amy closer and closer to the bins at the kerb. She wants us to know exactly how close we can get to obstacles without touching them. One day we might need to know. One day it might save our lives.

Amy winces as we pass the bin behind the charity shop. "I don't want to do a Dan!"

There are still lines of polystyrene balls in the gutters, and along the edge of the pavement. Charlie laughs.

"Don't worry. I'll tell you if you need to stop. Go slowly, keep moving, and watch your road position."

Amy drives with exaggerated care, past the bins and down to the barrier that separates us from the main road. The road is wider here, so she can swing the car round and drive back without having to reverse.

"OK, Amy. One more three-point turn, and we'll give Bex a go in the driving seat."

Amy guides the car carefully past the obstacles and executes a neat turn, keeping away from the kerbs and the bins as she drives. Even in the dark, she's figured out where to stop reversing, and how close she can get to the bins when she swings the front of the car round. I wish I could see how she's doing it. What she's seeing that I'm not.

Charlie turns back to me.

"Your turn, Bex."

Amy stops the car, pulls on the handbrake and turns the engine off. She sits back in her seat and taps the steering wheel with both hands, a satisfied smile on her face. I pull my hoodie forward over my face, open the door and step out.

Time to be brave.

*****

"…and then she just kept reversing! Back and back until we're crunching against the fence, and Charlie had to yell at her to stop!"

Everyone's laughing, sitting round the table over dinner. My driving skills are today's distraction from our detention in this tiny flat. If that's what it takes to keep us laughing, let them laugh. It's frustrating, not being able to learn this skill. Watching everyone else get it before I do. But as Charlie said, we've got time. I just need to keep practising.

"All three of us had to run up and down, pushing the bins back to the right shops. Bex rearranged them, all over the road!" Amy isn't getting tired of this story.

"Maybe Bex should drive the distraction vehicle. No one will be able to guess what she'll do next! The rest of us will be miles away by the time they start looking for us." Dan grins at me, and I make an effort to smile back.

Charlie smiles, and puts her hand on mine for a moment while the others laugh.

"Come on. Less of the teasing. You all had to start somewhere, and at least she's taking it slowly." Charlie glares at Dan. "No polystyrene snowstorms."

"Sorry, Bex." Dan nods. "You're doing OK. You haven't killed a beanbag yet, so you're doing better than me." He bows his head, dramatically, and holds up his hands for silence. "Rest in peace, slaughtered beanbag."

And we're all laughing again.

I hate this mental block that hits me when I sit in the driving seat. I hate that I can't think my way through it, and I can't tell when I'm getting it wrong. But at least I have the chance to try. I have the chance to learn, and I'm doing it for everyone round this table. They've depended on me before, they've followed my lead, and they might depend on me again. Until then, one of them can take the wheel. This is one skill I'm not in a hurry to use.

*****

"I don't think it's like that, Jake. She's not in this for the glory."

I'm standing in the corridor, outside the kitchen door. Jake and Dan are washing up, the sounds of water and clattering crockery punctuating their conversation. I'm not supposed to be hearing this. I came back for a glass of water, and now I can't move. I need to hear what Jake has to say.

"She still thinks she's running everything."

"What makes you say that? She's just trying to live with this – the same as the rest of us."

"She speaks for us. She tells other people what it's like to be us, but she hasn't bothered to ask if that's OK."

"Jake …"

"She hasn't asked me what it's like to live with all this. She just assumes …"

"I don't think that's fair."

The washing-up noises have stopped.

"Fair? What's fair about Queen Bex getting her own room while the rest of us slum it out and share? What's fair about all the sympathy she gets for her nightmares? What about mine?"

Dan takes a breath, and speaks with exaggerated calm.

"No one is saying you don't have nightmares, Jake. We all do. But no one else is screaming in their sleep. No one else is beating themselves up the way she is."

"But we've killed people! We've shot people. We have to live with that."

"And we'd do it again, to protect our friends."

There's an uncomfortable pause. I want to walk away. I don't want to be eavesdropping like this, but I want to know what's bothering Jake. I know he blames me for leaving him at Camp Bishop, and I know he hasn't forgiven me for handing him back to Ketty when we drove away. I can also see him, stepping up beside me in the gatehouse at the bunker, gun raised, standing with me in case the next person to come in wasn't Dan. I thought he was forgiving me. I thought he understood that we had no choice.

"There's a difference, Jake. We killed strangers. We killed people we'd never met, and we killed them to protect our friends. What Bex did – what she blames herself for – is losing people she was trying to protect. She feels responsible for Saunders. She thinks she should have rescued Margie and Dr Richards. She hates the idea of losing someone else that she cares about. The people she's failed to rescue – they're still alive. Because she let them go, they're wearing orange jumpsuits and waiting for the firing squad. Every night she gets to look for them on the news. Every night, they could be the headline. And to her, they're there because she failed."

"She failed me, too."

"And she knows that. She has nightmares about you, Jake. Leaving you at the gate with a gun to your head? How could you think that she was OK with that?"

"Didn't stop her."

"It didn't stop any of us! I was in the truck. Charlie was driving. Why is this her fault?"

"It was all her idea. And I was stupid enough to do what she asked me to do. She didn't have a plan. She wasn't going to take us with her …"

"Of course she was! But plans don't always work out, do they?"

Silently, I turn and walk away, treading softly on the wooden floor. This conversation can carry on without me. Jake hasn't forgiven me. I've lost him, as surely as I've lost Margie. But he's here, with me, hating me. A constant reminder of everything I've done wrong. All my worst decisions, reflected back at me day after day.

He's right. I'm not special. I'm not the only one in pain. But I won't stop speaking up for us when Caroline and Neesh ask for too much. I won't stop defending him when they try to use his story for themselves. And I know I won't stop dreaming about leaving him behind. His face as we drove away, the gun held to his head, Commander Bracken shouting for us to stop – that's an image I'll never forget.

And I shouldn't, because it reminds me that my actions have consequences, and my failures don't just affect me.

Questioning

Ketty

We're off site this morning. A car picks me up at eight, stops to pick up Bracken, and takes us on the 30-minute drive to Belmarsh prison. We're using dedicated military lanes where we can, so we avoid the traffic and arrive ahead of time.

"Worst of the worst in there," the driver says as we open the doors. "That's where they're holding the terrorists, isn't it?"

Bracken gets out, leaving me to mumble something about Top Secret information before I follow him into the car park. He's said nothing for most of the journey, and my first priority is getting him some coffee. He needs to be awake and on the ball for this.

I follow him through the entrance, and through security. We show our ID badges, walk through metal detectors, and hand over our bags to be searched before we're waved through. There's a prison officer waiting on the other side.

"Colonel Bracken? Corporal Smith? Follow me, please."

We follow her along a concrete corridor, through a door that she unlocks with a card and PIN pad, and down a set of metal stairs.

"Colonel, Corporal – I'm sure you don't need me to tell you that the existence of this area is Top Secret, and that anything you see or hear down here is not to be discussed with anyone without the correct authorisations."

"Understood." Bracken sounds tired.

Wake up, Sir. This is where you show them what we can do.

At the end of another bare corridor the officer shows us into a waiting room. It's surprisingly comfortable for a concrete box with no windows – arm chairs, tables, refreshments. A row of doors on the far wall.

"Make yourselves comfortable. Help yourselves to drinks. The brigadier will be here shortly."

She leaves us alone, closing the door behind her. I hurry to the refreshment table and track down the coffee, pouring two cups and taking one to Bracken.

"Drink up, Sir."

He frowns at me, but takes a sip before sitting down in one of the armchairs.

"What do I need to know, Ketty?"

I stay standing, sipping my coffee. "William Richards. Owner of Makepeace Farm and the bunker in the woods. Known terrorist. Apprehended with a group of accomplices on the night of the bunker raid, thirty miles away, ambushing a supply convoy. The group was wearing the armour they stole from the Camp Bishop recruits, containing our hidden trackers. Richards is believed to have been working with our missing recruits, as well as with the two women arrested at the farm, identities unknown. We're hoping he can tell us where our recruits ran to, after they escaped from the bunker.

"But this is a preliminary interrogation. So far he's given us nothing in basic questioning. We're just hoping to break the ice today. See what he says, what he doesn't say. Root out what he's got to hide."

Bracken nods and drains his coffee. I'm at his side, passing him a fresh cup before he can put the first one down. He gives me a sour look, but takes the second cup and keeps drinking. I pull a plastic bottle of painkillers from my pocket and hold a couple out to him. He rolls his eyes, but swallows them anyway.

"Better, Sir?"

"I'm fine, Ketty. Stop fussing."

"Yes, Sir."

I'll stop fussing when you stop coming to work drunk. I'm here thanks to your promotion, so looking out for you keeps us both in our jobs.

The door opens, and Brigadier Lee walks in, followed by a distractingly good-looking man in fatigues, corporal stripes on his shoulders. I stand to attention and salute as Bracken gets to his feet, my attention split between Bracken's attempt at sobriety, and the amused smile on the Corporal's face.

A smile that's making my stomach turn somersaults.

Concentrate, Ketty. Keep your attention on Bracken.

"Colonel Bracken. Corporal Smith. At ease."

Lee walks to the table and pours himself a coffee.

"This is Corporal Conrad, my assistant." He waves a hand at the man standing by the door, and turns to Bracken. "So. Are you ready for your first terrorist interrogation?"

Conrad's green eyes meet mine, and I have to remind myself to breathe.

This is pathetic, Ketty. Grow up.

"Yes, Sir." Bracken's voice drags my attention back. At least he's sounding more awake.

"Finish your coffee, and we'll go in. Conrad – can you handle the tech?"

"Yes, Sir." Lee waves Conrad away, and he crosses the room to one of the doors on the far side. I can't help watching as he walks past. He reminds me of Dan Pearce – posh-shabby-gorgeous. He's not as tall as Dan, and his hair is darker and regulation-short. His uniform is neat, and he has the same quiet confidence. The same sense that he fits, here. That he's earned his place.

I'm still watching as the door closes behind him.

Get a grip, Ketty. You're here for Bracken.

"Corporal Smith," says Lee, coldly, all the charm he once used on me vanished. "How's the hunt for your recruits going?"

I look back at him and force myself to smile. "It's progressing, Sir."

He looks at me for a moment too long, and nods, slowly. "Of course it is."

You don't think I deserve to be here. You don't think I can find them.

A hint of amusement on his face turns into a cold smile. "Would you like to observe the interrogation?"

"Yes, Sir." It takes all my effort to answer him politely.

"Follow Conrad. He'll get you settled in."

"Thank you, Sir."

I exchange a final glance with Bracken and follow Conrad through the door.

*****

The room is small and full of camera equipment and recording devices. I'm suddenly, awkwardly aware that we're standing too close together in the cramped space. I step back, and make myself watch carefully as Conrad sets up the equipment.

Come on, Ketty. Focus. Find out how this works.

I look around, pushing my attention away from Conrad. There's a large window in one wall, and on the other side is a room with a table and three chairs. Two chairs face away from us, but seated on the third chair, facing us across the table, hands in handcuffs, is the man from the raid on the coach. I catch my breath – this is the man who stood and watched me and Jackson and our recruits from the field as we drove past. This is the man who sent Ellman and Pearce onto my coach.

He's an older man, with grey hair and the lined face of someone used to spending time outside. He's tall, and slightly hunched over in the chair. And he's thin to the point of malnutrition. Thinner than he was when I saw him standing in the road, directing the raid on my recruits.

Don't do well in captivity, terrorist? Too bad.

My mind jumps to Jackson in his hospital bed, anger tightening in my chest. This is the man who coordinated the raid. This is the man who sent me and Jackson to hospital, and drove away with two of the kids we were trying to protect.

I'm staring through the window, and I realise my hands are clenched into fists at my sides. Conrad is watching me.

"Personal, this one?"

I take a deep breath and force myself to relax and smile.

"You could say that."

He waits for me to explain, and when I say nothing he waves me to a chair. He sits down next to me, his elbow brushing mine.

Concentrate.

"So – have you been in an interrogation suite before?" I shake my head, trying to focus on what he's telling me. "Basic one-way mirror setup. Of course the prisoner knows we're here, but he can't see us, so he doesn't know *who* is here. That can be useful. We're recording," he waves his hand at the cameras and stacks of black boxes, "visual and sound. Date-stamped, time-stamped – and one feed that isn't. Just in case we need to edit something. But officially that feed doesn't exist. The officer told you that this is all Top Secret, right?" I nod, still watching Richards through the glass. "So all this doesn't *officially* exist. But PIN needs footage of the terrorists, and we need our questions answered, so here we are."

I turn to look at him, his eyes meeting mine. He really is gorgeous.

Come on, Ketty. Do your job. Figure out what happens here.

"So what else is there down here that doesn't exist?"

"Another interrogation room. Holding cells. We can keep a whole team of terrorists down here, out of sight." He sounds proud. "The cells are pretty full right now. Lots of people for us to question."

Interesting.

"Where did they come from? Your other prisoners?"

He shrugs. "Here and there. Top Secret." He winks at me, and nods at the prisoner. "So what did he do to you?"

Trained the tiny fighters who put a bullet in my knee. Nearly killed my best friend. Harboured my fugitive recruits.

I take another breath.

Keep it professional, Ketty. He doesn't need to know.

"I'd rather not discuss it. Let's assume that I'd very much like to hear what he has to say."

"OK," says Conrad, holding up his hands and turning to activate the recording equipment. "Just asking."

There are red lights blinking on the boxes on our side of the mirror when Bracken and Lee walk in and sit down opposite the prisoner. There's a red light over the door in the interrogation room, too, so the questioners know that the cameras are running. At first, the two of them watch Richards without saying a word. Richards lifts his eyes to the window, and I can feel the icy sensation in my spine again as his eyes meet mine. I have to remind myself that he can't see me, and I move to one side to avoid his gaze.

There's an uncomfortable pause, and then Lee puts a folder down on the table.

"William Richards."

Richards ignores him, and stares at the window. Is he watching himself in the mirror, or does he know where the observers in here are sitting?

Lee opens the folder and turns over a sheet of paper.

"Former owner, Makepeace Farm. Forestry expert. Resistance Leader. Terrorist."

Lee and Bracken watch him again. He doesn't move.

"Nothing to say, Richards? No defence? No excuses?" Lee closes the folder again. "I suppose not, seeing as we caught you with stolen government property, raiding a government supply convoy. Not to mention the terrorist gang we found on your land, in your house, and in your secret nuclear bunker.

"So. Where would you like to start? The armour you picked up in a raid on a coach full of children? The fact that you sent children onto the coach to do your front-line work for you? The underground fortress in your backyard? Or your arrest in the middle of the night, crouching in the bushes next to a motorway? Your choice. You tell me."

He sits still, staring past me.

"Twenty pounds says he's not going to talk." Conrad folds his arms and settles back into his chair.

I shrug. "What can he say to that? Haven't we got anything to threaten him with?"

"Not that anyone's thrown at him yet. He must know he's on Death Row. What's the point of telling us anything if we're going to shoot him anyway?"

Lee is talking again, but Richards sits, calm and still, ignoring him.

Conrad shakes his head. "Lee's not going to be happy."

Neither am I.

Lee passes the folder to Bracken, who pulls out another sheet of paper.

"Mr Richards. How about telling us about your contact with the Opposition In Exile?"

No reaction.

"Come on, Richards. We know they run the terrorist cells in the UK. We know they're sitting in Edinburgh, laughing at us because we can't get to them." He leans forwards in his chair. "Well, here's the bad news. We're going to get to them. And we're going to get to them through you."

Richards blinks, and looks down at the table. Conrad sits forward in his chair.

"That's got him uncomfortable. What do you think he's hiding?"

"I don't know. What's the Opposition In Exile?"

He looks at me in surprise. "They think they're the legitimate government of the UK. The Scottish government agrees, and they're helping the OIE. Premises in Edinburgh. Armed guards. Government protection. Bodyguards, safe houses – the works. Lee thinks they're running the terrorist cells, and from Richards' reaction I'd say he could be right."

"Why haven't I heard of them?"

"You're new here. Do you still get your news from the Public Information Network?" I nod, and he gives me an unkind smirk. "That's why. You and everyone else out there. The government's trying to keep them hidden. When they took away the civilian Internet and the mobile phone signals, the government controlled our access to information like this. If we don't know about the OIE, they can't influence us." He waves at the room in front of us, his voice smug. "Top Secret, remember?"

It's a shock, to find myself being mocked. I try not to roll my eyes. I didn't come here to be patronised by someone with the same rank as me.

Back off, Conrad. And don't underestimate me.

Bracken is talking again. "Who's your handler, Richards? Who do you speak to in Edinburgh?"

Richards sags a little in his chair, but he doesn't look up.

"OK." Lee puts his hands on the table. "Let's talk about something else. Let's talk about Leominster."

The prisoner's head jerks up, and he looks right at Lee. Suddenly Conrad and I are on the edges of our seats, and Bracken is sitting up straight in his chair.

"Oh – guilty conscience, Richards? Perhaps you'd like to tell us how you did it? Wiped out an entire town – buildings, people, roads?"

I can feel the ice in my spine. I know Richards didn't wipe out Leominster. I know he had nothing to do with it. I know that, because I was there.

We did it. The army, the government. And we blamed the terrorists.

So why are they asking Richards about it?

"You bastard." Richards' voice is soft, with a lilting Welsh accent, but the hatred behind it is like a hammer. "You bastard," he spits again.

Lee leans forward. "Something you'd like to share with us?"

"That *atrocity* was nothing to do with me. The blood of Leominster is on your hands, Brigadier." He lifts his hands, palms outwards, the chain between the handcuffs taut. "Not mine."

Lee takes a moment to meet Richards' angry stare. I've been on the receiving end of Lee's gaze, and it's not a comfortable place to be. The two men lock eyes, and there's a smile in Lee's voice when he responds. "We'll see about that, Richards. We'll see who believes you, and who believes me. PIN already has you tried and convicted, and I've got the job of hunting you down." The prisoner breaks his gaze and bows his head. "I'd say those hands were looking pretty bloodstained right now. Wouldn't you, Colonel?"

"Public opinion would definitely send you to a firing squad for the attack on Leominster." Bracken sounds smug. "Good luck washing your hands of this, Richards. We can put your people on the ground in Leominster three days before the attack. We know they were there. You know they were there. Might as well come clean and admit to it."

But Richards sits still, eyes on the tabletop. He's silent, but his hands are shaking.

He says nothing for the rest of the interview.

*****

It's mid-afternoon by the time we get back to the office, and the telephone. I call the hospital, but there's no change.

I'm sorry, Jackson. We'll get him. He has to talk sometime.

When I get back to the flat, I change the bandage on my knee, pull on leggings and a T-shirt, and run. I have a route that follows the river up to Waterloo Bridge, along the South Bank, then back over Westminster Bridge, past the moth-balled Palace of Westminster. Lead Medic Webb would be shouting at me, but I'm stuck in an office all day and I need to run.

I try not to think as my feet pound the pavement, but in the evening light the image of Jackson is always there. Wasting away. Losing himself.

And Conrad's eyes, when he smiled at me. His unkind smirk when he realised he knew more than I did. When he tried to make me feel small.

The painkillers are waiting when I get home. I will not waste away. I will not forget who I am. I will not lose my-self in Bracken's weakness, or Conrad's smile. I will not lose myself in this overwhelming city.

Photos

Bex

Another day, another delivery. I'm on shift with Amy today, unpacking and stacking the boxes and bottles on the store room shelves. We've just brought the pallets in and hung up our hoodies when Caroline drives up outside. I take my hand away from the shutter controls and wait for her to duck underneath before I finish closing it.

"Morning, you two." Caroline walks past us and calls back over her shoulder. "Is everyone upstairs?"

I shrug. "As always."

"I'll grab Neesh and meet you up there."

I resist the temptation to salute, and Amy mimes aiming a rifle at her retreating back. She's smartly dressed, as usual, and coldly efficient. None of us enjoys being told what to do by Caroline, but she's the one with the direct line to Edinburgh, so we keep our heads down and listen to what she has to say.

"Come on." I start walking towards the stairs. "Let's get the kettle on."

*****

Charlie lets us in, and I send Amy to knock on the living room door. Dan and Jake will still be asleep, but if Caroline's coming up, she's going to expect everyone to be awake and waiting for her. Amy bangs on the door until Dan opens it, rubbing sleep from his eyes, his T-shirt crumpled.

"We've got company," I call down the hallway. "Get Jake up, and get in here. Caroline's coming."

Dan waves acknowledgement and closes the door.

In the kitchen, Charlie is already making tea. I pull the mugs from the cupboard and line them up on the work surface.

"Do you think they've thought about what we said? About not being their front-line dolls?"

Charlie shrugs. "I guess we'll see."

The alarm sounds – someone's coming up the stairs. Amy checks the grainy black-and-white image on the monitor in the hall, then starts working on the locks.

Neesh and Caroline are waiting when the door opens. Neesh gives us a smile and hugs Amy on her way through the door. Caroline walks straight to the kitchen and takes a seat at the table. Amy checks the monitor, resets the locks, and follows Neesh into the kitchen.

Caroline looks around. "Will the boys be joining us?" Her Edinburgh accent is clipped and formal, and it's clear she thinks Dan and Jake are wasting her time.

The living room door slams shut, and Dan marches into the kitchen. He's brushed his hair, and pulled on dark jeans and a smart shirt. He's rolling his sleeves up to his elbows as he strides through the door.

"Caroline! Neesh! What a nice surprise."

I try not to laugh at his obvious sarcasm, and I notice Neesh doing the same. Jake follows him in jeans and a T-shirt, his hair still tangled and hanging over his eyes. Caroline puts on a tight smile.

"Right. Well. Now that you're all here. I have a message from the OIE. Pull up a chair."

*****

"As you know, our superiors in Edinburgh consider themselves to be the legitimate government of the United Kingdom." We all nod. We learnt about the Opposition In Exile when we first arrived, and they've been trying to decide what to do with us ever since. The driving training is their idea, as is the safe house system the Newcastle cell is using. "They need to get their message into the UK. They need to make sure that people know who they are." She looks around at us, not hiding the disappointment on her face. She must have liked their heroic stories idea.

"Well, we fed back to them what you all told Neesh, and they've come up with another plan."

She pulls a roll of paper from her smart handbag and flattens it out on the table.

"They want to go head-to-head with the PIN TV appeals. They want to show that the resistance isn't a terrorist movement. They want to rebrand you lot into brave resistance fighters."

I stare at the poster on the table, and it's as if Caroline has punched me. It's me. It's the photo from Birmingham. The photo from the news. The photo on my wanted poster. This is the image that people in every town in the country see as they walk to work, or go shopping. Posters on bus shelters, advertising hoardings, community noticeboards. There's a version with small photos, where we're all lined up across the poster, and there are individual posters – one for each of us. My face, my image, being used to hunt me down.

Except that this one's different. Instead of a glossy black-and-white image, this one is screaming with colour. I'm shown in shades of grey, but the background behind me has been edited out, and in its place is a waving Union Jack in bright red, white, and blue. At the bottom, in bold red letters, is the word 'Resist', and in smaller letters underneath, "Support the Opposition in Exile".

My stomach drops. I can feel my knees giving way, my hands shaking. Charlie and I are standing – we don't have enough seats for seven – and I step away from the table and lean against the kitchen cupboards, putting my tea down and gripping the edge of the work surface to keep myself on my feet.

The others are talking, asking questions. I know I should hear Caroline out. See what the OIE are planning. I take some deep breaths, close my eyes, and try to follow the conversation.

"What's the point? What are they going to do with them?"

"This is a new task for the active resistance cells. Our priority will be getting these up everywhere, over the top of the wanted posters. We need people to see that there is a resistance, and that we're all over the country."

"Won't that be dangerous?"

"Very. But we all have to play our part."

"People could get shot for this."

"And you could get shot for walking out of the front door. We've got willing volunteers. We just need to give them something to do. Something that will make a difference."

"Is it all of us? Or is it just Bex who gets to be the face of the resistance?" That's Jake, sounding bitter.

"Just Bex for now. The OIE wants to see these going up, and they'll decide what to do next when they see how people respond."

"Anyway, it's better to have one face of the resistance. One person that everyone can relate to." Neesh, trying to calm Jake down.

"And Bex does have the best photo." Amy.

I can't believe this. I can't believe that the OIE wants to use this image that I hate – use *me* – as the face of their resistance. And I can't believe that my friends are calmly sitting around and discussing it, as if this is a good idea. As if this doesn't mean anything.

"It's better than using our stories." Dan, sounding thoughtful. "And it is a good photo."

"Just a moment." Charlie. Footsteps on the kitchen floor, and then there's a hand on my arm.

I don't need sympathy. I don't need help from people who are seriously considering saying yes to this. I push myself up from the work surface, open my eyes, and brush Charlie's hand away.

I'm angry with the OIE for thinking of this. I'm angry with Caroline for suggesting it. And I'm livid with my friends for discussing it. I try to find something to say, something to make them all stop talking, but I can't. I'm angry and I'm shaking and I can't find the words to explain.

"Bex ..." Charlie puts her hand on my shoulder. I can't handle this. I can't stand here and be reasonable with that poster on the table. I twist away from her. I'm out of the kitchen and down the corridor before I can think. I want to get out, go outside and walk away, but I can't leave the flat. I head to my room and slam the door behind me. I sit down on the bed, fists clenched, fingernails pushing into my palms. The pain helps me to focus.

I'm the front-line doll, all over again. A pretty face for their campaign – that's all I am to them.

But that's not who I am.

*****

Charlie knocks on the door, but I ignore her until she walks away. I don't need company. I wish I could cry, or argue, or run. I want to act. I want to fight. But there's nothing to act on and no one to fight with. Caroline isn't going to listen, and whoever came up with this idea isn't here to hear what I think.

I'm lying on my bed, face to the wall, when Neesh walks in. I try to say something, to send her away, but my voice is cracked and broken. She closes the door, and sits down on the floor behind me. In the tiny room, her feet slide under my bed and she has to cross her legs to fit into the space. I stare at the wall.

I'm expecting her to say something. I'm expecting her to sell me the idea, justify it, but she doesn't. She just sits, quietly, alongside me while my pulse slows and my hands relax.

This is what I need. Time to calm down, and someone on my side. Someone who isn't pushing me.

It's a long time before I can speak.

"Why do you work with these people, Neesh?" I'm still staring at the wall. I don't trust myself to look at her.

"Because they're our best hope for getting our country back."

I laugh, once, my voice hoarse.

"They think they're the good guys, right?" Neesh starts to answer, but I cut her off. "They didn't ask. They didn't talk to us. They've never even met us." I turn to face her. "We're not real people to them."

She nods, meeting my eyes, letting me speak.

"We're wanted by the government, who think we're traitors. And we're being used by the resistance, who think we're cardboard cut-outs. But we're not. We're real, and we're in danger, and we're hurting."

She waits for me to continue.

"What gives them the right to use my face? What gives them the right to assume it's theirs to use?" There are tears in my eyes now, and I blink them away.

"Nothing, Bex. Nothing gives them the right. Nothing gave the government the right to recruit you, either. Or the right to plant bombs and blame them on us."

I shake my head and lower my voice. "I did everything they wanted. I wore their armour and I patrolled their events, and I wanted to make a difference. But the whole time, I was just a doll. I wasn't protecting people. They were using me to put a pretty face on their war.

"I put my life on hold for that. They took me out of school and they dressed me up, and they used me to cover for the horrible things they've done. They used all of us.

Front-line dolls." I remember Jackson, taunting me just after that photo was taken. Calling me 'Soldier Barbie'. I remember my fury, and my helplessness.

"And now the resistance wants to do the same. To take *my* face, *my* photo, and use it as their pretty face." Neesh nods. "They don't know me. They haven't bothered to meet me. They haven't asked whether any of this is OK with me."

Neesh watches me for a moment.

"I know, Bex. And I know who you are. You got your friends out of the bunker. You got them out of Camp Bishop before that. You're loyal and you're brave and you don't give up." I brush tears from my eyes and will myself to stop crying.

Neesh leans forward and puts her hand on my elbow.

"But you know what? That makes you everything the resistance stands for. That makes you the person who *should* be on their posters. You're the recruit who witnessed Leominster. You're the recruit who decided to walk away. You're the recruit who saved everyone in this flat.

"Who else's face should we use?"

I close my eyes. "They should have asked first."

"They should." She squeezes my elbow and lets go. "You're right."

Neesh sits quietly for a while, waiting. I force myself to stop crying, and push myself up on my elbows. I sit up and face her, leaning my back against the wall, legs crossed. I brush the tears away from my cheeks with the heels of my hands.

"You asked why I work with them?" I nod, and she continues. "I'm everything the government hates. I'm everything they don't want to see. I'm Neesha Hasan – the child of immigrants. I'm a successful, educated, political radical. I want better links with the rest of the world, more immigration, more travel, more trade – I don't want to live in a fortress. I run a business in spite of their restrictions. I think for myself, and I notice what they're doing, even when they want me to look the other way. I don't believe what I hear on PIN, and I don't believe what I read in the newspapers. And I refuse to be afraid. I've opposed everything they've done – all the anti-terrorism powers. Taking away our freedoms. Taking away our votes. I've marched and I've protested, and none of it made any difference.

"So now I work with the OIE. And they're not perfect, Bex. Not at all. But they're free. The King is effectively under house arrest at Buckingham Palace – the Home Forces don't trust him. The Palace of Westminster is empty – we don't have MPs any more, or votes. But the OIE? They're outside the UK, they're away from the oppression and the false flag attacks, and they've got the support of all our neighbouring countries. Government soldiers can't stop them. They're our best hope for putting things right. For getting our democracy back."

"And there's no one else?"

"Not with this kind of power. The OIE runs the resistance cells. They're working to change everything. They're making a difference. And if we can put these posters up – tell people that there is a resistance, that we're fighting for them – maybe a few more people will take notice. Maybe we'll see fewer people in the firing squad crowds, and more people demanding an end to martial law. Fewer people taking everything they see on PIN and in the papers as the truth, and more people asking questions."

I nod.

"I hate the government as much as you do. And I want to make a real difference as much as you do. I haven't done anything as brave as you and your friends, but I'm doing what I can. And I really think this could help us."

I look round the room, and down at the blanket I'm sitting on. Everything we have here is thanks to the OIE. Neesh and Caroline, the shop, the safe houses – all of this is run by the resistance in Edinburgh. They picked us up when we had nowhere to go, and they've kept us alive, and hidden. None of us is standing on an execution platform, and that's thanks to them. We've given them armour and guns, and we've given them hope that there are more recruits like us, ready to walk away and fight for the resistance.

I don't want my face out there again. I don't want people getting shot for putting my poster up. I want to run again, and I want to hide. I want someone else to be in the spotlight for once.

But I also want to make a difference. I want to stop the people who took us from school, who trained us to be their front-line dolls. I want to stop the people who killed Saunders, the people who have Margie and Will and Dr Richards. I want to save the people I left behind.

I can't do anything, stuck in this flat. I can't go out there and save anyone. I can't stand up and tell people what happened in Leominster. I'm powerless, and I'm trapped.

But maybe I can do this. Maybe being the pretty face of the resistance isn't as bad as being the distraction for government atrocities. I hate it. I hate the photo, I hate the poster, and I hate the idea of my face being used by another army. But at least it feels like fighting back.

"Fine," I say. "Fine. Use the poster. If you think it will do some good, if you think it will make a difference, use it."

Neesh smiles. "Thank you, Bex. Thank you."

I'm exhausted. This feels like defeat. This feels like being used all over again. I need them to understand.

"Tell Caroline I want them to ask us before they use us like this. Tell them that we're real people – not just stories. We want to help, but we're not their soldiers. We need to be in the loop, and then we'll do everything we can."

She nods, standing up. "Absolutely. I'll let her know."

I lean my head back against the wall. Neesh walks out and gently closes the door, and I'm alone again. I'm exhausted. I want to scream, and I want to laugh. Jackson was right – I'm still the front-line doll. It doesn't matter what else I do – who I save, who I fight, and who I leave behind – I'll always be a toy in someone else's war.

Frustration

Ketty

We're back at Belmarsh this morning. Lee wants to see whether one of the other prisoners will give him something to use against Richards.

I'm sitting with Conrad behind the mirror, trying to ignore him while Bracken waits in the interrogation room. I haven't forgotten how he treated me last time we were here. Lee has called for help from the prison guards, and he follows two of them into the room, a man in an orange jumpsuit walking between them. The prisoner is walking with a limp, and the guard on his right is supporting his weight. The guards lower him into a chair, cuff him to the table, and leave, closing the door behind them.

Lee takes his seat.

"This should be interesting." Conrad finishes setting up the recording, and the light comes on over the door. "One of Richards' cell, from the bunker."

I take a closer look at the prisoner, and I realise I've seen him before. He was the guard on duty when we stormed the gatehouse. The guard who preferred taking bullets to shooting at children. For a moment I'm back in the tiny concrete room, the guard slumped against the wall, and Saunders trying to be brave as he refused to let me into the bunker. I can't help smiling as I realise that I'm responsible for the prisoner's injury. My bullet – my threat to Saunders – did the damage to his leg.

Still think taking bullets was the right choice?

I look at Conrad. "I thought he was missing?"

He shrugs. "We tracked him down."

"So he got away? He had several bullets in him, last time I saw him."

56

Conrad raises an eyebrow. "We think the terrorists took him with them when they escaped."

Mummy Ellman. Couldn't resist helping another soldier in need?

This will be interesting.

*****

The prisoner denies everything.

He claims not to remember what happened on the night of the raid. He claims that he doesn't know anything about the farm or the bunker. He says that he woke up in hospital with bullets in his abdomen and his leg, and that's all he can tell us.

Liar. You remember. And I bet I can jog your memory.

"Give me a moment," I say, standing up and heading out into the waiting room. Conrad protests, but I leave him with the black boxes and the blinking lights. I straighten my uniform, step up to the interrogation room door, and knock.

Bracken answers, and steps out, closing the door behind him.

"What, Ketty?" He sounds impatient.

"I can get him to talk. I can place him in the gatehouse."

"Ketty ..."

"Let me do this. Let me impress Lee. Let me do something, instead of sitting back there watching you ..."

He sighs. "You saw him there?" I nod. "And he saw you?"

"Very much so, Sir."

He looks back over his shoulder and shrugs. "It can't hurt." He looks past me, to the coffee, and I know he's going to let me in.

Get yourself some caffeine, Sir. Let me do my job.

He opens the door, and waves me through.

*****

Lee looks up in surprise, then waves me to Bracken's chair. I don't know what he's just been asking, but the prisoner is shaking his head. He looks exhausted.

I lean forward, put my elbows on the table, and wait for him to look at me.

"Last time I saw you, you weren't looking so good. Someone fixed you up nicely." I give him a smile.

His eyes widen as he sees my face.

"So, you do remember."

He shakes his head again.

"How's the leg? Still proud of taking bullets to protect children?"

He lunges at me across the table. He tries to stand, but his leg gives way and his handcuffs hold him at a safe distance. He collapses back into his chair.

"Murderer!" He growls, looking into my eyes. "Coward!"

Keep talking. Keep incriminating yourself.

I lean back in my chair, and smile at him again. "So, where were we, last time we met?"

His anger overrules his common sense, and he shouts, "You were in the gatehouse. You shot my helper. You shot a *child*, in cold blood."

"I shot a guard, who was refusing to help me. I shot you, too. As I recall, you didn't help me either."

"You had no right." His voice is calm. Quiet.

You've just admitted that you were there. Let's see if you'll admit resisting arrest.

I keep my voice calm. "I had a right to defend myself. Did you do anything to defend your helper?"

He slumps back in his chair. "I used my weapon. I did the best I could."

"Firing at me, and my team?" He nods. "Denying us entry to the gatehouse?" He nods again.

"I tried. I did my best."

"So you didn't surrender? You didn't drop your weapon and come quietly?"

His expression changes. He seems to realise what he's said. He tries to raise his hands to his face, but the handcuffs stop him and he looks at them, as if he's seeing them for the first time.

"Remind me. How many bullets did we hit you with? Two? Three?"

He looks down, shaking his head.

"I'd say you were actively defending the bunker. Actively defending the terrorist cell cowering in their underground hideout. How many of them were helping you? How many of them were ready to back you up?" I lean forward again. "I didn't see anyone helping you out. I'd say the cowards were the ones sleeping downstairs while you were on the front line. Wouldn't you?"

He hangs his head. There's nothing more for him to say. He's already confessed to defending the bunker.

I look across at Lee. He's watching me, a neutral expression on his face.

"Thank you, Corporal," he says. "I think that's enough for now."

*****

"Good job, Corporal Smith." Lee sounds as if he's paying me a genuine compliment, but he doesn't smile. "We've got his confession on record. We'll let him think about what he's said, and see what else we can persuade him to tell us."

The prisoner is back in his cell. Conrad has downloaded the recordings, and we're back in the waiting room. I finish pouring a coffee for Bracken and hand it to him before turning my attention to the brigadier.

"Tell me," Lee sits back in his chair and sips his coffee. "If you can inspire a confession like that from a known terrorist, why am I still waiting for you to bring in our missing recruits?"

I stand up straight, and I'm about to protest when Bracken jumps to our defence.

"We're doing everything we can." Lee raises his eyebrows, but says nothing. "We're tracking sightings, we're bugging the landlines of everyone we suspect of being part of the resistance. We don't think they've left the country, but they could be anywhere in the UK by now. We're working on it."

Lee watches me, waiting for me to speak. I glance at Conrad, but he's watching Bracken, a smug smile on his face. When I say nothing, Lee shrugs.

"I think you should work a little harder. Don't you, Corporal?"

I'm about to respond, but Bracken cuts in again.

"I'm sure we'll track them down, Brigadier. We know them. We know what they've done before, and what they'll risk to avoid being caught. They'll slip up eventually, Sir, and when they do, we'll be waiting."

Lee gives us both a cold smile.

"Don't wait too long, will you?"

*****

"We need to track them down, Sir. This has gone on long enough. Lee is laughing at us. He won't keep us here if we don't bring him results."

He's already tried to send me home once. I'm not going to let him try again.

I'm pacing in front of Bracken's desk, running my fingers over my hair in frustration. Bracken watches me, unsmiling.

"We're waiting for them to make a mistake, Ketty. We're waiting for them to give up their cell. When they do that, we'll raid their base and bring them all back to London in chains. You can have your five minutes with them then, and so can Lee, but not before."

I look up.

"What if I can pull one of them out of the group? What if I can bring one of them back here for questioning? They could give me the group, and all their connections."

Bracken shakes his head. "What are you suggesting?"

I pull up a chair and sit down. "I'll do some research. Find out which of those kids has a weak spot. Some way to drag them out of their safe place."

"What are you going to do? Read their school reports? Find out who their best friends were and hunt them down as well?"

I'm thinking this through as I speak. He's right – the schools would be a good place to start. Everything we know about these kids came from their school records. Time to make some visits.

I smile. "Something like that, Sir."

He shrugs, and throws his hands up. "If you think it would help, then see what you can find out. Report back to me if you find anything."

"Yes, Sir!"

"And Ketty? Don't take too long. We have other work to do."

"Yes, Sir."

He lets out a sigh. "Go on, then. Go and bother some teachers. Dismissed."

Navigation

Bex

"Let's focus on the basics, Bex. Don't worry about road position and three-point turns and complicated stuff. You're just going to start the car, drive, and stop. Start, drive, stop. We'll do that over and over, and see if it helps."

I nod, gripping the steering wheel. Neesh is right – maybe I'm pushing myself too hard.

"So. From the beginning. Are you in gear?"

I check the gearstick, and it moves freely.

"No."

"OK. So what's next?"

Neesh guides me through the process of starting the car. She's patient, and she's methodical. This is exactly what I need.

It's just the two of us in the car. Watching the others drive isn't helping my confidence, so we're working together while everyone else makes dinner and cleans the store room.

Start, drive, stop. Up and down the service road. Neesh talks me through the turns, and I struggle to stay calm and focused, but we're here to practice the easy stuff. The goal is for this to become automatic. Second nature. Just something I do without thinking about it.

That goal seems a long way away.

*****

"Swap seats."

I've pulled the car up outside the shop, and I'm ready to head back upstairs.

I give Neesh a confused look.

"Swap seats. I'm taking you for a drive."

"You're … what? You can't. My face is on posters out there." I wave at the end of the road. "There are posters everywhere. You can't take me out there." I'm starting to panic. The idea of leaving the safety of the service road is overwhelming. I don't want to go out there. I don't want to put the others at risk.

Neesh smiles. "Relax. Pull your hood up, and let me take you out onto the road. We'll drive around for a bit, and you can get the hang of watching for traffic. You can tell me what to look out for – spot hazards and traffic lights and obstacles." She sees the fear on my face. "It's dark, Bex. No one's going to look twice at a teenager in a hoodie in a car. Now, swap seats."

So I do. I strap myself in as Neesh adjusts the seat and the mirrors. I pull my hood over my face and slump down as far as I can in my seat. As Neesh starts the car and drives to the barrier at the end of the service road, I start to panic again. My fists are clenched, gripping the edges of the seat.

"Neesh, I …"

"I know, Bex. You'll be fine. Sit up, and tell me when it's safe for me to turn onto the road."

She drives towards the barrier, and it starts to rise. It feels like taking my armour off, or letting water into a sinking boat. My protection, everything that was standing between me and the world outside is lifting away, and I'm terrified.

"Bex? Take a look at the traffic. Both directions. When am I safe to move?"

I take a deep breath. I force myself to focus. I look out at the road, at the cars driving past. I make myself pay attention. I look left and right. I think about how fast the cars are moving, and I start to feel the rhythm of the traffic as they pass. I see the gap in the cars to the left, and another to the right.

"After the next car. Then you're safe."

Neesh checks, and pulls out, and we're on the road. We're outside.

I try to concentrate on the traffic. On the obstacles and the traffic lights, but I can't. I'm watching the shops. The cafés. The bars. The people. There are people everywhere – walking, sitting in restaurants, drinking, talking, waiting at the bus stops. People living their ordinary lives, people with no idea that we're hiding in the next street. I pull my hood further over my face, but Neesh is right. No one's looking at us. No one's seeing me. I'm outside, and I'm safe.

"Focus, Bex. I need you to watch where I'm driving. Tell me what's coming up. What I should do."

I sit up in my seat, watching the road ahead.

"That bus is pulling in. It's going to block this lane."

"Good, Bex! Yes. So what should I do?"

I look around at the traffic, watch what other people are doing.

"Stop behind it. Wait for it to move off."

"OK. That's what we'll do." Neesh is smiling. We wait while the bus picks up passengers and pulls away.

"There's a junction coming up, Bex. What can you tell me about it?"

I lean over to look past the bus, and I see traffic lights, just turning from green to amber.

"The lights are changing. They'll be red by the time you get there."

Neesh glances over at me. "That's great, Bex. That's really helpful." She pulls up at the traffic lights. "I think you're better at this than you are at driving the car."

Neesh takes us through the suburb and into the city, challenging me to make the driving decisions for her. She checks everything, but she seems pleased with most of my suggestions. By the time we're heading home, I'm paying attention to the road, and I'm hardly seeing the people and the shop fronts. I'm telling Neesh what to do, and she's correcting me when I make mistakes. We're both concentrating on the drive, and it feels amazing to be outside, watching people leading their ordinary lives. It feels free.

And then I see my face on a poster at a bus stop. We're only a street away from home, and there's my face on a wanted poster, life-sized. Everyone we've driven past tonight knows that poster. Everyone knows my face. And everyone thinks I'm a terrorist. I push myself down in my seat again, pulling my hood forward and shielding my face from the streetlights.

We're not free. We're not safe. And whatever we do, we're not in control.

*****

The others have eaten by the time we get back, and Dan sets himself up as our waiter as Neesh and I sit down at the table. He drapes a tea towel over one arm and affects a ridiculous French accent, offering us fine wines and exotic cuisine, then serving our reheated baked potatoes and cans of lemonade with flamboyant pride. We're all laughing as he pulls up a chair to sit with us.

"So? How was it? How's the outside world?"

"Good." I nod, eating my potato.

"Do they still have buses out there? Streetlights? Trainers?"

"Of course!" Neesh laughs, and rolls her eyes.

"Any new fashions I should be aware of? Green hair? Viking beards?" He scratches his chin, thoughtfully.

"Dan! It's been two months. No, no one's wearing green hair or weird beards."

"Do they still know who we are?" He's serious, suddenly.

"Yeah. Yeah – they still know that. We're still on the posters."

"Not just PIN, then. We're properly famous. Faces on every street."

He smiles, but he's not joking any more.

"Come on," he stands up when we've finished eating. "Time for Spot the Prisoner. Leave the washing up – I'll do that later."

We follow him into the living room. Everyone else is waiting for us – the TV is on, and it's coming up to the hour. The PIN bulletin will be on shortly. Neesh sits on the end of Jake's bed and I choose a spot on the floor next to the sofa.

"How was it?" Charlie whispers.

"OK," I say, smiling. Across the room, Neesh gives Charlie a thumbs-up. Charlie gives my shoulder a squeeze as the PIN news begins.

We watch the headlines. A bombing in Bournemouth. A food poisoning outbreak. Football results.

And a new prisoner.

We're watching the footage from an interrogation room. Plain white walls and floor. A man in an orange jumpsuit, handcuffed to a table. Someone in uniform asking him questions. The newsreader is talking over the footage, but we can all see the prisoner's face.

It's Charlie who shouts first, but then we're all shouting and pointing at the screen. Neesh looks confused.

"Who is it?"

"It's the guard. The guard from the gatehouse!"

"The one you carried out of Makepeace Farm?"

"That's him," says Charlie, shaking her head. "They've tracked him down."

There's a ice-cold feeling on the back of my neck. If they've found him, how long will it be until they find us?

"But we called the ambulance for him." Amy sounds indignant. "We made sure he got to hospital!"

"We made sure the ambulance came," says Dan. "That's not the same. And he couldn't exactly hide three bullet wounds, could he?"

Neesh holds up her hands. "Wait – so you called an ambulance?"

"At the first payphone we found."

"We called the ambulance and left him there."

"We kept walking. Charlie stayed close, and made sure the ambulance stopped for him."

Neesh nods. "OK. So you don't know what happened to him after that?"

Charlie shakes her head. "It's the best we could do. We had to get away, and he was badly hurt. It was his idea." She waves her hand at the screen, where the guard is shaking his head at the person sitting opposite him at the table. "And he's alive, so someone treated his injuries."

"So either the ambulance crew figured out that he was from the farm, or the hospital had to report the gunshot wounds." Neesh looks around at all of us. "What does he know? Can he tell them anything that could lead them to you?"

Dan slumps back against the wall. "I don't think so. We didn't know where we were going, so he can't tell them where we are."

"And they already know who we are. They've got our photos. He can't tell them anything they don't already know about us."

I think about the time we spent at Makepeace Farm. The guard was part of Will's group, but we didn't spend much time with him.

"Amy's right. There's nothing useful he can add to what they already know."

I feel cruel, assessing this man's interrogation in terms of what it means for us, but this is all we can do here, in hiding. Watch PIN and calculate the risks. It's frustrating that we can't help. We can't step in, and we can't rescue anyone. We're powerless, sitting in our top-floor flat.

And I can't shake the feeling that they're closing in. Tightening the noose around our hiding place.

Connections

Ketty

I start with Ellman and Pearce.

Posh boarding school just outside Macclesfield. They were the first to be picked up on their march, and the information the recruiters took from the school is limited. I book a car from the vehicle pool for tomorrow, and catch up with the commander's paperwork for the rest of the day, clearing his office of bottles as usual before I leave for the night.

In the morning, I'm out at seven, driving out of London before rush hour kicks in. It's a three-hour drive to the school, using the military priority lanes on main roads to avoid the traffic and the speed limits, and I'm pulling up outside as the kids are heading back to classes after a morning break. I'm wearing my service uniform, Corporal stripes on the shoulders. Smart, efficient, and instantly respected.

I park the car close to the public entrance. It's a marked military vehicle, so no one can complain if I park it outside the official spaces. It feels good to disrupt their perfect driveway, and the perfect, imposing main entrance. I pick up my document case, lock the car, and walk up the stone steps to an arched wooden door, doing my best to hide my limp.

The receptionist buzzes me in before I've pressed the bell.

The uniform got your attention, then?

I push open the heavy door, and walk into a wood-panelled hallway, a matching wooden reception desk to one side.

"Welcome to Rushmere," says a woman who looks as if she's just stepped out of a professional photoshoot. Perfect hair, perfect makeup, just the right balance of assertive and helpful. I walk up to the desk, give her a tight smile, and flash my ID card.

"Corporal Smith. I'm here to track down some student records."

"This is for our RTS students, I assume?"

I nod. The woman's cheerful mask slips for a moment, and I notice the disapproval in her eyes. She recovers quickly, smiles at me, and stands up.

"This way, please."

She leads me through a door in the wood-panelled wall, and into a room lined with filing cabinets. There are two desks in the centre of the room, one of them occupied by a young woman in a smart suit.

"Lesley," says the receptionist, "the Corporal is here about some RTS records."

Lesley stands, and offers her hand. I cross the room and greet her with a firm handshake.

"I'll leave you to it?"

Lesley nods, and the receptionist leaves us alone.

"So. Whose records are you looking for?"

"Rebecca Ellman and Daniel Pearce, and anyone else in their recruitment group."

She narrows her eyes.

"Are you from Camp Bishop?"

I nod. "I was one of the instructors there."

"Can I ask what happened? We heard rumours, but …"

I wave a hand to stop her. "I'm afraid I'm not at liberty to discuss RTS affairs."

Or any mistakes we may or may not have made, or any recruits we may or may not have lost.

She nods, and points to the empty desk.

"You'll want to work here. I'll fetch the records for you."

I sit down, and watch as she pulls hanging files from one of the cabinets. By the time she's finished, there are twenty-three beige folders stacked on the end of my desk.

"Thank you," I say, as I pull the first folder towards me. Lesley watches me for a moment, then sits down at her desk, facing me across the middle of the room.

I work my way through the records. The first few are all quiet, obedient recruits I remember from Camp Bishop. Nothing of interest in those, so I stack them at the other end of the desk.

And then I find Ellman. Mousy photo a few years out of date. Dull brown hair and an expression of vague surprise on her face, as if she wasn't expecting her photo to be taken. I think of Jackson, taunting her over the photo that's become her public image. She looks different, but there's a determination behind her eyes in both photos.

I look through her paperwork. Parental address in Stockport, both parents listed. Orchard House, which sounds posh until I realise it's a nursing home.

Really, Ellman? Who's looking after you if your parents are in there?

I check through the notes, and notice that she spent all her time at school. From the age of fourteen she lived here during the holidays, and apart from day trips to Stockport, she didn't spend any time with her family.

That is interesting. Your mother sent you away, and your response was to mother everyone around you. Filling a gap, were you?

I skim the rest of her file. Mother uses a wheelchair, father terminally ill. Only child. Middling grades, no outstanding achievements. A page in her handwriting where she manages not to commit to any particular plan for her education. She lists several career ideas, the first of which is 'teacher'. No surprises here. There's a note about a study group – her name is listed, along with Pearce, and someone called Margaret Watson. I scribble the name in my notes and move on.

Pearce's file is next. His parents are listed at a very expensive address in London. Only child, high-flyer, good grades, sporting success. A few minor disciplinary notes, but nothing worth calling daddy over. His career essay spans doctor, surgeon, lawyer, and politician. I'm sure daddy approved. His study group is listed, too. Rebecca Ellman, Margaret Watson. I underline her name on my notes.

I give the other files a quick read through, but there's nothing connecting our well-behaved recruits to any of the terrorists.

I check the notes I've made. Contact details for both families. Details of their subjects and grades. And the study group.

I look at Lesley.

"Do you have a file on Margaret Watson?"

She looks up suddenly, trying to hide the surprise on her face.

"We do," she says, but her voice is guarded.

"What's the story? Did she avoid conscription?" I indicate the files in front of me. "She seems to have been studying with my recruits before they came to Camp Bishop."

She thinks for a moment, as if she's trying to decide what to tell me. "It's complicated."

Sheltering deserters, are we? Hiding students from the RTS?

"Can I see her file?"

Lesley nods, and jumps to her feet. "Of course. Just … let me find it."

She searches in her desk drawer and pulls out a set of keys. She heads to the far corner of the room, and unlocks the bottom drawer in one of the filing cabinets. She flicks through, and pulls out another, bulging beige file, and hesitates before she brings it to my desk.

"We don't really know what happened," she begins. "We're not sure why she left." She puts the records down in front of me. "Maybe it will make sense to you."

I thank her, and open the file.

The first item is a copy of an official letter, addressed to the Recruit Training Service. It explains that while Margaret is still registered as a student at Rushmere, her whereabouts are currently unknown. It goes on to explain that, while she is eligible for conscription, this will not be possible as requested, as she is no longer in residence at the school.

A deserter before she even joined up. And a friend of Ellman and Pearce. This is interesting.

There follows a series of letters confirming her absence, and requiring the school to inform the RTS if Miss Watson returns, and another series of letters between the school and Margaret's parents. I check their address, and I'm surprised to find a PO Box in Kenya. I flick through the rest of her file. Younger sister, living in Kenya. Good grades, no misdemeanours. Her career essay is hopelessly idealistic, and apparently she wants to run a development charity or go into politics. I check the parental information page, and it seems that she's following in their footsteps. Their charity is listed, with a brief outline of its activities. Education, training, political activism.

The final letter is a formal submission to the school inspector, refuting the claim that Margaret absconded from school with one of her teachers, and claiming that there is no evidence to support this theory. I turn back through the letters, and there's one accusing the school of allowing an inappropriate relationship between a teacher and a student, which led to both of them leaving without notice or permission. They left on the same day, and the suspicion is that they left together. I'm trying to hide a smirk at the idea of Ellman's friend running away with her favourite teacher, when I find Margaret's photo.

Slim face. Dark eyes. Long dark hair.

It's our prisoner. This is the girl who walked into Camp Bishop, and the girl we took from Makepeace Farm.

Margaret Watson, who hasn't given us her name. Who hasn't said anything since the night in the farmyard.

Who went to school with Ellman and Pearce, and ran away to join the terrorists.

I turn back to the inspector's letter, searching for the name of the teacher.

Dr Richards.

Richards. There's a connection here, somewhere. I can't see it yet, but it's here.

"Lesley," she jumps at the sound of my voice. "Do you have a file on Dr Richards? A photo? Anything?"

She nods, and returns to the same locked drawer. She pulls out a blue file, 'Staff' stamped on it in large letters, and brings it to me.

"We really don't think there's a connection …"

I wave her away.

And open the file.

Doctor Sheena Richards smiles out at me from a full-page photo.

The woman from the farmhouse. The other prisoner from the raid on the terrorist base.

And the pieces fall into place. William Richards, owner of Makepeace Farm, currently sitting on one of our cells. Sheena Richards, possible relative, apprehended at Makepeace Farm, in the company of Margaret Watson. Margaret, the activist, who ran away from her school friends before the recruiters arrived – not because of any inappropriate relationship, but because she wanted to join William's terrorist gang. And the school friends, Ellman and Pearce, next on our terrorist Wanted list.

Gotcha.

*****

"I think we can do it, Sir. PIN puts out a recurring appeal for Ellman to come and see her dying father before it's too late. We'll get someone from the nursing home to take pictures of Mr Ellman. We'll show them on TV, stake out the nursing home and wait for her to arrive."

Bracken regards me over his steeped fingers. "What makes you think she'll come?"

"I can't see Ellman resisting, Sir. She didn't get to see her parents much before she joined the RTS, and I think she misses them. She won't leave him to die without saying goodbye, and then we've got her."

"But she'll know it's a trap, if we put it out on the news."

"She will, but I think she'll come anyway. The way she stormed the coach? The way she got the prisoner out of Camp Bishop? I think she does the obvious thing, and counts on us not expecting it. She'll walk in through the front door, and she'll expect to get away with it."

"And she might, if she's clever. If she catches us off guard again."

I shake my head. "I don't think so, Sir. Give me enough soldiers, and I can secure the home. Even if she gets in, there'll be no way out."

Bracken thinks for a moment. "So you want me to go to the Public Information Network, the only source of news and information in the country, and you want me to tell them to run a repeating segment on getting one girl to come home and see her father?"

I smile, thinking about the look on Conrad's face if I can make this happen. "I do. The terrorists are already putting her image on their posters. Why don't we offer a compassionate service to someone they've already claimed as their own?"

A smile spreads across his face. "That might just work. We get to look good and set a trap at the same time. And when we catch her …"

"When we catch her, PIN can report that she handed herself in, and offered to cooperate fully with the government. That will frighten the rest of her cell, maybe even push them into moving, coming out in the open. And then we've got them all."

Family

Bex

"It's horrible. It's horrible and it's on the news, every hour."

I'm shouting. I'm shouting at Charlie, who doesn't deserve it, but she's the one who's come to talk to me. We'd been out for more driving practice, eaten dinner together, and gathered in the living room to watch the news. We were expecting more footage of the guard, or maybe someone else from the bunker.

I wasn't expecting this.

"Bex. Bex. Sit down."

I stop pacing and sit next to her on my bed. She puts her arm round my shoulders.

"You're right. It's horrible. It's a cruel, unfair thing to do to you. You have every right to be angry."

"They put *my Dad* on TV. My Dad, who had nothing to do with any of this. He doesn't deserve to be on every TV in the country. Not like that. Not in a hospital bed. All thin and sick and dying." The anger turns to tears, and I'm sobbing into Charlie's shoulder.

"I know, Bex. I know." Her voice is gentle, but I can tell she doesn't have answers for me. I want to forget the images from the news story. The photo of me from the wanted poster. The horrible, sentimental appeal to me to come home, before it's too late. Pictures of my Dad, propped up on pillows, eyes closed.

"And it looks bad. It looks like he's ... like I don't have much time."

Charlie nods. "I think they're telling the truth."

I sit up. "About Dad, maybe. But not about letting me visit."

She shakes her head, sadly. "I think you're right."

"What do I do?" My face crumples again, and I can't stop crying.

She tightens her arm round my shoulders. "I don't know. And I can't tell you what to do. This is your call. No one can tell you not to go, but you need to understand what that means."

"Caroline will tell me not to go."

"Then we won't tell Caroline."

I push the tears from my face roughly with my hands. I've faced worse than this. I've been through worse, and I've got out alive.

"I want to go. I want to see him again. I want to say goodbye. But not like this. Not with everyone watching."

Charlie shakes her head again. "It's a trap, Bex. Don't forget that this is all a trap, and you're the prize. You, and everything you know about the resistance."

"I won't tell them anything!" I'm angry now. Why would I give up my friends? Why would I put anyone else's life in danger? This is about me and my family.

She puts her hands on my shoulders, and gently turns me to face her.

"You won't mean to, Bex. We all know that. But what about when they try to hurt you? What about when they threaten you, or threaten us, or bring your Dad into it again? Will you be able to keep quiet? And what about when you're facing a firing squad? You won't give us all up then, just to walk out alive?"

She pulls me into a hug, and I let her hold onto me while I fight the tears.

She's right. I know she's right. "This isn't fair."

She pulls back and looks me in the eye. "No, it's not. You shouldn't be in the middle of this. You got here by pro-tecting your friends, and following your conscience, and everything you did was brave and justified and right. Never forget that. Never forget that you got Margie out of the camp, and you got all of us out of the bunker. If we can help

76

you with this, we will. But you need to know what you're walking into."

"So I have to chose. See Dad, or protect the resistance." Charlie nods, and I feel my anger flaring. I'm shouting again. "That's too much. That's too much that's on me."

"I know, Bex."

"They've got my face. They've got my photo on that stupid poster. I've given them that."

"You're the face of their resistance. So they won't be happy if you end up on TV in an orange jumpsuit."

I feel sick. If that's the choice I have to make, then I won't see Dad again. Too much depends on us staying safe and staying hidden. But if there's a way for me to get to him, and get away safely – I have to use it. I can't let anyone take this from me.

"I'm their front-line doll." Charlie bows her head. She knows how I feel about this. "They get to dictate my movements. It doesn't matter how many times I escape – someone else still decides what I do. Were I go, where I live, who I see."

"I know it feels that way, but this is all to keep you safe. To keep all of us safe."

"And to beat the government. I know. And that's what I want." I close my eyes and try to see clearly through my anger. "But I also want to be me. I don't want to lose myself to their cause. I want to be more than a front-line doll. And I want to see my Dad."

"I know. And I understand." She puts her hand on my arm. "We're here for you, Bex."

"Yeah. Thank you. I know you're looking out for me." I shake my head, tears filling my eyes. "It's just that it's not enough. You can't protect me from this."

"No. But we can help you, if that's what you want."

I nod. I can't think about putting everyone here in danger, but I can't imagine not seeing Dad again. This isn't the gatehouse guard, or some stranger on an execution platform. This is different. This is my family.

"Get some sleep. Talk to me about it in the morning. I'll swap my shift so I'm here for breakfast." She takes my face in her hands and brushes the tears away.

"OK. Thanks, Charlie."

I crawl into bed as she leaves. I'm sure I'll be awake all night, thinking this through, but I'm out almost as soon as I lie down.

*****

I wake early, already knowing what my decision will be.

I get up, get dressed, and head to the kitchen. Charlie is waiting, leaning against the worksurface, a mug of tea cradled in her hands. She watches me walk into the room, looks me in the eye, and nods.

"You're going, aren't you?"

"Yeah. I'm going."

She sits down at the table and waves me to the chair on the other side.

"We can't let you go by yourself. You can't do this on your own. We need a plan." She thinks for a moment. "I think your driving skills might be needed sooner than we thought."

Insult

Ketty

"That's good work, Corporal Smith."

Brigadier Lee settles back into his chair in front of Bracken's desk, a page of notes in front of him from my report. Bracken can't hide his proud smile, and neither can I.

"Thank you, Sir."

"And you're sure about the background on Margaret, and the Richards woman?"

I nod. "I am, Sir. It makes sense."

It also explains why none of them will talk. No one wants to incriminate the people they care about.

"We'll take this to the interrogators. See what progress we can make."

"Yes, Sir."

He lifts another sheet of paper from the table in front of him.

"And what about this Ellman situation? Has anything happened there yet?"

"No, Sir, but we're expecting Recruit Ellman to show up in the next few days. I think she'll try to stay away, but I'm sure she'll come eventually. And we've offered her safe passage, so that should help to persuade her."

"Not that we have any intention of letting her walk away."

I shake my head, smiling. "No, Sir."

"The soldiers are in place?"

"Yes, Sir. Guards on the nursing home entrance, and constant patrols of the grounds. We're ready for her."

He nods. "Good, good." He pauses, and gives me one of his piercing stares. "And you, Ketty? How are you? How's the knee?"

My smile fades.

You know exactly how my knee is. Broken and twisted and you could be helping, but you won't.

I grit my teeth. Bracken shifts awkwardly in his chair.

"Good, thank you, Sir. Still improving."

Still limping. Still on painkillers. Still hoping for another Brigadier Lee miracle package.

I give him an insincere smile, and he matches it.

No hope there, then.

He watches me for a moment too long, and then waves a hand at Bracken. "The Colonel and I have things to discuss. Thank you for your time, Corporal Smith. Keep me posted on the nursing home stake-out." There's a sneer in his voice as he dismisses me.

*****

I take my frustration out on the firing range. I'm supposed to complete ten hours of firearms practice every month, and as I check in I realise I haven't been spending enough time here. I take the ear protectors and bullets from the Private on duty, and make a mental note to practice more often.

I pull the gun from its holster on my belt. I load my target and my gun, and spend a moment with my eyes closed, controlling my breathing.

Focus, Ketty. Nothing else matters. Fire the gun, hit the target.

I open my eyes and raise my weapon. The target hangs at the end of the range, a silhouette waiting for my actions.

I push everything else from my mind, and line up the sights.

Aim, and fire. Aim, and fire.

I channel all my frustration into the bullet, and let it rip into my target.

Stay calm. Stay focused. Do your job.

Every bullet pierces the silhouette. Every shot is a hit. I'm calm as I aim my gun.

I can't control the pain in my knee, and I can't force Brigadier Lee to save me again. But I can shoot. I can defend myself. I can use my skills.

I can survive.

Iron fists and steel toe caps.

The target comes back to me, shredded.

*****

"I'm not putting up with this any longer. I'm not going to let him mock me any more."

I meet Bracken in his office first thing in the morning, and I'm angrier with Brigadier Lee now than I was last night. I've had a chance to think about what he said.

"He thinks this whole nursing home plan is a joke. He thinks he knows Ellman better than I do. He thinks we won't get anything out of it." Bracken puts his head in his hands. "He's laughing at me, Sir. This is all a joke to him. All of it."

Bracken doesn't move. He's heard enough of my anger at the brigadier to know it's best to let me shout it out. We both know Lee's not going to send me another PowerGel, even though he knows what sort of pain I'm living with. And now he's laughing at my plan to catch him a terrorist.

"He thinks the bunker was my fault. He thinks everything that failed at Makepeace was my fault. And he won't trust me again, until I prove I can do what he wants." I stand up and pace the room. Bracken sits back in his chair and glances at the filing cabinet where he hides his whisky, but he doesn't get up. He catches me watching him.

"Are you done, Corporal? Are you finished for today?"

I sink back into the chair. My knee is aching, and I shouldn't be walking on it. "Yes, Sir. Sorry, Sir."

He leans forward, elbows on the desk.

"Don't be sorry," he says, deliberately. "Be angry." I look up at him, and he must see the confusion on my face. "It's fine to be angry, Ketty. It's perfectly understandable, with everything that's happened. But what are you going to do about it?"

I shake my head. I'm not sure what he's getting at.

"You don't like Lee's attitude?" I shake my head. "Then change it. Do something about it. Prove him wrong."

"Sir?"

"You think the nursing home trap is going to work? Put your back into it. Make it work. Make Lee see what you can do."

Are you telling me to get involved? To lie in wait for her myself?

I think it through. If Ellman turns up, if we catch her, that all happens without me. I'm hundreds of miles away in Bracken's outer office. Lee doesn't have to give me any credit at all. It was Bracken who sold him the plan, and it will be the soldiers on the ground who make the arrest. Lee can shut me out of my own plan, and carry on ignoring me.

I need to be there. I need to make this happen.

I smile at Bracken.

"I think it's time I had a chat with Bex Ellman's mother."

Delivery

Bex

Neesh drives us down the next day, in a car borrowed from a friend. She bought a map of Stockport, and we realised they didn't need to teach me to drive – they just needed to teach me to mind the traffic, turn left, and stop. Charlie and Neesh have been over the basics with me for hours. We've been out on the road again, Neesh waiting for my instructions, and I've stopped and started the car more times than I can count. On my own in the car I can drive for a short distance, and I can pull up and stop without stalling. My hands shake and I'm terrified, but I can do it. That's all I'll need, if everything goes to plan. We're all hoping it's going to be enough.

Charlie leaves us in the car, and goes to wait near the rendezvous point, a baseball cap pulled down low and a scarf round her neck to hide her face. Neesh drives me to a car park two streets away from the nursing home, and gets out without cutting the engine, holding the driver's door open for me. I take a deep breath, step out, and walk round the car. Neesh gives me a hug, and grabs the parcel and the clipboard from the boot while I'm getting in and fastening my seatbelt. She drops them on the passenger seat, and reaches across the car to put her hand on my arm.

"You can do this, Bex. You can make it in and out. Just be quick, and stick to the plan."

I grip the steering wheel, willing my hands to stop shaking. I lean over to take a final look at my face in the rearview mirror. The long, black wig streaked with purple. The contact lenses that make my eyes a muddy shade of green. The heavy-rimmed glasses and the peaked baseball cap pulled low over my forehead. The weight I've lost, that makes my face look pinched and thin. The dark circles under my eyes.

I nod.

"Sure. Sure."

She closes the door, and comes round to my side of the car. I open the window, staring straight ahead and pushing the fear away.

"Just like we practised. Watch the traffic. Be careful. In and out. I'll move the car, and see you at the meeting point."

"Yeah. Thanks, Neesh."

This has to work. We don't have a Plan B. This is it – I'm going to see Dad. And I'm terrified.

I close the window, plant my feet on the pedals, release the handbrake, and concentrate on driving the car.

*****

Left out of the car park. Left onto a main road. I'm lucky – the traffic is light, so I'm not dodging cars and buses on this short drive. I drive slowly, keeping the car in the middle of the lane, and then turn left into the nursing home drive-way. I nearly bottle out when I see the troop carrier parked outside, and the two soldiers guarding the door, but I clench my teeth and turn in, looking as confident as I can. Those troops are here for me.

I pull the car into a space near the road. I remember the handbrake. I ease my feet from the pedals, and I switch off the engine. I take the keys from the ignition, and drop them out of sight under the seat.

I've done it. I've got myself this far. This is happening.

There's no going back now – not without making the soldiers suspicious.

One more deep breath, then I pick up the clipboard and step out of the car. I walk round to the passenger door and grab the parcel, feeling the eyes of the guards on me with every move I make. I need to slow my breathing. I need to be able to talk.

I put the parcel on the roof, blocking their view of my face. My hands are shaking. My knees are shaking. I need to start believing in my own disguise. I close the door, closing my eyes for a moment and willing myself to smile. I pick up the parcel, and walk confidently towards the entrance, clipboard in hand.

"Delivery?" Asks one of the guards. I do my best to look surprised.

"Yes. I just need to drop it off and get a signature."

"ID, please," says the other guard, making it clear that this isn't a request. I unclip the ID badge from the clipboard and hand it over. It's genuine – Neesh had a friend at the delivery company make it up for us. It should stand up to a security check. The only lie is the fake employee name.

The guard stares at the grainy photo, and at me. I keep my chin angled down so the peak of the cap shields my face. I'm wearing the wig loose to match the photo, and the dark hair falls forward, to hide any familiar features he might recognise. This is the first failure point. If I fail here, I'm going to London in handcuffs, and everyone I care about will watch me face a firing squad on live TV.

He takes an age, checking the photo. I try not to panic. My grip tightens on the clipboard as I wait.

"Who's it for?" He nods towards the parcel. I make a show of reading the label. There's no name on it, and it's addressed to a random room number.

"Room 68," I say, with an apologetic shrug.

The guards exchange a glance, and the first guard shrugs. The second guard hands me my badge, and I stuff it into my pocket.

"Go on. Don't take too long." And he opens the door for me.

I step into the porch and wave at the young woman on the reception desk, who presses a button to release the second set of doors. I turn and push one open with my hip, then walk in, trying to keep my feet on the ground. I'm past the guards, and I feel as if I might float away. I glance around as I walk. The entrance hall is just as I remember it – patterned carpet, fresh flowers on the tables, security doors to other parts of the building.

I step up to the desk. Second failure point. It would be easy for the receptionist to call for help, if she suspected anything.

"Hi," she says brightly. "Delivery?" She already has a pen in her hand, ready to sign for the parcel. I pretend to consult my clipboard.

"I'm sorry, but this needs to go to the recipient. Some sort of insurance issue? I can't take a signature from anyone else." I shrug, apologetically.

"OK," she says, putting the pen down. "That's unusual. Let me check that with the supervisor." She reaches for the phone.

I lean over the desk, before she can pick up the receiver. "Sorry," I say, as casually as I can, "would you mind if I used your toilet?" I jerk a thumb at the car. "You know what it's like, driving round all day." I give her a reassuring smile.

She looks at me, appraisingly. I do my best to look embarrassed.

"OK," she says, eventually. "Through those doors, and on the right." She reaches for the button to override the locks. I pick up the parcel, and she gives me a surprised glance. "You can leave that with me," she says.

"I need to keep it with me." I'm fighting to keep my voice steady. If she makes a fuss, the guards will come in. I force another smile. "My boss would kill me if I let it out of my sight." She looks uncertain, and reaches for the phone again. "Tell you what – I'll leave the clipboard with you. That way I've got to come back." I manage a grin, and she smiles back and nods. "Thank you so much!" I call, as I walk towards the doors. "I appreciate it!"

The doors are unlocked when I reach them, and I push through and turn into the Ladies' toilets. I make for the end cubicle and lock myself in, fingers already pulling at the tape on the parcel.

I can't believe this is working. And I can't afford to stop and think about it now. I've got maybe two minutes to change and walk out of here before the receptionist is watching through the doors.

I tear open the parcel, pulling off my hat, wig and glasses, and fishing the ID badge from my pocket. My hands are shaking again, and I keep fumbling as I peel off my jeans and sweatshirt. I can't afford to screw this up. Not now that I'm so close.

I pull out the nursing home uniform from the parcel. Pale green scrubs and a pink tabard. I put them on as quickly as I can, then run my fingers through my hair and catch the ponytail in a hair elastic. I wince as I pull my eyelids up and take out the contact lenses, dropping them into the sanitary products disposal bin. Finally, I pull out the bundle from the bottom of the parcel, and unwrap the handgun. I slip it into the back of my waistband, and stuff everything else back into the box, pressing the tape down as I go. I step out of the cubicle and check my reflection in the mirror, combing out the ridges in my hair with my fingers before turning to the door. Brown hair back in a ponytail, blue eyes, nursing home uniform. I hope it's enough to avoid detection for now.

I pause by the door, listening for noises in the corridor outside. I can't hear anything, and as much as I'd like to stay here, leaning against the door, paused between the dangerous parts of the plan, I have to move. Every second makes the difference between success and failure. Every second is another second I could spend with Dad before I have to run again.

I push open the door.

*****

The corridors are clear as I make my way to Mum's room. I'm shaking. I need to breathe, and I need to walk. One foot in front of the other. Calm and confident. My fingers are crushing the cardboard parcel.

And here it is. Room 50. Ellman, Liz and Peter. A wave of relief crashes over me. There are tears in my eyes, and I'm sobbing before I can stop myself.

Deep breath. I brush the tears away with my sleeve and step forward to knock on the door.

Someone calls out from inside the room, and I grip the door handle. Another failure point. If there are guards inside, I'm cornered. But at least I'm armed.

I push the door open.

And there's my mother in her wheelchair, turning herself to look at me. There's their sideboard, framed photos of the three of us crowding the top surface. And there's my father in a hospital bed in the living room, plugged into tubes and wires and machines.

Mum turns and looks at me, and first she sees the uniform, but then the polite smile on her face turns into a look of astonishment, and it's as if the sun has come out from behind a cloud. She gives me a huge, warm smile, and opens her mouth to say something, but I raise my finger to my lips, and close the door gently behind me. I glance around the room, but there are no soldiers waiting. No trap ready to be sprung. For a few moments, I really am safe, and I really am home.

I drop the parcel. I walk over to Mum, hardly believing that this is real. I kneel down, and reach out to her. She leans forward in her chair and wraps me in her arms. I hold her as tightly as I can.

I could stay here forever, but I need to move. I don't have a lot of time. Gently, I break free, holding myself up on the armrest of her chair, my whole body shaking.

"Bex!" She says, taking my face in her hands. "My beautiful girl. What are you doing here? How did you get in?"

There are tears on her cheeks, and mine.

"They said …" I take a ragged breath, and fight to keep my voice above a whisper. "Dad. They said I should come."

She raises her head and looks across the room at my father in his bed, and she nods.

"He won't … he doesn't respond to much any more. Don't get your hopes up." She takes my shoulders. "Go on. I know he's been waiting for you to visit."

I nod, and brush away the tears again. I stand up, and walk slowly over to the bed.

Among the tubes and wires and drips, my Dad is lying, utterly still save for his shallow breathing. I perch on the edge of the bed, and reach over to take his hand. He looks so small and fragile against the pillows. His face is pale and thin, and I can see the shapes of the bones under his skin.

"Talk to him," says Mum. "Tell him what's been happening."

"I'm sorry, Dad. I'm sorry. I've been away. I've been busy." He doesn't move. "I'm not at school any more. The army came and took us away. We've been training and fighting and patrolling. You might have seen us on TV, keeping people safe from the terrorists." I can't help laughing at that. Dad clearly hasn't watched TV in ages, and the last thing I've been doing is keeping people safe.

There are tears on my face again as I speak. "Actually, Dad, I ran away. I'm not with the army any more." I glance up at Mum. "I'm working with some people who want to get our democracy back. I'm kind of a fugitive right now.

"I can't stay long. I don't want to put you two in danger. But I wanted to come and see you." I squeeze his hand, and for a brief moment, I'm sure he squeezes back. I laugh, and lift his hand, and he squeezes it again. It's not much more than a twitch, but I'm sure it's there.

And then I'm holding him, carefully, around the wires and the tubes, and I'm sobbing. Tears are running down my face and neck, and soaking into his pillow. Mum comes up behind me and puts her hand on my shoulder, and there I am, for the last time, in the safety of my parents' arms.

When I sit up, there are tears on Dad's face as well. He knows I'm here.

I reach out to stroke his cheek. And I know that this is goodbye.

I've been here too long.

I tear myself away, and stand up. "I need to go." Mum starts to protest, but I cut her off. "I need to get out of here. There are guards outside, and they're looking for me. When they work out I'm here, they'll come after you." My voice starts to crack. "I'm sorry, Mum."

She shakes her head. "When we saw you on TV, we thought it was a mistake. We thought you were at school. But then we heard what the government was saying, about their young recruits, and we realised they'd taken you. And then you were on a wanted poster, with that horrible gun."

She points at the TV. "Then they showed that nasty appeal, asking you to come here. Asking you to visit your father. And we knew it was a trap.

"It wasn't us, Bex. We didn't ask you to come. We didn't give them permission to take those awful photos. If there are guards out there, they're not going to let you walk away."

"It's OK, Mum. If I go now, I might make it out before they realise I'm here."

"Do you know what you're doing?"

"If I can't get out, I'll set off the fire alarm. I'll make sure I'm near an exit and I'll get away. I promise."

"When we saw you with that gun and that armour …"

"Mum, I …"

She holds up a hand.

"I don't care what you've done, Bex. I know you'll do what you need to do." I nod, and my face is wet with tears again. "You got away from the army?" I nod. "Good. They had no right to take you from school. It makes me sick, what they've done." She takes my hands in hers. "You're worth more than that. You want to fight for us? For yourself?" I'm sobbing, loudly now, and all I can do is nod in agreement. "Then you do what you have to do. Look after yourself, Bex. Be careful. But if it takes a gun, if it takes everything you have to protect yourself from the people ruining this country, then you do it. You hear me?"

"Yes, Mum." My voice is a rough whisper.

"And don't think about us. We're the past. You're the future. Fight for yourself, and make a future worth living in. Don't give up." She grips my hands tightly as she speaks.

"I'll try."

"And you have friends?" I nod. "Good friends? Then look after them, too. And never give up on them." She looks down at her wheelchair. "Find happiness where you can, Bex, even in the middle of the fight. Don't wait for this to end before you give yourself permission to live."

She pulls me into another embrace.

"You're a hero, Bex. You always have been. Don't give up."

I hold tight, my arms round her shoulders.

And my whole body tenses as we hear noises in the corridor outside. Shouting. Someone barking orders.

I freeze. I've been here too long. I stand up, and look around the room. There are net curtains at the window, but outside I can see the shapes of two guards in black armour, blocking my only escape.

There's a cold feeling in my stomach as the panic hits. I'm trapped. Mum grabs my hand again.

"In there!" She hisses, pointing at the door to her bedroom. "Get under the bed. There are boxes under there – get behind them. Take your parcel with you."

It's my only option. The noise in the corridor is getting closer. They've figured out that I'm here.

"And Bex? Don't move. No heroics. I'll make sure you get out. I can trigger the fire alarm from here." She points at a red box on the wall – the kind where you break the glass to set off the alarm.

"But …"

"I couldn't protect you at school. Let me protect you now. Don't try to help me – you'll only get yourself caught." She shakes her head over my objections. "You're getting out of here today – back to your friends. Back to *your* fight. This is *my* fight. Let me make a difference. Let me look after you."

I'm shaking my head, tears on my cheeks. I hadn't meant to put her in danger.

"Promise me. Promise me that what I do here will make a difference."

"Mum …"

"Promise me."

I nod, through tears. I step away, dropping Mum's hands, and pick up my box. I run through to the tiny bedroom, leaving the door ajar, and crawl under the bed. I pull myself up from the end, the action I learnt under barbed wire on the assault course. I hide against the wall behind the boxes, pulling the valance down behind me and kicking my parcel into place against my feet. I pull the gun from my waistband, push myself onto my side, and take aim at the door.

Conversation

Ketty

We pull into the car park, and I'm amazed to see that Ellman's registered address really is an ordinary nursing home. A long, two-storey building set back from the road, a tree-lined car park in front. Nothing special. Nothing posh. We drive past a line of parked cars, and pull up behind the troop carrier at the entrance.

I step down from the passenger seat and walk up to the guards at the door. I wait for them to salute me first, then I return the gesture.

"Any trouble?"

"No, Sir."

"Patrols in the gardens?"

"Yes, Sir."

"And no sign of our recruit?"

"No, Sir."

"Good work."

I reach out for the door, and one of the guards sweeps in and opens it for me.

"Sir!"

I walk into a glazed entrance porch. The double doors ahead of me are locked, and I knock on the window to attract the attention of whoever is manning the desk. I shield my eyes with one hand and look through into the hallway. There's a group of people in pale green uniforms at the desk, huddled together in conversation. I knock on the window again.

One of them looks up, gives me a wave, and presses the button to unlock the door. I push it open, and walk across the hallway towards them. The conversation falls silent.

"Can I help you?"

The receptionist eyes my fatigues and tries to hide the look of concern on her face.

"Here to see Mrs Ellman. Government business." She nods. I look around at the staff, sensing the guilty silence in the air. "Something wrong?"

"We've had a small problem. Nothing to worry about." She flashes me a nervous grin. I fix her with a recruit-scaring look, and raise an eyebrow. "We … err … we've lost a delivery driver. They came in, asked to use the toilet, and now we can't find them." She waves a hand dismissively. "I'm sure it's nothing. We'll sort it out. No one's raised an alarm."

I can't hide my smile.

Ellman. Here already? Couldn't resist the Daddy bait?

I pull the radio from my belt and activate it.

"Francis."

"Sir."

"I want patrols around the building. Take a member of staff and put guards outside the Ellmans' windows, and next to all the exit doors. Now."

"Yes, Sir."

I look up at the group, watching me in silence. I pick a young woman with streaks of pink in her hair.

"You. Can you find their room from the outside?"

"Yes." She sounds nervous.

"Go outside to the soldiers, and show them where to go. Quietly. Don't let anyone inside the building know you're there."

"Yes," she says, and hurries off. The receptionist lets her out of the doors.

I lift the radio again.

"Francis, get me four guards in here."

"Yes, Sir."

I put the radio back on my belt, look back at the receptionist, and give her an unfriendly smile. "I'm sure you'll get it sorted." I check my watch. "I'm sure it won't take you

94

very long. And if you find the driver, make sure you hand them over to the guards outside."

"OK, if you think that's necessary."

"I do. And while you're searching, would you direct me to Mrs Ellman's room?"

She nods, distracted. "Absolutely. Absolutely." She looks at her colleagues. "Pat. Could you take the officer to Liz's room?"

Pat steps forward, a friendly smile on her face. "Come with me."

I follow her through a set of double doors. There's a ladies' toilet on the right. The door is open, and as we walk past I can see a caretaker on a ladder, pushing up sections of ceiling tile and shining a torch into the space above.

Good luck finding her in there. That's not what she's here for.

Something on the floor of the room catches my eye.

"Excuse me," I say to Pat, and step into the toilets.

It's an ID card, for a delivery company. The name is wrong, and she's wearing glasses and a ridiculous wig, but the face is Ellman.

Got you.

I step into the corridor as the armoured guards arrive. Pat waves us on, and we follow her together. I turn to the guards on my left.

"I want you two outside the door. No one comes out, unless they're with me. Detain and restrain anyone else leaving the room. I don't care if they're 90 years old and they look like your granny. Understand?"

"Yes, Sir."

"And you," I wave at the guards on my right, and hand the ID card to the woman in armour walking next to me. "I want you two patrolling up and down this corridor. Anyone answering this description, I want them detained. Defend yourselves if you have to, but I want her alive."

The woman nods, showing the ID card to her partner. "Yes, Sir."

All four guards draw their guns.

Pat looks terrified as we walk up to room 50. "Here we are," she chirps, trying to be cheerful.

"Thank you, Pat. Now, get yourself back to reception and get rid of the crowd of people there. Get yourselves out of the way. All of you. Hide in the office or the dining room – I don't care. Just leave the entrance hall empty." She looks as if she's going to protest. "It's for your own safety." She nods, and hurries away along the corridor.

I pull the radio out again.

"Francis? Take over at reception. And don't let anyone in or out of the building. Wait for my clearance."

"Yes, Sir."

"And if I'm not out of here in ten minutes, send someone in."

"Sir. Will do."

The guards position themselves, one on each side of the doorway. I clip the radio to my belt, and step between them to the door.

*****

"Mrs Ellman?" I put on my best commander-charming smile. "Pleased to meet you." I walk into the room and hold out my hand. She pushes her wheelchair towards me, and stops to shake my hand. I can't help remembering the feeling of being trapped in a chair like hers. Of relying on other people to look after me. Of powerlessness. I force myself to keep smiling. The door closes behind me as I step inside.

The room is small. There's a chair for guests, a sideboard covered in framed photos, and a couple of bookshelves. Nowhere for a disguised delivery driver to hide. Two doors to other rooms, one slightly open. Across the room, under the window, is a hospital bed. The man lying in it is small and frail, and the monitoring wires and needles in his arms are uncomfortably familiar.

Jackson. I'm so close to catching her.

His eyes are closed, but his hollow cheeks are wet with tears. He doesn't react as I walk towards him.

"And this must be Mr Ellman."

I turn back. She's watching me, arms folded. She's smiling, but there's steel behind that smile. She wants me to understand whose space I'm in.

"Won't you sit down?" She indicates the chair beside her.

"Thank you." I stand for a moment longer, looking around the room. The books on the shelves. The paintings on the wall. The photos in frames on the sideboard. I lean in to take a closer look. Every photo is of the Ellman family. Mum, Dad, Bex. Baby Bex, toddler Bex, Bex enjoying the beach, Bex sitting on a donkey, Bex holding a medal for some sporting achievement – all with mummy and daddy beside her. I feel an unexpected stab of jealousy for this impossibly happy family, until I remember the wheelchair, and the hospital bed. The feeling of power, when I pinned Bex against the mud with Jackson and gave her the bruises she deserved.

Not so happy now, are you, Bex?

I hide a smirk, and sit down.

"Mrs Ellman," I begin, watching her carefully. She watches me back, her gaze steady and defiant. "My name is Ketty Smith. I was a Senior Recruit at your daughter's training camp. I'm here to find out whether you know anything about her disappearance."

She raises her eyebrows, arms still crossed. "Disappearance? From where? Army camp? As far as we knew, she was at school. I wrote letters, but the school started returning them unopened. The first we heard about an army camp was when those posters started showing up on TV. We assumed there'd been some sort of mistake."

Of course you did.

I shake my head. "No mistake, Mrs Ellman. I was one of her commanding officers, and it was on my watch that she chose to leave the camp without authorisation. I'm here to see if I can clear up some of the confusion. Do you know why she ran away?"

There's a pause, as she takes in what I've said. She leans forward slightly, and looks me in the eye. "Sorry for not understanding the complexities of this situation, Miss Smith, but wouldn't *you* run away if you'd been taken somewhere against your will?"

I allow myself a smile. "Desertion is a very serious offence, Mrs Ellman. We'd like to know what drove Bex to it, and what we can do to make sure it doesn't happen again."

She smiles. "I'd think it would be rather hard to stop it from happening again, if she's not currently under your command."

I'm losing ground in this discussion. This broken woman thinks she holds the power here, and she doesn't like me threatening her family. I glance around the room again, at the photos and the hospital bed. Maybe she thinks she has nothing to lose. Nothing I can take from her.

I stand up. "So you haven't seen Bex since she left the camp?"

She shakes her head, and points at the faint silhouettes of the guards outside the windows. "Why would she come here? If she really is a deserter, then why would she walk into this?"

Good question. And I think you know the answer.

"So she isn't crouching in a cupboard somewhere, listening to us?"

Her mother laughs. "Really, Miss Smith? In here?" She spreads her arms to indicate the small room.

I roll my eyes. "It's Corporal Smith. And you won't mind if I take a look around."

She waves her hand at the doors. "Please do."

I watch her for a moment. Bex is here. I'm sure she is. And yet here's her mother, inviting me in. Inviting me to look around.

I meet her eyes as I pull the handgun from the holster at my waist and turn towards the closed door. She gives me a disapproving look.

"Is that really necessary, Corporal?"

"I believe it is, yes." I wave the gun in her direction. "Stay where you are, please."

I step over to the door and rest my hand on the handle. I lean my ear against the wood, but there's no sound coming from inside. Carefully I pull the door open and swing the gun to cover the room. It's dark, but there's a light pull on a long, dangling cord. I aim the gun at chest height, and pull the light on.

There's no one here. A wheelchair-accessible bathroom with plenty of space, and nowhere to hide. The shower curtain is pulled back, so there are no hidden spaces. I switch off the light and turn back to the living room.

Mrs Ellman shrugs at me. I step to the second door. This one's already open, and the room is lit by another window. I look back into the living room, at Mrs Ellman's infuriating smile, and then turn and kick the door open. It smashes into the wall with a satisfying crack.

It's a bedroom. Single bed, bedside table, wardrobe, dressing table. I circle into the room, gun ready. There's no space to hide under the dressing table. I step across the room and pull open the wardrobe doors – first one, then the other, keeping my gun trained inside. I reach in, past the clothes, and grab handfuls of bags and shoes, throwing them onto the floor. No one hiding.

I step over to the bed. There's a valance hanging from the mattress to the floor. As I reach down to pull it up, there's a sound of breaking glass from the living room, followed by the impossibly loud wail of the fire alarm.

That was your plan? Get me out of the room and hit the alarm? Evacuate the building? How does that help?

I think it through. What if Bex isn't in the bedroom? What if she's hiding somewhere else in the building? What if she's slipped in and out of this room already? This could give her the chance to walk away with everyone else as they leave. I pull out my radio.

"Francis!"

"Sir!"

"Get guards to the doors. Cover all the exits. Check *everyone*. Ellman's using the fire alarm to get out of the building."

"Yes, Sir!"

And then I realise that all the security doors will be automatically unlocked. The staff will respond. The fire engines will arrive, and the chaos will swamp me and my guards. All the exit doors will be crowded, with people rushing to leave the building. No time for security checks. No ID controls. We can no longer control this situation.

I pull up the valance, gun ready, and find a row of boxes. I try the end of the bed, but the boxes go all the way back to the wall. I pull one out, near the foot of the bed, but its too dark to see what's behind. More boxes? Bex isn't here. She's already making her way to an exit.

The fire alarm is wailing. I'm running out of time.

And I know what to do.

If I can't take Bex back to London, maybe I can take her mother.

Rendezvous

Bex

The fire alarm screeches and it's all I can do to stay still. I've listened to Ketty threatening my mother, and I've watched as she stalked me through the bedroom, kicking the door open and dumping Mum's belongings on the floor. I'm cramped, I'm hurting, and I'm angry.

But I promised Mum, and now she's got control of Ketty. She's got a plan, and I've promised to let her fight for me.

I want to shoot. I want to burst out from under the bed, gun blazing. I want to pin Ketty to the wall and watch her bleed.

But if I do that, whatever Mum has planned won't save me. Ketty has a gun. Right now, she doesn't know I'm here. If I try anything, Mum's plan fails, and we both take bullets. Ketty wins.

Ketty pauses as the fire alarm sounds. She's on her knees next to the bed, and she turns towards the door. She pulls out a radio and orders guards to cover the exits. I relax a little. She doesn't know where I am.

And then she turns back, and lifts the valance.

I hold my breath. If she finds me, I have to shoot, and then she'll shoot back. I'm trapped here and my aim is blocked, so I can't stop her. I'm pinned down by boxes and I can't move. I'm trapped, and I'm an easy target. If she finds me, she can kill me, and then she won't need Mum and Dad any more. She can shoot them as well, and blame it on me, or say they were helping me. And then no one gets out of here.

I shouldn't have come. I've put my parents in danger. I should have stayed away.

But Ketty isn't here for me. She didn't storm in here with backup. She didn't know I was here. She's still searching.

She would be here, with or without me.

I can let this play out, find out what she wanted. I can still get out of here. We can all still walk away.

She moves to the foot of the bed and lifts the valance again. My parcel blocks her view of my feet.

She comes back to the side of the bed and starts to pull one of the boxes out. I feel it move away from my knees, and I tighten my grip on my gun. I'm holding my breath as she pulls the box all the way out, drops her head and looks under the bed.

My pulse is a hammer, shocking my entire body with every heartbeat. The fire alarm seems to slow as the sound rises and falls. I'm seconds away from discovery.

And then she stops. She pushes the box back, drops the valance, and stands up.

I let myself breathe again.

She walks out, back into the living room.

"Mrs Ellman," she shouts above the noise of the fire alarm. "I think its time we were leaving."

"I think so, too." There's a smile in my mother's voice, and I can't help smiling as well. Ketty as evacuation nurse. Mum has her completely under control.

But Ketty isn't finished with us yet.

"I think I'm going to take you for a ride, Mrs Ellman. How would you like a trip to London?" Ketty's voice is clearer now. She's sounding confident. And she's taking Mum.

Before I can move, before I can react, Mum shouts across Ketty. "That sounds lovely. Take me anywhere you like, as long as it's away from here. Now let's get out of this burning building, Corporal. The nurses will be here in a second, so if you want to decide where I go, you'd better make a move."

My mind races. Can they accuse Mum of helping me? Can they put her on trial? Do they have any evidence?

I promised. I promised I would get out, that I would carry on fighting. I can't save her without giving myself up.

"If you want to decide where I go, you'd better make a move."

She's giving herself up. She's trading herself for my freedom. The nightmares are coming true, and there's nothing I can do to stop her.

The fire alarm screams as Ketty pushes Mum away.

*****

The door to the corridor slams shut, and my mother is gone. I listen for movement in the living room, but there's nothing louder than the fire alarm. I think about my next move.

I'm wearing a staff uniform, and they don't know I changed my clothes and hair, so I should be able to walk out with the evacuation. The building isn't on fire – I heard the glass break in the living room. Mum set off the alarm. But the firefighters will come anyway, and check the rooms. Someone will come and rescue Dad. The chaos will definitely work in my favour. But if they know the building is safe, they'll leave guards to watch for me.

There's a sound from the next room. The door opens, and someone walks in, calling Mum's name. Then someone else is talking to Dad, and shouting instructions. I can hear three, maybe four voices in the living room. I nudge my parcel out of the way with my feet, and push myself out from under the bed. I step away, into the corner of the room, push the gun back into my waistband and straighten my clothing. I open the box, and pull out the glasses, then shake out my pony tail. It's not much, it will help to cover my face.

I need to get my clothes out of her room. I can't leave evidence that I was here. I kick through the pile of bags on the floor, and find one large enough to hide my clothes, but smart enough to be mistaken for a handbag. I make sure it's empty, and throw everything from the parcel inside. I pull the box apart, and push the pieces of cardboard into the bag as well. I close the zip, and put the strap over my shoulder.

I'm just about to leave, when I see a pile of letters on the dressing table. Stamped, franked, and marked 'Return to sender'. Letters to me. Letters from Mum. I grab the pile, and cram it into the bag as well.

I step out into the living room. Four carers are standing round Dad, hooking his wires and cables up to a mobile battery unit. One of them looks up as I walk over.

"Who are you? What are you doing?"

"Just checking the bedroom," I shout over the siren. "No one there. Can I help here?"

The woman gives me a hard stare, then hands me a bundle of cables. "Keep this tidy while we get ready to move him."

I take the cables from her, and lift them out of the way as she leans over and checks the connections.

One of the other carers elbows me out of the way.

"You're not supposed to go back for personal belongings," she shouts, pointing at my bag.

I give her a guilty smile. "I was on my way back from the bathroom. You know. Seems silly to leave it behind."

She ignores me, and takes the cables from my hand.

"Ready to move?"

"Ready."

The four women take up positions around the bed, and I put one hand on the guard rail as they start to move Dad. We're walking towards the door, and in the corridor I can see soldiers in armour. I put my head down, and walk with the team. Out through the door, right onto the corridor, and out towards reception. If the soldiers see me, they don't notice that I'm not supposed to be there. We keep walking. I keep a tight grip on the bed rail.

Out through the security doors, wide open now for the evacuation. Out into the car park. The troop carrier is still parked in front, and there's a pickup truck outside the entrance. No sign of Mum or Ketty. I look out to where I parked the car, in time to see Neesh opening the door and climbing in, ducking down to find the keys under the seat. I feel a rush of gratitude, that there are people looking out for me today. Neesh has been watching from across the road. Like me, she's decided that chaos offers us the best chance of getting out.

I look around. The sirens of fire engines are starting to sound in the surrounding streets. The carers around Dad are pushing the bed away from the entrance, leading me towards the far side of the car park, far away from where I need to be, and I realise that I don't want to leave him. I'm walking with them, and I'm starting to panic. Images from my nightmares are running through my mind – losing Dad, losing Mum. Letting go of him will be the hardest thing I do today. I can't say goodbye. I can't even touch his hand as I leave. And I can't stop and let myself think about what I'm doing. I have to let him go.

The carers push him further into the car park, and I'm still walking with them, still holding on to the bed. I can't let the soldiers see me – not after what Mum's done for me. I close my eyes and will the nightmares to stop. I force myself to let go of the rail. I lift my hand, and before I can think about it I turn my back on him and walk away.

I blink back tears. He knows I was there. He knows.

I make my way along the front of the building, walking quickly, head down, as if I have somewhere important to be. I force myself to walk past the guards as they check everyone leaving through the emergency exits. I want to turn round, to run back and tell him I love him. To say goodbye. To rescue Mum. To have a happy ending.

But I can't. I have to meet Charlie and Neesh at the rendezvous point. I head towards the end of the building, past the kitchens, and into the service yard. Access to the yard is from a side street, away from the chaos and the streams of people moving to safety. I check over my shoulder that no one can see me as I cross the yard, and walk into a tree-lined residential street. I ditch the tabard and the top of the scrubs in one of the bins as I pass, so now I'm wearing pale green trousers and a white T-shirt. There's no reason for anyone to connect me to the nursing home as I walk to safety past the rows of terraced houses.

Two fire engines tear past me, lights and sirens splitting the air of the quiet street. I don't look up. Keep walking. Don't stop.

Charlie and Neesh are waiting in the car outside a supermarket. I walk up, open the door, and crawl into the back seat. Neesh looks at me in the rear-view mirror, waiting for my signal. I'm sure I haven't been followed, and I raise my hand where she can see it. She nods, and starts the car. Charlie turns round when we're on the road.

"You OK, Bex?"

I try to speak, but all I can do is rest my head against the back of the seat as the tears rush down my face.

"Did you see your Dad? Did you say goodbye?"

I nod. Charlie reaches back and puts a hand on my knee.

"Well done, Bex. You did it. You got in and out, and you slipped through their fingers."

I try to speak. I try to explain, but my voice dies in my throat. Charlie needs to know what happened. I force myself to whisper.

"Ketty was there."

"Ketty? At the nursing home?" I nod again. "Did she see you?"

"No. Almost, but no. But I think she knew I was there."

"What makes you say that? You got away, didn't you?"

I find my voice again. I need to tell her. I need her to know what it cost to get me out.

"Ketty took my Mum, Charlie. She's taking her to London." I'm sobbing again. "Mum went with Ketty so I could get away. She traded herself for me. I've just given them another prisoner."

Another prisoner, to go with Margie and Dr Richards. I think about Bracken, holding Margie by her hair in the farmyard. Dr Richards, pulling away from me as I tried to save her. Saunders, lying still on the cold concrete floor. Mum, punching the fire alarm. All the people I couldn't save.

And all the way back to Newcastle, I'm inconsolable, sobbing and crying and shouting on the back seat.

Captured

Ketty

We've radioed ahead, and Bracken is waiting as the troop carrier turns into the driveway of Belmarsh Prison.

"Welcome to your new home, Mrs Ellman."

She closes her eyes and takes a deep breath, ignoring me. She's been quiet since we drove away from the nursing home. I'm not sure she understood where she was going, but she can't avoid it now.

Did you think this was a game? An empty threat?

The vehicle comes to a stop in front of the entrance, and two of the guards open the rear doors and jump out. I stand up, and step round the wheelchair, releasing the brakes. I take the handles and push the prisoner to the open doorway.

It takes four guards to pick up the wheelchair and lower her down onto the road.

Bracken strides over, a look of thunder on his face.

"Corporal Smith! What on earth …?"

"Sir. Meet Mrs Ellman. Bex's mother. I think she prefers 'Liz'." And I can't hide my grin.

*****

"Ketty – you realise I need to get clearance for this? I can't just waltz in here and stash a prisoner in a Top Secret cell – a prisoner who's done nothing wrong."

I look around the empty waiting room, the door to the cells propped open on the far side. "It looks as if that's exactly what you've done, Sir."

Bracken rolls his eyes. "Give me a few minutes to get this sorted out with the brigadier."

"Yes, Sir. And don't forget we have reason to believe she helped her daughter escape."

"Thank you, Ketty. I think I'll try to play that angle down, seeing as we don't yet have Bex in custody."

I shrug. "Liz is the bait, Sir. This is how we'll get to Bex."

He gives me a long, furious stare, then marches out of the room.

I stand in the waiting room, a very satisfied smile on my face. If Ellman risked turning up at the nursing home to see her father, what will she do to get to her mother? She won't get in here. She won't even know that this place exists. All she knows is that I've got her mother – and she knows what I'm capable of. The feeling of power is back. I can do what I want to the woman in that cell, and no one will stop me.

Afraid yet, Bex?

*****

We start with an interrogation, the morning after the fire alarm.

The prison doctor visits Mrs Ellman in her cell, checks her medical status, makes a note of the drugs and assistance she needs, and then I'm cleared to run her through whatever questioning I choose. Technically it's Bracken who has the authority here, but I've worked with him long enough to know how to take the lead. Brigadier Lee is turning a blind eye. He doesn't want her here, and he's made it clear that he thinks I failed again when I let Bex get away.

Too bad, Sir. I rescued the nursing home operation. This is going to bring us our missing recruits.

A nursing team transfers her to the bed, gets her up in the morning, and dresses her for the interview in an orange jumpsuit. I talk Bracken through operating the recording suite, remembering the steps Conrad went through to set up the equipment, and I push Mrs Ellman into the interrogation room. I snap the handcuffs onto her wrists and make sure they're threaded through the loop on the table. She looks past me, at the mirror. I close the door, and take a seat, my back to the cameras. The recording light comes on over the door, and I lean back in my chair.

"Elizabeth Ellman," I say, slowly, watching her face.

She looks at me across the table, her eyes cold.

"That's *Mrs Ellman* to you, *Corporal* Smith."

I shrug. "I don't think so." She holds her gaze steady, and says nothing.

I consult the file on the table in front of me.

"Elizabeth Ellman. Formerly of Orchard House Nursing Home, Stockport." I look up. "I understand there was a fire at Orchard House yesterday. Or was that a prank? Some irresponsible person sounding the alarm, calling the fire brigade – wasting everyone's time?"

A smile tugs at the corners of her mouth, but she controls it.

"All those poor people, evacuated to the car park. Crutches. Wheelchairs. *Hospital beds.*"

That wipes the smile away. She closes her eyes and breathes deeply.

"Nothing to say?"

"Not to you."

I pull Bex's Wanted poster from the file.

"Rebecca Ellman. Your daughter?" She sits still, eyes still closed.

Starting to understand this, are you?

"Tell me, Elizabeth. When did you last see your daughter?"

She opens her eyes and shakes her head.

"When do you think I saw her, Corporal Smith?

I raise my eyebrows. "I think you saw her yesterday." I put the Wanted poster down on the table. "I think she walked into Orchard House disguised as a delivery driver. I think she asked to use the toilet, changed into a nursing home uniform, and ditched the disguise. I think she came to your room, said goodbye to her father, spoke to you, and then left. You punched the fire alarm to give her a chance to escape past my guards." There's a look of surprise on her face, as if she's just figuring out how Bex got in. "And I think that makes you guilty of aiding and abetting a known terrorist."

That's like a slap in the face. She sits up straight.

That's right, Elizabeth. Life in here if you're lucky, firing squad if you're not. Regretting breaking that glass yet?

"Anything you want to tell me? Anything you want to correct about my theory?"

She glares at me, and there's the steel behind her eyes. She speaks slowly and clearly.

"I don't know what you're talking about."

I sit for a moment, returning her glare, then I lean forward and take something out of the file. I flip it over and over between my fingers.

"That's disappointing, Elizabeth," I say, turning the ID card towards her and placing it in front of her on the table. I wave my hand, dismissively. "I know the hair is ridiculous, and the glasses are just plain funny, but under that disguise, I think we can both figure out the identity of the missing delivery driver."

She looks down, and reaches out awkwardly to pick up the card, restricted by the handcuffs. She sighs, and hunches over in the chair.

"I found that in the ladies' toilet, Elizabeth. Next to reception at Orchard House. Just before I came to your room." She takes a long look at the card, and throws it back onto the table. I pick it up and slip it back into the file. "So. Let's try this again. When did you last see your daughter?"

She hesitates for a moment, slumped forward in her chair. Then she sits up straight and fixes me with a determined stare.

"I don't remember."

"Is that so?" I let a smile spread across my face. "You're sure about that? Because I'd hate to have to jog your memory."

Her voice is quiet, but determined, her gaze unwavering. "I don't remember."

"Well. I think we're done here. Don't you, Elizabeth? I think I'll give you some time to sit and think about everything we've talked about. See if you remember anything you might want to tell me." I smile.

She glares back at me, defiant.

*****

I join Bracken in the recording suite.

"Anything we can use?"

"Ketty Smith. You are one hard-nosed, determined, scary woman."

I smile. "Thank you, Sir."

"Is that how you used to run my camp?"

I shrug. "Didn't need to, Sir. The kids were much easier to scare."

He laughs, shaking his head. "What are you planning to do with the footage?"

"I thought we might turn The Bex Ellman Slot on PIN into a recurring feature. What do you think, Sir?"

He shakes his head again. "That might just work."

Mrs Ellman is back in her cell, the cameras are offline, and our encounter is backed up on several of the boxes in the recording suite. All we need to do is choose a section of the recording to put out on the news tonight, and Bracken can take it to PIN.

Bracken plays the footage back, and we watch as Elizabeth refuses to talk. There's the dramatic change in body language when she realises what we're accusing her of, and the resignation when she sees the ID card. We pick a suitable section, transfer it to a memory stick, and head back to Whitehall to run it past Brigadier Lee.

*****

It's after lunch when the car drops us back at the office. Bracken takes the memory stick to Lee's office while I make sure there's nothing urgent in today's briefing papers.

Back at my desk, I call the hospital again.

"Nevill Hall Hospital, High Dependency Ward."

"Corporal Ketty Smith, calling about Liam Jackson. Is there an update?"

"Corporal. We were wondering when you'd call." I wait, my breath catching in my throat, for the nurse to say something else. "He's not so good today. There's an infection in his lung. We've started him on antibiotics, and we're doing everything we can. We should have an update for you in the morning."

My throat is dry, and my breath comes in shallow gasps. I force myself to thank the nurse and hang up the phone.

Keep fighting, Jackson. Keep fighting.

Fear

Bex

I haven't slept. Charlie comes in after the morning delivery and brings me a mug of tea, but I don't want to talk. I lost two people yesterday, and it was worse than the nightmares. Letting go of Dad – that wasn't a panic dream. That was real, and it was final. I don't get to try again. I don't get to say another goodbye.

And Mum. Ketty has my mother, and the thought of what she might do makes me sick. I think about Ketty, pinning me down in the woods while Jackson punched me over and over, every blow bruising my ribs and crushing the air from my lungs. Margie's face when they'd beaten her up, too. The things Jake told us about his imprisonment at Camp Bishop, after the rescue. Mum needs nurses and carers and medicine. The things that Ketty could do, just by withholding her care – I realise that my nightmares are only just beginning.

Ketty has my mother. Ketty is cruel and violent, and she'll use Mum to get to me.

I couldn't save Mum. Like all the other people I've lost, I couldn't hold onto her. I couldn't protect her.

Charlie comes back maybe an hour later. I haven't moved. I haven't touched the tea. She looks at the full mug, shakes her head, and sits down on the bed. She puts a hand on my knee.

"Bex," she says, quietly. "Bex, I'm so sorry."

I close my eyes and take a deep breath.

"Bex? You've got to keep going. Let me get you some breakfast, while you get up and have a shower. You'll feel better."

I want to shout. I want to show Charlie how much this hurts, but I can't move. My arms and legs are too heavy. My eyes are swollen and puffy from crying. My head is full of black thoughts and I can't lift it from the pillow. There's a weight like a rock in my stomach. All I can do is lie here and think about Mum.

"Hey, Bex." Amy is standing in the doorway. "Come and have some breakfast. Dan's talking about making sandwiches."

Charlie turns to look at her, shaking her head, and Amy's expression changes. She hesitates for a moment, then she walks in and kneels down on the floor in front of me. I'm staring across the room at the wall, and she kneels in my eyeline, sitting back on her heels. When I don't react, she leans forward and pushes one arm under my shoulder, wrapping the other round my back and holding me tightly.

It's as if something inside me thaws. I reach out and hug her back, clinging to her. It's like finding a life raft after swimming for hours in an empty sea. She doesn't move. She doesn't ask anything of me, but for the first time I feel as if someone understands.

*****

"Charlie says you were amazing yesterday." Dan puts a plate in front of me, loaded with one of his trademark sandwiches. He sits down across the table and waits for me to take a bite. It's past lunchtime, and I've dragged myself to the kitchen. Charlie's right – I do feel better after a shower and a change of clothes.

I shake my head. "Not amazing enough."

"Oh, come on. You got in and out, right under the noses of the guards. You gave Ketty the slip. It sounds as if you called out all the fire engines in Stockport to do it, and you walked away! That's amazing, Bex."

I look at him for a moment. I need him to understand. My voice is a whisper, but it gets stronger as I push myself to speak.

"Ketty took my Mum. My Mum is in London with the person who beat me up, and beat up Margie and Jake. The person who shot at all of us when we drove out of camp, and tried to gas us in the bunker. She came for me, and she took Mum instead." I can feel the tears starting again. "If she doesn't have me, what do you think she's going to do to my Mum?"

"Your Mum saved you, the way Charlie tells it. Gave herself up to let you walk away. Your Mum's a hero."

"She is a hero. But she's a hero who needs carers and nurses and doctors. What if Ketty doesn't give her those things? What if they take away her medication and her carers and her wheelchair?" I shake my head and brush away tears. "That's on me, Dan. That's my fault."

"She had a choice, Bex," Dan says, gently.

"No, she didn't. I stayed too long with Dad, and I made this happen. If she hadn't gone with Ketty, I'd be in handcuffs in London right now. They'd be parading me around in an orange jumpsuit. You'd be seeing my face on the news tonight." Something is twisting inside me. There's a pain like a knife in my back, and I can't fill my lungs. "I couldn't sleep. I've been going over and over what happened yesterday, and everything comes down to me. I lost Mum. I gave Ketty another prisoner. I stayed too long, and I dragged my family into Ketty's war." I push the plate away, my stomach too knotted to eat.

Dan thinks for a moment. "So Ketty was there to catch you?"

I shake my head. "I don't think so."

"She didn't know you were coming?"

I shrug.

"So what was she doing in your parents' room?"

"Asking my Mum questions. Being a bully."

He leans forward. "Bex. If she was there anyway, and she was questioning your Mum, who's to say she wasn't planning to take her back to London, whether you were there or

116

not? Maybe that's what she was there for – to take your Mum away." He puts his hand in mine. "Maybe there's nothing anyone could have done."

"I could have stopped her. I could have turned myself in."

"And now you'd both be in London. The face of the resistance, on TV with her mother, in matching jumpsuits." He takes my other hand. "Come on, Bex. Don't blame everything on yourself. Sometimes the bad guys win, and there's nothing you could have done." I shake my head, but he carries on. "You got in, you got out. That's the story of yesterday. What happened to your Mum – that's part of a different story. You got to see your Dad, he knows you were there, and you got away. Hold on to that." He gives my hands a squeeze.

I think about what he's saying. Maybe Ketty wasn't there for me. Maybe she was after Mum all along. Maybe it wasn't my fault – maybe Ketty was always going to take her away.

I don't know what to think. I hold Dan's hands as defeat hits me and tears stream down my cheeks.

Jake is right. I'm no hero. I'm a pawn in the game, and it doesn't matter what I do. Someone else always wins.

*****

I'm still at the table when Amy comes in to ask about cooking dinner. I've eaten the sandwich – I let Dan persuade me to take a bite, and realised how hungry I was. I hadn't eaten since yesterday morning. Dan and I have been drinking tea all afternoon, and we're talking about going back to school. He's doing a good job of keeping me distracted, asking what I'll do on my first day back. Which lesson I'll look forward to most. Which teacher will be most disappointed to see us again.

I know we're not going back, but it beats thinking about Ketty.

He turns to Amy, and I sit back and listen as my friends talk about normal things. An everyday conversation that makes me wish I had nothing else to worry about. I'm smiling as they discuss what to cook.

And then Jake is running into the room, shouting my name. His face is white, and he's breathless.

"She's on TV, Bex. She's on TV."

Dan's asking who he's talking about, and Amy's asking him to repeat himself, but I already know who it is.

I feel as if I've been dropped into icy water. I'm shaking, and I can't move. Amy and Dan are talking to me, but I can't hear them over the sound of my own heartbeat, drumming in my ears.

Amy sits down next to me, her hand on my arm. I'm looking at her, but I can't make sense of what she's saying. Jake is standing in the doorway, looking lost. Dan is talking to him, and looking across at me.

Slowly, I push myself to my feet. Amy stands with me and takes my arm. I force myself to walk to the door, where Jake steps aside to let me pass. Down the corridor, through the living room door. Step after step. Charlie is waiting, her hands reaching out to me.

The TV is on, PIN headlines scrolling across the bottom of the screen. But I'm not reading them. I'm not seeing them at all.

I'm seeing Mum.

Mum in an orange jumpsuit. Mum handcuffed to a table.

Mum facing Ketty in an interrogation room.

I don't know what happens next. I think I cry out. I'm on my knees on the living room floor and all I can see is Mum, her face moving from defiance to fear as Ketty speaks.

There are gentle hands on my shoulders and arms, lifting me up and sitting me down on the sofa. I can't take my eyes off the screen. Charlie and Amy sit with me, arms around my shoulders, holding my hands, as we watch the report. Jake sits on his bed and Dan stands in the doorway.

PIN cuts back to the newsreader, who flashes up a photo of me and calls me a wanted terrorist. She praises the arrest of my mother, and announces the charge against her.

She's charged with aiding and abetting a known terrorist.

That's a firing squad offence.

She's being held for helping me.

"They can't!" My voice rasps in my throat. "They've got no proof! Ketty didn't see me. She can't prove I was there."

And then the screen changes, and there's a photo of my ID card. The fake ID from the delivery company. The ID I put in my pocket at the entrance as I walked in, before I changed my clothes. ID I must have dropped as I stuffed my clothes into the box.

Proof.

I slump back on the sofa. Charlie and Amy tighten their hold on my shoulders. The news report runs the footage of Mum again, her face changing as Ketty accuses her of help- ing me.

The newsreader returns, and introduces studio guests who want to talk about the arrest. They're there to discuss what will happen to my mother now. Discuss her life, as if it's just another political story. As if she doesn't matter.

Dan steps over to the TV and turns it off.

I can't breathe. I'm taking tiny, painful gasps of air, but I can't seem to get enough. My vision is blurring, and the sofa seems to be falling backwards. Charlie wraps both arms around me, and I push my head into her shoulder. Amy strokes my hair and Dan kneels down in front of me and takes my hands.

No one speaks. There's nothing to say.

We don't move for a very long time.

Debrief

Ketty

"So where's our missing recruit, Corporal?"

Lee lounges in one of the chairs in front of Bracken's desk and watches me as I stand in the middle of the office. Bracken sits behind the desk, staring at the paperwork in front of him. It's early, so he hasn't had time to balance his whisky breakfast with coffee.

Thanks for the support, Sir.

"As far as I can see, your entire Nursing Home plan was a waste of time. Ellman got to see her father with no consequences. You let her slip through your fingers, and you cost us money, resources, and reputation while you did so." I try to protest, but Lee holds up his hand. "I have not given you permission to speak, Corporal. I think it would be good for you to listen for a change." He smirks at Bracken, who gives him a brief smile, but doesn't look up at me.

Lee spreads his hands in an extravagant shrug.

"It seems to me that what you got out of this episode is one more prisoner. A prisoner who, as far as we can tell, knows nothing about the resistance and nothing about the terrorists. She might – *might* – know where Ellman was hiding while you were on your knees scrabbling around under her bed, but I fail to see the relevance of this information, now that we know Ellman left the premises during the fire alarm. I'm sure it fills you with great satisfaction, locking up a woman who needs round-the-clock care, just because she called half the firemen in Stockport to confuse you and your guards, but I have yet to see any real benefit from this whole affair."

I wait for permission to respond, but he holds up his hand again.

"I haven't finished. Corporal, can you explain to me why it took all those soldiers and vehicles and weapons specialists to bring one wheelchair-bound woman from Stockport to London? If all you wanted was Elizabeth Ellman, why not just walk in and take her? All you'd need is a car and your own two hands."

I can feel the warmth rushing to my face as Lee details my failures. I stand up straight and stare at the wall above Bracken's head while Lee takes my decisions apart.

"And how *did* Ellman get in and out so easily?"

It was hardly easy, Sir.

"It seems to me that she drove a vehicle she's not licenced to drive," he starts counting his accusations off on his fingers, "up to the door of the home. She blagged her way past your guards with a false ID card, waltzed through several sets of security doors, vanished into thin air and reappeared in her parents' room. From there, she vanished again, and then walked out of the front doors, past the fire crews who were running in. Past your guards, past the nursing home staff, and past you – but you were too busy kidnapping her mother to notice. She walked out of the car park, and – correct me if I'm wrong – but that's where we lost her. No one has any idea where she went next. Oh – and the car vanished, too. No one seems to know when that happened.

"Am I close, Corporal? Any of that ring any bells?"

My mouth is dry, and I'm focusing on slowing my breathing. I want to fight back. I want to explain, but I'm in enough trouble without disobeying a direct order.

"Corporal?"

"Yes, Sir."

"So you're happy to accept responsibility for the disasters of the last couple of days?"

That's not fair.

"Sir, I …"

"Katrina Smith! You will answer the brigadier's question!" Bracken brings his fist down on the desk, hard. Lee gives him an amused smile, then turns to look at me. I feel like a specimen under a microscope. I feel utterly exposed.

I clear my throat. "I'm not, Sir."

Lee looks at me in mock surprise. "You're not?"

"No, Sir." I stare hard at the wall behind Bracken.

Lee spreads his hands again, in an invitation.

"Given the facts, perhaps you would be good enough to tell me why you don't think that any of this is your responsibility?"

I take a moment to put my thoughts in order.

"Sir. If I could explain." Lee nods. "The trap we set for Ellman was planned with your approval, and the approval of Colonel Bracken. I judged that Ellman's father provided us with a temptation that Ellman would not be able to resist. I know Ellman, and I know how she thinks. And I was right."

Lee sits back in his chair and watches me, faint amusement on his face.

"The decision to bring her mother back to London was taken in the moment when I realised we had lost track of Ellman. I had no plan to use her mother – I was hoping her father's condition would be enough to put her into our hands. But the opportunity presented itself, and I realised that Mrs Ellman is a weapon we can use against her daughter. A weapon we can continue to use for as long as we need to. While we have Elizabeth, Bex will be living in fear. Any move she might be planning to make against us will be tamed, in case we punish her mother for her actions. Any direct action the terrorists decide to take will be with the knowledge that Mrs Ellman could be harmed."

I'm warming to my subject now. I'm beginning to think that this could work.

"And all we need to make this happen is one cell, time in the interrogation room, and a slot on PIN whenever we need it. I guarantee you that, if Ellman and her friends weren't watching every minute of PIN news coverage before today, they'll be glued to the screen after today. It's the only way for Ellman to know whether her mother is still alive.

"We've got her, Sir – Ellman, and her friends. We haven't caught them, but I think we can control them."

And it will be my very great pleasure to take responsibility for that, Sir.

Lee doesn't move. He keeps his eyes fixed on my face, waiting for me to say something more. To say too much. Then he starts to clap, slowly. I can feel my cheeks flaming as he mocks my defence. I keep my gaze fixed on the wall.

"Very good, Corporal. Very good." The clapping stops. "Don't you think?" He turns to Bracken.

The Colonel nods. "It's an interesting suggestion."

Lee turns to me and grins. "It is. It is." He pauses, and looks down at his hands.

"OK, Corporal. I'll give you this assignment. Manage Ellman by putting her mother on TV. Monitor the terrorist chatter, and use Elizabeth to keep the resistance in line. The goal is still to bring in our missing recruits, but while we don't know where they are, this is the next best thing."

I have to focus on standing up straight. The sense of relief is making my knee shake.

"Thank you, Sir."

"And to make sure you're up to speed on everything that happened at Orchard House, I'll have the CCTV sent down for you to look at. See if you can spot your missing recruit – or anything else that might be useful."

"Yes, Sir."

"Dismissed, Corporal."

As I turn to leave the room, I try to catch Bracken's gaze, but his eyes are fixed on the desk in front of him.

Thanks for all your help there, Sir.

*****

Back at my desk, I make the call to the hospital. No change. Jackson is fighting the infection, but he's still hooked up to the machines. He still hasn't woken up.

Jackson, where are you when I need you? I could use some friendly respect right now. I want to tell you what happened. I want you to be impressed. I want you to be the one mocking me – not Lee, not Conrad, and not Bracken. I want you back.

Dangerous

Bex

I'm sitting at the table with Amy when Caroline and Neesh arrive. It's early, but we're all awake. We threw all the mattresses together on the living room floor last night, and Amy and Charlie slept next to me, stroking my hair and comforting me when I woke up screaming, time after time.

There's a mug of tea in front of me, and I'm drinking it slowly. I can't think about eating. Charlie opens the front door and shouts down the corridor for Dan and Jake to join us.

Caroline sits down opposite me, without looking at me. She concentrates on pulling sheets of paper out of her handbag and stacking them on the table.

"Well," she says, when everyone is crowded into the kitchen. "Does anyone want to explain what I saw on PIN last night?" Her voice is cold, and there's anger in her eyes. She still hasn't looked at me.

When no one speaks, she starts turning over sheets of paper and arranging them on the table. Printouts of CCTV footage, from the nursing home.

Me. Neesh. Ketty. Mum. Soldiers and nurses. A car park full of people and fire crews.

"How did you …?" Charlie begins, but Caroline holds up her hand.

"That's hardly important. What is important is that these images exist. If we have them, you can be sure that the government has them." She looks round the table, still avoiding my eyes.

"As far as I can piece together, your cosy little group took an unscheduled field trip two days ago. You went to Stockport, you infiltrated a nursing home that was surrounded by government guards, and you engineered a fire alarm to get yourselves out again." She stops, and takes a deep breath, her voice spitting with anger. "And the first I hear about it, the first clue I have that you've been making decisions behind my back, is a report on the evening news."

Jake starts to protest, but Caroline cuts him off. "I don't care which of you was there, and which of you was here. I don't care who knew about this, and who didn't. As far as I'm concerned, you're all guilty, and more importantly, you're all in danger."

"We took every precaution, Caroline." Charlie sounds apologetic. "We knew it would be dangerous, but we couldn't let Bex go alone."

Caroline turns towards her, her anger barely controlled. "My question, Charlie, is why did you let Bex go at all?"

"Come on, Caroline. You saw the news appeal."

"I did. And I also saw that it was a blatant attempt to lure a member of this group into custody. I assumed that you did, too. I assumed that all of you had more sense than to run head-first into a government trap."

Neesh shakes her head. "It wasn't like that. Bex's father really is seriously ill. We just wanted …"

"I don't care what you wanted!" Caroline slaps her hand onto the table, shouting, looking round at all of us. "I don't care what PIN bribes you with. *You do not leave this flat.* Do you understand?"

She's talking about me, as if I'm not here. She's talking about Dad as if he isn't real. About Mum, as if she's just a face on a screen. The heavy, black feeling comes back, and I have to put my elbows on the table and rest my head in my hands.

"We got away with it, Caroline." Neesh holds out one hand in a pleading gesture.

"Did you?"

"Bex got herself in and out."

"Without her ID card, or so PIN informs me."

Neesh bows her head. "Bex is safe. We got her back here."

"Oh? And which car did you use?"

Neesh looks surprised. "I borrowed it."

"From who? From someone who lives round here? From someone who could lead the soldiers right to our door?" She stabs one of the CCTV images with her manicured finger. "That car?"

Neesh looks at the image, and nods, her shoulders slumping.

Caroline takes a deep breath. No one else moves.

"Right. Well. Never mind who did what." She starts gathering up the images from the table. "I need you all to go and pack."

She wants us out of here. Out of the safe house. I sit up straight and look at her. "You're throwing us out?"

She looks directly at me for the first time, and I notice that her hands are shaking. "I should be throwing you out. You've put all our lives at risk. You've put Neesh's business at risk. You've put the entire safe house network at risk. I should be dumping you in a field somewhere with bullets in your heads and letting the government take you off my hands."

I can feel myself starting to panic. We're safe here. We're protected. We're hidden. I can't believe that this safety is ending.

"You can't …" Dan sounds indignant as Caroline speaks over him.

"I can. This is my safe house, and my network. I'm protecting you, and the people who came with you from the bunker, and two more flats full of people who want to help the resistance. Your actions," she looks at me again. "Your *stupid* decisions – they put everyone at risk. All the people I'm keeping safe. Not just you. Not just Bex. Everyone."

My hands are shaking. I clasp them together on the table and try to control the panic.

"Where are you sending us?" Charlie's voice is calm.

Caroline pushes the pile of paper back into her bag and places it carefully on the floor before she answers. She looks around the table again.

"Edinburgh. The OIE wants you across the border and away from anyone who might be tracking you."

Relief hits me in a wave. I slump back in my chair, gripping the edge of the table with my fingers. I close my eyes and take deep, calming breaths. We're safe. We're still safe.

And we're on the run again.

"I need you all packed and ready to leave by …" she consults her watch, "… twelve. No later. We'll take you in two groups. One rucksack each. Nothing that could connect you to here, to the shop, or to me or Neesh."

*****

I'm stuffing clothes into my rucksack. I don't have a lot of things to take with me, but we've all been provided with jeans, T-shirts and fleeces from the local charity shops, and I'm struggling to fit them all in. We're not carrying armour or guns – we handed those over to the cell when we arrived – but the extra clothes are filling my bag. The frustration is keeping me from thinking about what I've done.

I concentrate on packing. I reach up onto the bed for the next handful, and my fingers close round the pile of letters from Mum. This is everything. When these are in the bag, I'm packed. I'm ready to walk out and keep running.

I check the time. I've still got a few minutes before Caroline comes back for us. I pick up the letters and pull one out from the pile at random, pushing the others into the bag. I tear the envelope open and pull out a thin sheet of paper, covered with Mum's neat handwriting. I sit down on the floor, my back against the bed, and read.

My darling Bex,

We've been so worried. All the letters I've written since the start of term have been returned to me. Has the Recruit Training Service taken you away from school? Rushmere won't tell us anything – only that you're not in residence, and not expected back any time soon. I'm going to keep writing, and keep hoping that my letters make it to you.

I'm so sorry. I thought we could protect you. I thought we could make your life better, by sending you to Rushmere. I thought you'd have a chance to study and make friends and live a life that was about you, not about me and Dad.

Bex, wherever you are, I want you to know that we love you. You're our hero. You're our helper and our sunshine. Don't give up. This fighting can't go on forever, and when it's over you need to be ready to pick up your life and make it yours again. Don't let them define you. Don't let them change who you are.

We love you, Bex, and we're thinking of you. Wherever you go, and whatever happens, we'll be thinking about you. Be strong, beautiful girl.

Love, always,

Mum.

I read the letter over and over. I force myself to think about where Mum is now. What's happening to her. How my actions, and my mistakes, put her there.

The letter is smudged with tears when Charlie comes to the door.

"Ready to go?"

I wipe my eyes with the back of my hand and put the letter back in its envelope, and back into the pile in my bag.

"Yeah."

I stand up and pull the rucksack onto my shoulders, my hands shaking. I pause in the doorway and look back at the tiny room. Another place I've almost felt safe, and another place I have to leave. My fault, this time. I'm not the hero of this story – I'm the reason we have to move on. I screwed this up.

"I'm sorry," I say to the empty room, when Charlie is out of earshot. "I'm so, so sorry."

And I'm not sure who I'm talking to.

Location

Ketty

The CCTV footage arrives at ten. Lee sends me a flash drive that I can plug into the screen in Bracken's office, but he also sends a folder of still images that someone on the Terrorism Committee has already pulled from the footage.

I start with the stills.

Ellman, walking up to the door in her laughable disguise. My guards, letting her through. There's a shot of me walking out with Elizabeth, and several shots of the evacuation. Nothing useful.

Bracken waves me into his office, and I pull one of the chairs over to the screen.

"Anything interesting yet?"

"Not yet, Sir. I'm hoping the film will show me more than the stills."

Reviewing the film takes hours. There are ten different cameras, and at least forty minutes of footage from each location. I sit in the chair with a notebook on my knee, pausing the footage where it might show something interesting. Bracken leaves the room to fetch drinks for both of us while I stare at the images until my eyes start to hurt.

"Anything?" Bracken asks as he hands me a coffee.

"A few sightings of Ellman. Not much else." I take the cup and take a grateful sip. Staring at film of empty corridors isn't the best way to stay awake.

"Do we know how she got from the toilets to her parents' room?"

I smile. "Actually, we do. She seems to have changed – taken off the disguise, gone back to her natural hair colour – and put on a nursing home uniform. There's a shot of her walking down the corridor with the box she brought with her. That's where she must have hidden the clothes."

Bracken nods. "So she put some planning into this. Any idea where she bought the uniform?"

"None, Sir. But I don't think it was local. It's standard nursing scrubs – she'd be able to buy them in any major town."

"So no leads there?"

"I doubt it, Sir."

We both watch the screen. It's footage of the corridor outside Elizabeth's room. I've watched Bex go in, and I'm waiting to see her walk out, but the next person on screen is me. Me and my guards.

I rewind and watch the whole section again, just to make sure.

Where are you, Bex?

She never left the room. She was in there all the time. I think back to my search – where was she? I checked the living room and the bathroom, and there was nowhere for her to hide.

She must have been under the bed. Behind the boxes.

I was inches from catching her when her mother broke the glass on the fire alarm. I can feel my cheeks warming with the memory of Lee's assessment of my actions. Bracken looks down at me and points at the screen.

"So Ellman was in the room …?"

I clear my throat and try to sound unconcerned. "It seems so, Sir."

He looks at the images – at me opening the door. "Probably not a good idea to draw the brigadier's attention to this section of the footage."

"Probably not, Sir."

When she leaves the room, it's with the nursing team around her father's bed. I replay the footage several times until I'm sure of what I'm seeing. She's let her hair down, and she's carrying a bag instead of a box, but it has to be her. I note the time stamp on the camera, and track her progress until the bed is out of shot.

Now I know what to look for, it isn't hard to track her out of the front doors and into the car park.

Two minutes after she disappears from the corridor, she's heading out of the building, still holding the rail of her father's bed. The footage gets confusing here, with firefighters running past, blocking the view from the camera. The next time we see the bed, Bex has vanished.

I search for another car park camera to see whether I can track were she goes, but there's always someone in the way, or a vehicle blocking the line of sight.

Come on, Ellman. Just one more star appearance, and we'll know how you got away.

And then I notice the car. As Ellman leaves the home, another camera shows something strange. Someone crosses the street towards the evacuation, and instead of offering help or asking what's going on, they climb into one of the cars at the edge of the car park and drive it away.

Using the evacuation as a distraction?

I play the footage again, double-checking the time stamps. The driver has time to watch the chaos in the courtyard, notice Bex coming through the doors, and then let themselves into the car and drive away.

I play it again, and freeze the image. A short woman, dark skin, short dark hair. No one we've seen before, but we'll add her image to the wanted list. I move the film on until the car turns onto the road, and right in the corner of the screen I can pick out the number plate.

I can't help smiling. We've got the car. We've got the driver. Maybe that's all we need to find Bex.

*****

I phone the number plate through to the Police Liaison Office, and wait for their response. I'm back in my office with another coffee, leafing through the folder of still images. Bracken has his office back, and he couldn't wait for me

133

to close the door before heading to the filing cabinet. I left him to his whisky, and brought him a coffee to wash it down.

In the back of the folder there's a photocopied sheet showing the front and back of the ID card we found at the nursing home. I'd assumed that the delivery company was a fake, that the whole thing was a fiction, but there's a telephone number on the back of the card. I don't recognise the dialing code, but it can't hurt to give them a call.

I dial the number, and the phone rings twice.

"Roker Couriers, how can I help you?"

So far, so professional.

"I hope so. Can I drop off a parcel with you for delivery?"

"You certainly can. We accept parcels at several locations in Sunderland."

Bingo.

"What sort of parcel are you looking to send?"

"It's an awkward shape. I'm not sure how to package it. Maybe I should bring it in. Would you be able to help me?"

"Of course. Do you have a vehicle?"

"I do."

And he gives me an address in Sunderland.

*****

The Police Liaison Office calls back while I'm checking the location on the map opposite my desk. If the courier company is local to where Bex and the others are hiding, we need to focus our search on the North East. Sunderland, Gateshead, Newcastle. I just need to trace the car to the same area, and I'll have something useful to report to Brigadier Lee.

"Corporal Smith?"

"Yes. Do you have a trace for me?"

"We've located the vehicle. Do you have something to write with?"

I grab my pen and notebook from the desk and turn to a fresh page, cradling the phone under my chin.

"Go ahead."

"The car is registered to an address in Jesmond, Newcastle Upon Tyne."

It's my lucky day.

*****

I'm smiling when Bracken calls me into his office.

"You've found them?"

"I've narrowed down the search."

"And?"

"They're in the North East. Newcastle, probably – but we should look at the surrounding areas."

"Any leads?"

I lean over his desk and put two sheets of paper down in front of him.

"Courier company, and the car from the nursing home, Sir."

He raises his eyebrows. "This is good, Ketty. Two addresses, and that's before we've taken anyone in for questioning."

I nod, and I can't hide my smile.

"It looks as if Ellman has made her big mistake." He pushes the notes back to me across the desk. "Take this to Lee – he'll want to know where to start looking."

"Yes, Sir."

It's a relief to have something positive to report.

Sit tight, recruits. We're coming for you.

Running

Bex

Caroline hands us each a black hoodie and sends us downstairs. There's a car waiting in the service road – a big SUV with tinted windows to keep our faces hidden. We put the hoodies on and pull the hoods up, then Charlie and I step outside and climb in with our rucksacks. The driver is a man we've never seen before. He nods to us in the mirror, but doesn't introduce himself.

"Caroline's passengers?"

"That's us."

"Buckle up. We'll be about an hour and a half."

Dan gives us a wave from the storeroom as he brings down the shutter, and we're leaving. Leaving the flat, leaving the shop, leaving the service road. Everything we've known for the last two months, and everyone who's kept us safe.

Charlie catches my eye as the car turns out onto the main road.

"You OK, Bex?"

I take a deep breath. "I'm OK." I've been outside before, with Neesh. This should be no different. I'm hidden in the car, and no one can see my face.

But this is different. This time, we're not going back.

Charlie puts her hand on my arm. "I know these last few weeks have been rough. But this is good." She waves her hand at the car, and the city streets around us. "We're getting out of danger. We're going somewhere really safe."

I think about Mum, sitting in a cell in London. About Margie and Dr Richards and Will. About the risks we took going to Stockport. About everything I've done wrong.

"What right do we have to be safe?"

Charlie sighs. "None, Bex. None at all."

"Then why …?"

"Why are we leaving? Why am I happy about it?"

I nod. I don't want to be angry with Charlie, but I want her to understand.

"Because we can. Because we're still free. Because all those people we've lost – they need us, fighting for them. And we can't do that from here."

I shake my head. This all seems so unfair. How do we get to walk away, to get ourselves to safety, when our friends are locked up in London? When Ketty is holding my Mum?

"I should be in London."

Charlie takes her hand from my arm.

"No one should be in London. Least of all sixteen-year-olds who should be at school." She looks at me, frustration in her voice. "You're not responsible for everything, Bex. You didn't make this happen – any of it."

"I went to see Dad."

"And you had every right to do so! It was dangerous, but we made a plan, and we made the best of a horrible situation."

"We screwed up."

"And Caroline is fixing it for us."

I stare out of the window and watch the traffic on the dual carriageway. Why doesn't she see? Why can't she understand how many mistakes I've made?

It's a while before she speaks again, and when she does, I'm not ready.

"What's happened to you, Bex? Where's the fearless girl I met at Camp Bishop? Where's the girl who didn't think twice about borrowing a kitchen uniform and sneaking into a prison, just to talk to her friend?"

I stare at her. I have no idea what to say.

"Where's the calm leader who took us all safely out of the bunker? Who went straight from finding her murdered friend to walking like an avenging angel through a farmyard full of soldiers?"

I shake my head, trying to understand what she's saying to me. She raises her voice.

"Where's the recruit who walked into the middle of a government atrocity, just to see what was happening? Who stood up to Ketty and Bracken, protected her friends, and took the bruises without telling anyone?"

She looks at me, searching my face for an answer.

"Where did the fight go, Bex?"

I'm numb. I'm trying to find an answer, but there isn't one. She's asking me to be strong again, when everything's been taken away. Mum, Dad, Saunders, Margie, Dr Richards – I've lost them all, and I'm supposed to keep going? To keep leading people and rescuing people and finding a way to put it all behind me?

"I can't save them. I can't save anyone." I start to turn away, but she won't let me. She catches my elbow and pulls me back.

"Rubbish, Bex. *Rubbish*. Stop feeling sorry for yourself."

She's not going to stop. She's not going to let this go.

"So you couldn't save Leominster. Did that stop you saving Margie? You couldn't save Saunders – did that stop you saving the rest of us?"

I want to curl up and hide. I want to lie down and never get up. I want to forget all the things I've done, and I want to stop feeling responsible for everyone else.

But I am responsible. My friends wouldn't be here if I hadn't planned Margie's escape. Mum wouldn't be in London if I hadn't gone to see Dad. And Saunders … Saunders would be alive if we'd stayed at Camp Bishop.

"I'm sick of losing people!" I shouldn't be shouting, but I can't stop myself. "I'm sick of everything I do ending in someone else's pain." I brush tears away from my eyes. "Whatever I do, someone gets hurt. Whatever I do."

Charlie's voice is calm. "Everything you've done has helped people, too. What about the people you've saved?

What about your Dad – he knew you were there. You did a good thing for him, Bex."

"But I hurt …"

"It was a risk. We all took a risk for you."

"And now we have to run again."

"Now, we're getting to safety. Real safety. We're going to be OK."

She's watching me, carefully. Waiting to see what I say.

I let out a breath, and try to keep my voice calm. "So we can keep fighting."

She nods. "So we can keep fighting."

She puts her hand on my arm again, gently.

"I get it. Some terrible things have happened. You feel responsible." I nod. "That's OK. You need time to process what's happened. To work out what you did wrong, and what you did right. To come to terms with the people you've lost, and think about the people you could still save." She looks down for a moment.

"It's been hard, in the flat. We haven't been able to do anything useful. We haven't been able to save anyone or help anyone, and we've been focused on each other. You didn't need that. You needed time to be yourself – to look after yourself. And time to figure out what happened to us. Who you are without school, or Ketty, or Will, or Caroline demanding things from you. Who you are when you're not just surviving."

I nod, looking down at my hands. "Everyone wants to tell me who I am. But I'm not this hero that everyone talks about. I just did stuff. I did what I needed to do."

Charlie laughs. "That's what makes you the hero. You didn't run away. You didn't put your head down and keep yourself safe. You looked after your friends, and you allowed yourself to see what was going on around you. You got involved."

I can't help smiling back at her. "That was stupid, wasn't it?"

She grins, and gives me an awkward hug round the seat-belts.

"Maybe," she says, "but it wasn't wrong."

She sits back and takes my hands.

"Promise me, Bex. When we get to Edinburgh, you'll take some time to figure out who you are, and what you need. You'll stop. You'll get help if you need it. You don't need to be the soldier and the hero all the time – that's a hell of a weight you're carrying. We've got your back. Let some of this stuff go – give yourself a break, and give yourself a chance."

I hold onto Charlie's hands. She's right – safety in Edinburgh will give me time to figure out what all this means. To stop. To think about what happens next.

And I realise that it's not all up to us any more. We won't be hiding, and we won't be alone.

We're about to be part of something bigger.

*****

The car pulls into a car park on a narrow country lane. There's a light rain falling from a grey sky, and everything outside looks cold and unwelcoming. I want to stay in the car, where it's warm and dry, but the driver passes a plastic bag into the back seat.

"Put those on. You'll need them."

We pull two sets of waterproofs from the bag – coats and trousers – and two pairs of gloves. Charlie's waterproofs are purple, and the smaller set is black. We take off our seat belts, pull on the gloves, and shrug our shoulders into the coats.

"You're going to keep walking from here." The driver points along the road, towards the sea and a low island in the distance. "The tide is in at the moment, but when the water clears, you walk. The road goes all the way to the island. I'll fetch the others, and we'll catch up with you on the other side." He hands us a map, and points to a junction of roads in the village on the far side of the island. "We'll meet you there, in about three hours." He looks back at us. "Keep your hoods up, and keep your voices down. It's not busy today, but there will still be people around. Don't get caught."

We thank him, and climb out of the car, pulling our coats and trousers on and taking our bags from the back seat. As soon as the doors close, he drives away, and we're left in the car park in the rain.

Invitation

Ketty

It's after three when I climb the stairs to Lee's office. Conrad is at his desk in the outer office, and he smiles as he sends me through to see the brigadier. I'm smiling as I walk through the door.

"Found them already, Corporal?" Lee raises an eyebrow.

"Not yet, Sir, but we have two leads that you'll want to know about."

He takes the papers from me and looks them over.

"The car and the courier?"

"Yes, Sir."

"I think we can look into these two." He checks the map on his wall. "I've got troops on stand-by at the camp in Morpeth. I'll send them down this afternoon to ask some questions. Maybe take some prisoners. Rattle a few cages." He looks at me. "Good work, Corporal."

"Thank you, Sir."

He puts the papers down on the desk. "Any news on the recruits?"

What do you think, Sir?

I shake my head. "No Sir – not yet. I'm hoping these leads will help point us in the right direction."

He looks at me as if he's about to dissect me.

"I'm hoping so, too, Corporal."

I wait for him to dismiss me, but he doesn't break his gaze.

"How's Bracken, Ketty? How is he holding up?"

I try to hide my surprise.

I thought we were through with this game.

"He's fine, Sir." I stare at the wall above Lee's head, keeping my voice neutral.

"Is that so?"

"Yes, Sir."

Lee smirks. "You're bringing him plenty of coffee?"

"When I can, Sir."

"You should probably get back to him." Lee waves at the door. "Dismissed."

I do my best to leave calmly, without slamming the door.

*****

"Corporal Smith!" Conrad jumps up as I march through his office.

"Corporal Conrad." I stop at the door and turn back to him.

Are you blushing?

"I was just … I was wondering …"

"Yes?"

"Are you busy, later?"

"Later, when?"

I don't have time for games. Get to the point.

"After work, later. For a drink?"

I almost laugh. The brigadier is mocking Bracken for his whisky problem, and now his assistant wants me to go out for a drink.

Conrad sees the look on my face and shakes his head. "Sorry." He holds his hands up. "Sorry – that was inappropriate."

I nod. "It was."

But I don't move. It's been ages since I've had the chance to let my hair down. To let off steam. And I don't know anyone in London, outside these offices.

Why not? I've just figured out where our recruits are hiding. Lee is sending troops to the leads I uncovered. Ellman has made her move, and we're acting on it. I can handle Conrad – outside work, he's just eye candy.

And Jackson. I need a distraction from thinking about Jackson.

Why the hell not?

"OK." I give Conrad a recruit-scaring grin. "I feel like celebrating. Meet you out front at seven."

He blinks at me in surprise. "Yes. OK! Seven." He takes a deep breath. "See you at seven."

I'm smiling as I close his door behind me. Confident Corporal posh-shabby-gorgeous actually sounds nervous. This could be fun.

*****

I pick up two cups of coffee on my way back to Bracken's office. He's on the phone when I arrive, so I step out and wait for him to finish. He calls me in, and I put the coffee cup on his desk.

"Thank you, Ketty." He looks at the phone. "That was Brigadier Lee. The Terrorism Committee has made a breakthrough with the prisoner profiles."

"Sir?"

"It's good news. It means we've got some leverage for the next interrogation."

"Anything I should know?"

He looks up at me. "We've got a family connection. The Committee confirmed it."

"William and Sheena Richards?"

He nods. "Father and daughter."

A smile spreads over my face. "That will be useful, Sir."

Let's see you keep quiet when you find out who's sitting in the next cell.

*****

"Corporal Smith."

"Sir!" I stand up straight and salute as Major General Franks walks towards me in the corridor, the door to the firing range slamming closed behind her.

"At ease, Corporal." She glances over her shoulder. "Here for target practice?"

I clasp my hands behind my back. "Yes, Sir."

She nods, watching me. "Good, good. It's important to be prepared."

"Yes, Sir."

"And your recruits?"

"Still searching, Sir, but we've narrowed the search to the North East. Brigadier Lee is following up a couple of leads."

She nods again. "Good work, Corporal. I like your attitude. No fuss, no hesitation. You get things done." She smiles. "We need more of that attitude around here. Keep it up, and you'll go far. We need soldiers like you."

"Sir."

"Dismissed, Corporal." She walks past me, patting my shoulder before she walks away.

I can't help smiling as I open the door to the firing range. Lee might not appreciate me, and Bracken might not see past my role as his assistant, but with Franks on my side? If the Major General wants to promote me, all I have to do is give her a reason. Find the recruits and bring them to London. Keep my eye on the target. Keep the pressure on Bex and her friends.

It's not Lee I have to impress. It's not Bracken.

It's Franks.

And I can do that.

I collect the bullets and ear defenders from the Private on duty, and clip up a target. I hold the gun in my hands, feeling the power it gives me.

I take aim, and fire.

I've traced the owner of the car.

I fire another shot.

I've traced the courier company.

Another bullet hits the target in the chest.

Bex and her friends can't stay hidden for long.

Fire. Fire. Fire.

145

I've got you, Bex. I'm closing in.

I bring the target back, and admire the six neat holes punched in the the centre of the silhouette.

I've got this, Jackson.

Forgiven

Bex

We walk, Charlie and me. As the tide goes out, we follow the road towards the island, stepping aside for cars and thankful for our waterproofs. It's windy out on the causeway, and I've pulled the drawstring on my hoodie tight. I can hardly see the road ahead of me, so I'm sure no one can see my face. The hood of the coat is pulled down as far as it can go, and every time the wind blows I'm holding it in place. When it blows back, the rain blows in, and the neck of my hoodie is already soaked through. It's wet and cold, and walking is what keeps us warm.

It's impossible to talk. The wind is too loud, and with two hoods up neither of us can hear what the other is saying. It's a mile across the causeway, and another two miles on the other side before we reach the meeting point. My face is freezing, and rainwater is dripping from my nose and down my neck.

And I'm outside.

There's no one looking for me. There's no gun in a biscuit tin on the fridge. No locks on the door. I'm in the middle of nowhere, in a rainstorm, and it feels amazing.

Charlie catches me laughing, and she grins back, turning round and walking backwards at the edge of the road, arms open wide to the sky.

I know we're not free. I know we can't take our hoods down and dance in the rain. But this is still the best day we've had in months. I think about the others, crossing to the island by car, and I'm sorry that they won't experience this freedom. This astounding open space.

I'm smiling as I walk into the rain.

*****

We arrive at the meeting point with hours to spare. The rain has eased to a light drizzle, and we're sheltered from the wind. There's a bench to sit on, and a view towards what a signpost tells us is Lindisfarne Castle, and the sea. It's beautiful, even with the grey clouds and the rain.

We sit for a while, watching the view. While it's raining, we won't draw attention sitting here with our hoods up, but as the rain eases I start to feel conspicuous.

"We should keep walking. Make it look as if we're covering our faces against the wind."

Charlie nods, and we pull on our backpacks again, heading towards the castle.

It's amazing to be walking in this wild and open place, and it's wonderful to be outside for so long. We follow the path past the harbour and up to the castle, then down onto the beach. It's windy and cold, and I'm enjoying every minute. The wind on my face, the cold pushing into my gloves, the sand under my boots. Walking to keep warm, watching the scenery change around us. Not looking at the same four walls. I feel as if we've walked for miles when we realise it's time to head back to the village and meet the others. It's a relief to be able to do something so normal, so unimportant. To feel so alive.

We're both smiling as the SUV stops at the junction, and we hurry over to help with the bags and waterproofs.

When everyone's dressed, the driver gets out and gives Dan a hand-held searchlight and another map.

"Don't forget – light off until you see the signal. No point attracting attention." He looks around the group. "Good luck. All of you."

This time, he takes a moment to shake our hands before climbing into the car and driving away. I watch his tail lights disappear in the fading light.

"What was that? He hardly spoke to us when he dropped us off."

Dan and Amy exchange a glance.

"We should get moving. We're too obvious in the village." Dan sounds worried. He consults his map, then sets off along a narrow road, heading away from the houses. We follow in silence, hoods still up in case anyone sees us.

Past some farm buildings, the road becomes a muddy track. The wind has dropped, and there's no more rain. It's possible to walk with our waterproof hoods down, keeping the hoodies over our faces. I speed up my pace until I'm walking next to Amy.

"What was that about?"

Amy looks around, and raises a finger to her lips. "Not now. We'll explain on the beach."

"Did something happen?"

She nods, finger on her lips again.

I put my head down, and follow Dan.

*****

It must be a mile to the end of the track, and then Dan is consulting the map, picking out a route for us through the dunes towards the sea. The sky is getting darker, and if we don't move quickly, we'll lose the light.

"Watch out. The driver said it's really easy to turn an ankle or fall out here. Stay close behind me, and look out for each other. We're about five minutes from the beach."

Dan picks a direction and walks into the grassy sand dunes, and we follow.

Walking gets harder and harder as the sun sets and the clouds change from grey to near-black. The ground is uneven, the sand is soft under our feet, and the paths appear and disappear between the dunes. We keep Dan in sight, and walk as carefully as we can, holding each other's hands when the path gets rough.

When we make it to the beach, he checks his watch, and checks the map again.

"This is it. Make yourselves comfortable."

He sits down on the sand, and we sit down with him. The beach is cold, but our waterproof trousers keep us dry, our coats protecting us from the wind. I look out from the beach, but it's too dark to see past the breaking waves. The sound of the surf is like the sea, breathing. It's a comforting rhythm as we sit here in the dark.

*****

We sit, quietly, listening to the sound of the waves. The dark presses in around us. There are no lights, anywhere – only a gentle glow from the clouds. I can hardly see my hands in front of my face. Dan has the searchlight, but he won't switch it on until we need it. I can hear the rustling of waterproofs, and I'm overcome with gratitude that my friends are here with me, that we're safe. But in the darkness, just out of reach, I can feel the presence of all the people I've left behind.

I stand up, and walk away from the group, down to the edge of the water. The sea moves and retreats, moves and retreats, washing the toes of my boots. I pull off my gloves and kneel down in the sand. I push my hands into the icy water, and I can feel the tears on my face.

There are things I need to say. People I need to leave behind. Their absence is a weight, pressing down on me in the cold and the dark. I need to draw a line under the guilt and the nightmares. I need to be brave again.

I spread my fingers in the surf and make myself feel the cold. I focus on the people I've lost.

Saunders.

You saved us. I'm so sorry I couldn't save you.

Margie.

I saved you once, and I tried to save you again. I'm sorry.

Dr Richards.

I was so close to rescuing you, in the farmyard. I'm sorry I couldn't get you out of there.

Will.

I'm so sorry about the trackers in the armour. I didn't know.

Dad.

I love you. Be safe.

Mum.

I'm so sorry. We're trying to reach you. I'm sorry.

In the breathing of the surf it's as if they're here with me – all the people I've let down.

And I can feel forgiveness.

But they're not here to forgive me. This isn't my friends or my family talking.

This is me, starting to forgive myself.

The cold burns my hands, but I make myself feel it. I make myself let go.

I tried. I got involved. I did my best to save my friends. I have to stop blaming myself for things I couldn't control.

Charlie is right. I need to put down this weight. I need to stop beating myself up, and start fighting again. I need to stop reliving my failures, over and over. I need to let myself be brave.

I kneel in the surf, feeling the water wash my hands clean. The wind chills my cheeks, but when I reach up to brush them away, I find that the tears have gone.

Drink

Ketty

I head home at five, after sending another clip from Elizabeth's interrogation to PIN for tonight's news. I've got time for a run if I push myself. I change out of my uniform and follow my usual route, ignoring the pain in my knee. Back at the flat, I grab a quick shower, and think about what to wear.

I haven't been out since Camp Bishop, when Jackson and I used an evening permit to go to a pub in Leominster. I got to watch him hitting on other women all night, and he pretended to protect me from the attentions of the local men. We insulted each other all evening, and told tales about it afterwards. It was perfect.

But this? Going out with Conrad?

What are you doing, Ketty?

I pull out three or four outfits, and settle on skinny jeans with a cream satin blouse and a bold blue necklace. Classy, professional, respectable, and untouchable. I scrunch-dry my hair and pull on a pair of flat shoes. I'd love to wear heels, but without a PowerGel, that's not going to happen.

It's cold as I walk down the stairs, a long winter coat over my blouse and jeans.

Conrad is waiting outside the Home Forces building, neat and good-looking in jeans and a padded jacket. He does a double-take as I cross the road towards him, my hair spilling over my shoulders, painkillers helping me to walk without a limp. He's only ever seen me in uniform – my hair scraped back in a regulation style, army boots on my feet, and my jacket buttoned up. His face is a picture.

"Corporal Smith!" He says, eventually.

"Corporal Conrad."

He blinks and shakes his head. "Call me David."

"Ketty."

"Ketty. How about we go and find that drink?"

*****

"Is this allowed? You and me?" I'm shouting over the music in the bar, and pointing across the table between us to emphasise my point. There's a beer in my hand, and David is drinking some whisky cocktail with too many ingredients. It's loud, and it's crowded.

"Is it allowed? I don't know!" He shrugs. "I guess so."

"So no rules about socialising with colleagues?"

"Not that I know of."

"That's useful."

He nods. "Yeah."

We listen to the music for a while, watching the people around us.

"So you're the person who taught the missing recruits everything they know?"

I look back at him, surprise showing on my face.

"At Camp Bishop?"

"Yeah. I heard you were Lead Recruit."

I nod. "I was."

"So – how does that happen? Five recruits breaking out of camp?"

If he's going to mock me about this, I'm going to make him understand. I shake my head. "That's not what happened."

"So you didn't lose five recruits?"

"Oh, yeah. We did. It just took two goes to get them all out."

I take a sip of my beer, smiling at the look on his face.

He laughs. "Two breakouts?"

"Not exactly. There's a bit more to it than that."

"I think you should explain!" He waves his drink at me.

"Three of them broke out of camp." I hold up three fingers, aware that I'm competing with the music.

"OK."

"And they had a prisoner and a member of staff with them. They needed someone to drive the truck."

"They broke out in a *truck*?"

"Smashed their way out of the gates, yes."

David laughs again. "OK. That's a proper breakout."

I smile. "It was."

"So? What happened next?"

"So then two of them came back and rescued their friends. During the raid on the coach."

"I heard about that. You didn't come out of that well." There's the ghost of a sneer on his face.

I blink. I can't follow this conversation. This was David's idea, coming out for a drink, and now he's insulting me.

Laughter, and insults.

He's competing. He thinks I'm a threat.

He's right.

I hammer my finger into my chest. "I was hardcore, Corporal. Hardcore. I fixed up my own bullet wound, and got all the other kids rescued. I deserve a medal for that."

And so does my friend.

So much for distracting me from Jackson.

David makes a face. "I guess if being a target and losing two more recruits gets you a medal, I agree."

"Hey! Hey! You weren't there. Don't look at me like that. You weren't there."

He holds up his hands, fending me off.

"No, OK. I wasn't."

"You weren't. You don't get to comment."

"Sure."

"So what about you? What did you do to deserve Brigadier Lee?"

He shrugs, and flashes his gorgeous smile. "Just lucky, I guess."

I nearly choke on my beer. "Lucky?"

He swirls his drink in his glass. "Access to Top Secret information? Making footage for PIN? Front row seat at the prisoner interrogations – what more could a Corporal want?" He grins at me, over his cocktail.

I shrug. "I guess. It seems like a lot to put up with to get all that."

He shakes his head. "He's not all bad."

"He's a snake! He tortures people for fun."

"That's unfair."

Not from where I'm sitting.

"If you say so."

He nods. "Yeah." He pauses, then looks up at me. "So how are you finding London? I mean – it must be different from Camp Bishop."

Changing the subject?

I watch him for a moment, trying to work out what to tell him.

"It's different. Everything is bigger. Louder." I wave my hand at the crowded bar around us. "And what we do means something."

"No recruits?"

"No recruits. Actual, real work. I feel as if I can make a difference here. Track down some terrorists. Keep people safe. Keep the bombers away so this lot," I wave at the bar again, "can carry on as normal."

He smiles, but there's a look in his eyes that reminds me of Lee. "That's idealistic, don't you think?"

I lean across the table. "That's my job, David."

He laughs. "I thought your job was keeping Bracken on his feet."

Ouch.

I can't help fighting back.

"Bracken's not the one doing the work. I am. I'm tracking terrorists and finding their weak spots. That's what I do, every day. I'm on the trail of my missing recruits. If I find them, I find whoever's protecting them, and we have a target for Lee and Bracken and the Terrorism Committee to take down." I lean back in my seat. *"That's* what I'm doing. *That's* what my job is."

He smiles again. "Looking for a promotion, are we?"

I smile back, enjoying the eye candy, and take a sip of my drink. "Always."

He puts his drink on the table and looks at it for a minute before meeting my eyes.

"Watch out, Ketty. There's more going on here than you know." His smile is gone.

This sounds serious. Pay attention, Ketty.

"So what don't I know?"

He shakes his head. "I can't talk about it. Not here."

"Really? You're going to drop that nugget of information, and then you're not going to tell me?"

He shrugs. "I can't. But keep your ear to the ground, Ketty. Be careful. And keep an eye on Bracken."

I roll my eyes. "When do I not keep an eye on Bracken?"

"I'm serious. There are concerns that he won't handle what's coming."

I'm suddenly sober. My head clears. I don't like the sound of this. "What's coming, David?" He shakes his head, and downs his drink. I lean across the table and look him hard in the eyes, shouting over the music. "What's coming?"

He holds a finger to his lips, and shakes his head, a cold smile on his face.

"I think we're done here. You and me." He points between us. "Just … keep your eyes open. Don't go down with Bracken."

The bar is too crowded. The music is too loud. This isn't a celebration – he's cornering me. Offering me information and then pulling it away. He wants me to chase him for it. He wants to keep me at a disadvantage, to have me on a leash, and I was stupid enough to listen. Stupid enough to fall for the eye candy.

He stands up. "Walk you home?"

So I can ask you again in private? Coax the information out of you? Play your game?

I put what's left of my beer down on the table and pick up my coat. "No, thanks. I can look after myself."

And find my missing recruits, and take care of Bracken.

I leave him standing in the bar, a look of confusion on his face.

I'm not other girls, Corporal. Don't make that mistake.

Flying

Bex

I walk back up the beach to my friends, and the sound of my footsteps seems to break the spell of silence. I sit down next to Jake.

"So what happened on the way here?" Charlie's voice seems loud in the darkness.

"There were soldiers, driving into Newcastle. We passed them on our way out."

"That's not unusual …"

"Soldiers in black armour. Troop carriers full of them. Not patrols in fatigues."

No one speaks. If those soldiers were coming for us, we've left Neesh and Caroline and the others from the bunker behind to face them. I think again about the guns in the kitchen, and they seem laughable against troops in armour. I wonder what Neesh has to protect her flat, and her shop. I wonder what's going on, while we're out here, waiting.

I feel the cold wind on my hands. There's nothing we can do to help. The best thing we can do for everyone is get away. They've risked a lot to get us out here, and more to get us to safety. I take a deep breath. I need to let this go.

And then Dan's on his feet, switching on the searchlight and holding it up, the beam directed out over the water. I search the night in front of us until I see a white light, low over the sea. And there's a sound, getting louder, thudding over the breathing of the waves.

We're all on our feet, rucksacks on, waiting for rescue.

*****

The helicopter is impossibly loud as it hovers over the beach. Sand and water whip up around us as the wind from the rotor blades batters our faces and tugs at our water-proofs. In the searchlight, the pilot beckons, and we follow Dan to the door, climbing in as the landing skids sway above the sand. Inside, we crawl into seats and strap ourselves in, rucksacks on the floor. Charlie slides the door shut behind us and straps herself in as the pilot waves a headset at us, and points at the ceiling. I reach up and unclip a pair of head-phones, and settle them onto my head, relieved to be push-ing my hood down for the first time today.

The noise fades to a loud hum, and I can hear the pilot's voice. I pull the microphone down to my mouth, and listen to her instructions.

"Is everyone strapped in?"

Charlie checks that we're all in our seats. "Yes."

"Can everyone hear me? Names, please. One at a time."

We call our names, and we can all hear each other.

"This is everyone?"

"This is everyone!" Calls Dan.

"OK then. Hold on!"

The helicopter turns, and heads out to sea, the beach dropping away behind us in the dark, the sound of the waves replaced by the roar of the engines. I close my eyes, and feel the icy water on my hands.

We're leaving. We're really leaving.

*****

We fly through the night, lights from the coast visible as we turn north. The sea is black below us and the sky is black above. It's dark in the cabin, and we're flying low to avoid detection.

The motion and the noise are hypnotic. I'm warm and safe. I've spent the day in the fresh air, and I'm exhausted. I don't know when I fall asleep, but Amy touches my shoul-der and wakes me, pointing out of the window.

In the middle of the dark sea, there's a light. A boat, or an oil rig – I can't tell at this distance. And on the horizon, another, and another.

"Oil Rigs!" Dan's voice is loud in my ears. "We'll be landing soon."

I watch, resting my head against the window as the light grows larger. A spotlit tower, metal framework and lines of glowing windows in the dark. We slow down as we approach, and the pilot radios ahead. Someone turns on the lights on the helipad, and I watch as we circle the rig, the pilot lining us up with the platform.

We're touching down, in the middle of the North Sea, in the middle of the night. I feel as if I'm still dreaming.

*****

We land on the pad, the rotor blades strobing in the spot-lights. I keep my head against the window. None of this seems real.

"OK, passengers. It's been my honour to transport you. Your next ride will be here in a few hours. I need to leave again as quickly as I can, before anyone notices I'm off-course, so please get yourselves out of the cabin, and make sure you take everything with you."

I hang up my headset and I'm unclipping my harness when someone slides the door open and offers Charlie a hand down to the pad. Amy follows, then Jake. Dan waves me forward, and I pick up my rucksack and step to the door. I take the hand of a tall, red-headed man in day-glo yellow overalls and jump down to the landing pad, ducking under the battering wind from the blades. Dan jumps down behind me, and the man leads us to the edge of the platform.

"Hands on handrails at all times!" He shouts, holding his hands in the air. "Follow my instructions, keep out of the way, and we'll all have a happy ending." He turns, and waves to the pilot, who waves back and starts to lift the skids from the platform. In the downdraft from the helicopter and the wind from the sea he leads us down a set of metal stairs and across a walkway to a metal door.

I watch as the helicopter lifts off from the pad and tilts away from us, into the night.

Our guide opens the door, and waves us inside. He closes the door behind him, shutting out the freezing wind, and turns to us as we stand, packed together in the brightly lit corridor.

"I'm Greg. I'm the manager here." His face breaks into a grin. "Welcome to Scotland!"

Threats

Ketty

Another early trip to Belmarsh. Bracken doesn't look too bad this morning, and it's me who needs the coffee when we arrive.

"Late night, Ketty?"

"Something like that, Sir."

Lying awake, wondering what Conrad was trying to tell me. Trying to keep you in your job.

I hand Bracken a second coffee and pour another for myself. "So who's first this morning, Sir?"

"We're talking to Sheena first, then William. See what he'll say to protect his daughter."

I nod. "This should be interesting."

*****

"Sheena Richards." Lee leans back in his chair. "We haven't spoken. I'm Brigadier Lee, this is Colonel Bracken. We're here to ask you some questions about your activities at Makepeace Farm."

The prisoner sits up straight, hands cuffed to the table in front of her. Her long hair is tied back, and she watches Lee carefully as he speaks. I'm watching from behind the glass with Conrad, who is treating me with exaggerated formality, and hasn't mentioned last night.

Good decision, Corporal.

"We found you," Lee consults his notes, "in the farmhouse. Protecting the base, were you? Holding the fort? In charge?"

He waits for her to respond, and she returns his gaze.

"As I recall, Brigadier, I was asleep. Your soldiers dragged me out of bed, tried to poison me in the yard with an illegal chemical weapon, then abducted me and brought me here." Her voice is calm and assertive. "I've been waiting to talk to someone in authority ever since."

Lee spreads his hands. "It's your lucky day. What do you want to tell me?"

Sheena leans forward, her arms resting on the table. "I'd like to request a lawyer. I'd like to know what, exactly, I'm being charged with. I'd like to know why I'm being held here." She looks around the room. "I'd like to know where I am."

"Talkative, isn't she?" Conrad adjusts the recording levels on one of his boxes.

Lee starts to respond, but she holds up a cuffed hand. "No, wait. You stopped all that when you used your attack on Leominster as an excuse to put us under Martial Law. I don't get a lawyer, because you've decided that I'm a terrorist. You've used that definition to take away all my rights, and you've locked me up in this hole in the ground." She looks at Bracken. "You were there. Tell me – what bomb-making equipment did you find in the house? What terrorist plots did you unearth? What is it that makes me so dangerous that I have to be locked away?"

You were at Makepeace. That makes you a terrorist. Stop talking.

Bracken shrugs, and Lee pulls some photos from his folder. He lays them out on the table in front of her.

"Bomb-making equipment, maps, diagrams," says Conrad. "There's even one of a missile launcher in the barn." He sounds amused. "Lee brought it all in for the raid. Made sure we got photos. She's going to love this." He grins, and watches the prisoner.

She picks up the photo closest to her, and her shoulders slump.

"You have evidence. Of course you have evidence." She drops the photo, and looks at the others on the table. "Did you bring this lot with you? Drive it all up from a warehouse in London? Something to plant in case you didn't find what you were looking for?" She sits up straight again, and looks up at the mirror. "I want it on record that I have never seen any of this stuff before. This equipment was not at Make-peace Farm before your raid. I'm sure you enjoyed setting it up and taking your photos, but this is a fiction."

Conrad laughs. "Good luck using that defence on TV."

"So you deny the existence of the bunker on the proper-ty? You deny that it was being used by a terrorist cell?"

"As you have already stated, Brigadier, you found me in the house. My clothes, my property – everything was in the house. And I can tell you that none of this was in the house." She holds out a hand towards the photos.

Lee turns to Bracken. "Plausible deniability. Interesting." Bracken nods, and Lee turns back to the prisoner. "But I think you'll find that when we air this on PIN, no one will care where we found you. No one will be interested in the difference between sleeping in a farmhouse, and sleeping in a terrorist's nuclear bunker." He waves a hand at the photos. "I think the images will speak for themselves. Don't you?"

She takes a deep breath. "Let me guess. You're charging me with terrorism. Or at least with aiding and abetting. Both are firing squad offences." She glances down at her orange jumpsuit. "So, tell me. Why am I still here? Why have I been here for nearly three months, waiting for this conversa-tion? Is it because you've only just figured out who I am?" She leans forward again, her voice still calm. "Why haven't I been sent to a firing squad? Why am I not just another face on PIN? What is it that I've got that's so important to you?"

Lee watches her. I can imagine the look on his face. He reaches into his folder, pulls out another photo, and places it in front of her. It's William, sitting where she's sitting, hands cuffed, orange jumpsuit.

This time, she closes her eyes and shakes her head.

"It's not about what you've got that's important to us. It's more about what we've got that's important to you." He places another photo in front of her. Margaret Watson. Orange jumpsuit, handcuffs, being held by two prison guards.

She slumps back in her chair and glares at Lee.

"What is it you want from me?"

"From you?" Lee waves a hand. "Nothing. Just sit in your cell for us. Behave. Be nice. Don't make any trouble." He looks at the photos. "From Margaret, here?" He glances at Bracken, smirking. "Some entertainment. Some sound-bites for PIN before she meets the firing squad. A little Enhanced Interrogation."

She shakes her head. "You're a monster."

Lee ignores her, picking up the photo of William. "But from Daddy? We want everything. Everything he can do to protect you."

Bracken nods. "We want his cooperation. If he helps us, you stay safe. We won't bother you."

She looks at them both, eyes flicking between them.

"He won't help you. He won't fall for this." She tugs at her handcuffs. "You might as well shoot me now."

"She's trying to convince herself." Conrad points through the window. "She's just realising that she has no power. It doesn't matter how brave she is, and how much she talks back to Lee, there's nothing she can do to change this."

Lee puts the photo down and leans his elbows on the table.

"I think he'll help. I think he'll do anything to protect you. You're all he has left to protect." He sits back. "Anyway. It's not important. It's all up to him now. Firing squad. No firing squad. Nothing you can do about it. Either he helps, and you live, or he doesn't, and you die. Before or after Enhanced Interrogation – that's up to him, too." He watches her carefully. "I'd relax, if I were you. This is out of your hands. This is all up to your father."

She tugs again at her handcuffs in frustration, and when she looks up at the mirror there are tears on her cheeks.

Did you think this would be easy? Did you think you could outsmart Lee? That being brave would help you? Think again.

*****

Father and daughter meet in the waiting room, handcuffed and restrained. She's being taken back to the cells, and he's being brought out for questioning. Conrad and I watch from across the room as the guards hold them apart.

William's face crumples when he sees his daughter. He holds out his hands, but the guards hold his elbows and keep him at a distance. She shakes her head, tears streaming down her face.

"Don't listen, Dad. Don't do what they want."

He stares at her, and says nothing. The guards take his elbows and lead him to the interrogation room.

"Twenty pounds says he lets her die to protect the resistance." Conrad hisses in my ear as we hurry back to the observation room.

We settle into our chairs behind the window. William refused to answer questions last time, but I saw his face when he looked at her. I don't want to talk to Conrad, but I know he's wrong.

"Twenty pounds says he gives up without a fight."

Conrad raises an eyebrow, and sets the recordings running. The light comes on above the door.

The prisoner sits, slumped forward in his chair, hands chained to the table.

"William Richards. Welcome back." Lee can't hide the delight in his voice. "We've got some more questions for you."

William's voice is quiet, but the force behind it sends ice down my spine. This is the man who sent my recruits onto the coach. The man who planned the attack. The man responsible for my pain, and Jackson's. Last time he sat here, he was defiant. Silent.

As far as we can tell, he ran the terrorist cell. He was in charge. But now he hangs his head, and there is pain and defeat in his voice when he speaks.

"What do I have to do?"

I can't hide my smile.

We got him, Jackson.

Journey

Bex

Greg leads us to a lounge area with sofas, and a line of windows looking out at the rig. There are cans of drink and bottles of water, and someone brings us sandwiches and hot soup. I sit on the sofa, hands wrapped round my mug, trying to understand where we are. This morning we had a home. We had food in the fridge and beds to sleep in. It was dangerous, but we knew where we were. We knew what Neesh and Caroline expected from us.

And tonight? Tonight, we're in the middle of the North Sea, half way through our evacuation. I should be asleep, but I can't relax. I haven't had time to process this sudden change.

We've all peeled off our waterproofs, and we're sitting in our hoodies and jeans. Jake is snoring, his hood over his face, curled up at the end of a sofa. The rest of us have our hoods down, and I'm fighting the feeling of exposure. The knowledge that showing my face could lead to arrest.

I can't shake the feeling of responsibility.

I look around at my friends – the people I've cared for, and the people who've cared for me. I want to keep them safe. I want to show them that they're not alone. I want to get us all through this.

I take my empty mug to the table, and pick up my rucksack from the floor. Mum's letters are still tucked into the top, and I pull one out of the bundle before putting the rucksack down. I push it into my pocket, and find my waterproofs in the pile by the door.

"Bex?"

"I'll be back."

Dan nods, and leans back on the sofa.

I ease my boots into the waterproof trousers, pull the coat on over my hoodie, and head out into the corridor, fishing my gloves from the pockets. I retrace my steps, down a set of stairs and along another corridor, until I can see the helipad. I zip up my waterproof and step out into the night.

There's a strong wind blowing across the platform, and I keep my hand on the handrail for balance. It's cold, and the wind on my face is the only thing that feels real. Inside, it's just another room. Just another place for us to hide. Out here, there's freedom and danger and connection. The air rushes past me, blowing from the north. I walk to the edge of the platform, and in the distance I can pick out more platforms, more oil rigs. More lights in the dark sea. The deck is brightly lit and the machinery around me is humming, the night shift working the rig. Out there, other night shifts are working other rigs. There's a buzz, and an energy that I haven't felt in months. People, working together. Working with us. Keeping us safe.

I pull Mum's letter from my pocket, keeping a tight hold on the paper as I lean against the railing. She wrote this just after we left school, before she knew we'd been recruited. She talks about Dad, and how he's doing. She writes about a day trip she's been on, to Manchester. How much she enjoyed the Science and Industry Museum, and the meal they all had before the minibus took them back to Orchard House.

Mum, doing ordinary things. Making the most of the opportunities she had. Giving herself permission to live. I try not to think about Dad, lying in their room without her. Mum, locked up in London. Ketty, using Mum to get to me.

And I smile when I realise that Mum can handle this. Mum can handle Ketty. She's been in her wheelchair for as long as I can remember, and she's never let it stop her. She fights for me, she fights for Dad, and she fights for herself. If Mum decides to do something, she makes it happen. She organised the nursing home, she got me into Rushmere. She knew when we couldn't cope at home any more, and she made a plan. I'm laughing as I imagine Ketty trying to bully my Mum. Ketty's used to intimidating her tiny fighters, not tough women, twice her age.

I think about it. Ketty's not going to hurt Mum while she's trying to get to me. She's not going to put Mum's health at risk – she's too valuable, as bait to manipulate my actions. To keep me in line.

Mum's going to be OK, and as long as she gets her medical care, she's going to wipe the floor with Ketty Smith.

There are tears in my eyes, but they're tears of relief. There's a feeling of elation. A feeling that I really did leave a weight behind on the beach. That I can get through this – that we all can. I shout into the wind and pump my fist in the air. Mum's fighting for me, and she's going to win.

*****

Charlie finds me, just after dawn, still standing at the edge of the platform. I've watched the clouds lighten from black to grey, the rigs in the distance fading as the light spread across the sky. I'm freezing, and my hands are numb, but I'm smiling.

Charlie puts her hand on my shoulder, and looks out at the grey sea.

"You've been out here all night?"

I nod.

"It's beautiful." I point out the rigs on the horizon. "All this activity, in the middle of the night. All these lights, where it should be dark."

She smiles, and gives my shoulder a squeeze. "People can do amazing things, when there's nothing to stop them."

I look down at my hands on the railing.

"Yeah. Yeah, they can."

"We're past the darkest hour, Bex. Things will get better from here."

I give her a smile. I hope she's right.

"Come on. Come and grab your things. The helicopter will be here soon."

*****

The lounge is busy when we get back. Jake is awake, and pulling on his waterproofs. Everyone else is dressed and ready to go. I open my rucksack and slide Mum's letter back into the bundle, then close it up and shrug it onto my shoulders.

Greg leads us back outside. Our helicopter is waiting on the pad, rotors still.

"Best of luck," Greg calls, over the sounds of the wind and the rig. "I know the OIE is waiting for you."

"Thanks for your help," Dan says, shaking his hand.

Greg smiles, and stands at the edge of the pad while we climb on board. I fasten my harness, pull my headset onto my head, and watch as the rotors start to turn. Greg waves as the pilot lifts us into the air over the grey sea.

We're running again, but this time we're running towards something, not running away.

And that feels better.

Expendable

Ketty

Margaret is next. They bring her out of her cell when they've finished with William. Sheena Richards is safe for now, but William knows that her life is in his hands. If he goes back on his agreement to help, she'll get the justice she deserves.

Lee settles into his chair again, and watches as the guards lock Margaret's handcuffs to the table. Conrad waits for the guards to leave, then starts the cameras.

"I understand that you haven't said anything to the people who've questioned you so far." Margaret stares straight ahead, ignoring Lee and Bracken, just as she did at Camp Bishop. "We've asked for your name. We've asked what you were doing at Makepeace Farm. We've asked who you were with, and what you could tell us about the bunker in the woods. But you've chosen to keep your mouth shut." Lee shrugs. "OK. You don't want to talk to us." He opens the folder in front of him, and looks up at her. "But here's the problem, Margaret – we really want to talk to you."

When he uses her name, it's like a body blow. She jolts backwards in her chair, and her head snaps round to look at him.

Conrad laughs. Lee cocks his head to one side, and I know he's smiling.

Don't be so surprised, kid. You weren't that hard to track down.

She closes her eyes, takes some deep breaths, and looks back at the mirror in front of her.

Lee picks up his folder, and pulls out a series of images. He places them in a line across the table. From behind the window I recognise the wanted posters for the missing recruits. The prisoner stares straight ahead.

"We'd like to ask you about your friends." Lee sits back and crosses his arms. "Where you think they are. What they might be planning." No reaction.

"Margaret Watson! Look at the photos on the table. Answer the question." Bracken smacks his fist into the tabletop, and Margaret turns to glare at him, before looking down at the images in front of her. She scans the photos, taking in the wording on the posters. A smile tugs at the corners of her mouth.

"You don't have them. You don't know where they are." It's the first thing she's said since the night at the farm.

We're close, Margaret. We're very close.

She slumps back in her chair and looks up at the ceiling, blinking back tears. "They got away."

She looks back down at the table, and reaches out with one cuffed hand. She rests her fingers on Dan's poster, then looks up again, eyes on the mirror.

"So you can place them at Makepeace Farm? You can confirm that they were there?"

She closes her eyes, smiles, and shakes her head.

Bracken leans his elbows on the table.

"It's very simple, Miss Watson. You can help us, and we can talk about your future. Or you can stay silent, and your future will end on an execution platform, on live TV. Your decision."

"Bear in mind, Margaret, that we can send you for Enhanced Interrogation. No tables and chairs and formalities, there. No cameras, either. What's it to be?" Lee waits for her answer, but she sits up straight, fingertips touching Dan's photo. She fixes her eyes on the mirror, and says nothing.

Protecting Dan, are we? Interesting.

She can't keep the smile from her face.

*****

"What's Enhanced Interrogation?"

Conrad is switching off the recording boxes and uploading copies of the footage.

"You really are fresh from the countryside, aren't you?"

Really, Corporal? Still messing with me?

Still competing?

I stare at him as if he's an incompetent recruit. "I'm here to do a job, and I can't do my job if I don't have all the facts. Are you going to answer my question? Or do I have to wait until you feel like telling me?"

He meets my gaze, and looks away, hands up. "OK." He points through the window at the empty room. "That's interrogation. Table, chairs, people asking questions."

"Uh-huh."

Get on with it.

"Out that way," he points to the other side of the recording room, "there's a room with no cameras. No table, no chairs. The people who ask the questions don't sit down with the prisoners. They get to use their fists. They're very good at making people decide that talking would be the best option."

I smile. "Iron fists and steel toe caps?"

He gives me a puzzled look. "I guess. Why?"

"It's a technique I'm familiar with."

He raises his eyebrows. "Really?"

Don't look so shocked. And don't underestimate me.

"You find difficult prisoners everywhere. Even in the countryside."

He stares at me for a moment. "Camp Bishop?" He sounds incredulous. "Wasn't that kids?"

I nod, smiling. He blinks, and looks away.

Don't ever underestimate me.

*****

"So. What do you think?" Lee and Bracken are sitting in the waiting area when we leave the recording room, cups of

174

coffee in their hands. Lee looks up and waves us over. "Put Margaret on trial? Show William what we can do to his daughter if he doesn't toe the line?"

Conrad shrugs. "That could work. Put it on TV. Show him the footage."

Bracken steeples his fingers. "We'd have to follow through, though. We'd have to send her to the firing squad. Otherwise the message loses its power. Is she really expendable?"

"Ketty." Lee gives me a cold smile. "You did the research on our prisoners. What do you think. Can we do away with Margaret?"

What do you want me to say, Sir? Is this a test, or a trap?

I think it through. "Margaret is our link with the missing recruits, Sir, but there's not much more she can tell us. We've already placed them somewhere in the North East – I'm confident that we're close to tracking them down." Lee smirks, and takes a sip of his drink. I have to force myself to stay calm. "She's also a link to Sheena and William, but we've got both of them. She's only a kid – she probably doesn't know much about the operation at Makepeace. Plus if we put her on TV, Ellman and Pearce will have to take notice." I shrug. "Maybe see what she'll tell us under Enhanced Interrogation, and then use her to show William we're serious. Giving her a few bruises and introducing her to the firing squad can only increase his motivation to behave."

Lee gives Bracken a look of approval. "Margaret's days are numbered. Corporal Smith has spoken."

Bracken smiles. Conrad smothers a laugh.

I think about the room at Camp Bishop. Margaret, trying to fight back. Jackson and me, working together to keep her on the ground, using our fists to persuade her to talk. And the way she looked through me, while Jackson threw his punches, as if the bruises were happening to someone else.

Let's see how you handle the real thing, when it's not just five minutes alone with me and Jackson.

*****

"Do we have some footage of Mrs Ellman for tonight, Ketty?"

We're in the car, on the way back to the office. Bracken checks his notes and looks up at me.

"I think so, Sir – enough for a couple of days. There's still some footage left from the interrogation. I'll send it over to PIN when we get back."

He nods. "Good."

"And Sir? I was thinking. Could we blame Bex and her friends for one of the bombings? Bournemouth, maybe?"

He looks at me, a smile spreading across his face. "I think we can. I think that's a very good idea."

"Shall I prepare some wording for the news report?"

"Write something down, and we'll run it past the brigadier." He nods again. "Good thinking, Ketty. Let's build up some evidence against Ellman and her gang."

I sit back in my seat, and watch the traffic as we speed past in the military lane.

Back in the office, I call the hospital, but the phone rings and rings. No one answers, so I hang up.

I can't tell whether I'm worried or relieved to have no news.

I need you, Jackson. Keep fighting. I'll call again tomorrow.

DECEMBER

Exile

Bex

We're driven into the OIE compound at lunch time. Three cars with tinted windows were waiting for us at the airport, pulled up close to the helipad, and we've had a police escort of cars and motorbikes for the half-hour journey round the Edinburgh bypass. The traffic has stopped and waited for us to drive through every junction, and I've been pushing down a feeling of panic as we move through the streets, all eyes on our cars.

We should have been interviewed at the airport, and assessed for refugee status, but the OIE has fast-tracked our applications. The immigration officers will be coming to us, behind our razor-wire fence and armed guards. For the next few days, everything we do is in someone else's hands.

Amy takes my hand as we drive through the gates of the compound, past soldiers with rifles and armour. I have to remind myself that these are Scottish troops, protecting the OIE. They're on our side.

"We're here, Bex. We made it." She rests her head on the back of her seat, staring at the ceiling. I watch from the car window as we're driven behind the main building, out of sight of the road. The police cars wait on the road outside until the gates close, then drive away, blue lights flashing.

I want to respond. I want to say something positive, but all I can think about is how far I am from home, and from Mum. The excitement of the journey is wearing off, and the exhaustion of the last few days is sinking through me. I rest my head against the seat and squeeze Amy's hand.

The door opens, and a woman in a smart suit is calling my name.

I nod, and she holds out her hand, helping me from my seat. I climb out of the car, and she shakes my hand, smiling.

"Rebecca. Welcome to Edinburgh. My name is Gail, and I'm your liaison here at the Opposition In Exile. Come on inside. We've got some papers for you to sign, and then I'll show you to your room." She has a London accent, and her manner is kind, but efficient.

I turn to look for my rucksack, but the driver is opening the boot and passing our bags to another member of staff to carry inside. I look around, at the other cars, and at my friends. We've each been met by a smartly dressed liaison officer, and everyone's being brought inside the building. There are so many people in this small space around the cars, and I can't stop myself from pulling my hood up over my face.

Gail looks amused. "Don't worry. You're safe here. Everyone here," she waves her clipboard at the people around us, "they're all OIE. We're all here to look after you." She puts a hand on my shoulder and guides me towards the door. "Come inside, and let's get you comfortable."

*****

"Sign here … and here … and here." Gail picks up the form, and puts another on the table in its place. "And on this one, it's here," she points with the end of her pen, "and here."

She checks my signatures, and replaces the form on her clipboard.

I look around the room. We're in a conference room, the tables laid out like a classroom. We're all sitting at different tables, all signing declaration forms and immigration requests and asylum applications. We've each got our liaison officer, guiding us through the process. Someone brings two mugs of tea to our table, and I take a grateful sip as Gail explains the next form.

"So this one's up to you. Education up to 18 is compulsory in Scotland, but we'll provide you with that education here, and you can choose to take a vocational route. This form is for you to make your wishes clear.

"If you choose the academic route, we'll provide a tutor, and six hours of tutoring every day. But the route we recommend is the vocational option. If you request that, we'll continue your training from Camp Bishop, and we'll take it further. We'll train you in the use of weapons, communications, tactical scenarios, and military planning. We'll turn you and your friends into a fighting team. And when you're ready, you'll have the chance to fight with us.

"I'll give you some time to decide. Speak to your friends, choose what you'd like to do." She pushes her chair back from the table and sorts through the papers on her clipboard, waiting for me to stand up, to ask everyone what they think we should do.

But I don't move.

"I don't need to talk to anyone. And I don't need any more time." Gail looks up in surprise.

"Are you sure?"

I nod. "The government has my mother in a cell. They have my friend, and my teacher, and the person who ran the terrorist cell that saved our lives. I'm not going to run away from that. I'm not going to sit in Scotland, studying for exams, while they wait for their trials."

I'm talking, and I'm making my decision as I speak. I didn't know this was going to be asked of me. I didn't know what would happen when we reached Edinburgh, and safety. But I know that I can't let Mum sit in her cell, and Margie, and not train myself to get them out. My life isn't starting over. I have a chance to help, and I'm going to take it.

"I'm sure."

Gail nods her approval. "OK, then. Tick this box, and this box, and sign here."

I scribble my name, and set the course for my life in exile.

They give me a room, like a one-person hotel room. I've got a single bed, a desk and chair, some bookshelves, a wardrobe, and a chest of drawers. I've also got my own bathroom, stocked with towels and toiletries. It's much larger than my room in the flat, and when I've taken everything out of my rucksack, it still looks empty. There's a pinboard on the wall, and I've pinned Saunders' sketch of us in our armour in the corner over the desk. I sit on the bed and look around at the empty, cream-painted walls, and my view of the compound through the windows.

It would be easy to feel at home here. I could buy some books, and some posters. I could decorate the room and make my own space. I could put cushions on the bed, and a rug on the floor. It could be mine, in a way that nothing has been mine since Mum sold the house.

But I can't get comfortable here. Mum and Margie and the others are in London. I've asked the OIE to train me, and I know I'm going back to fight. I'm not staying here. For now, I have permission to remain in Scotland, and the OIE is working on getting us citizenship and passports.

I'm a refugee.

But I don't want to hide here. I want to go back, and I want to save the people I care about. I want to change my country.

I'm grateful. I'm safe for now. But this isn't where I belong.

*****

"En suite showers! Real beds! Single rooms! We've gone up in the world."

Dan leans back on the sofa, hands behind his head, shirt sleeves rolled up. The four of us are sitting together in the common room at the end of the corridor. We've had time to shower and change, and it feels great to be out of the clothes we were travelling in. There's a kitchen area, tables and chairs, and a couple of sofas. There's a TV, for the nightly news. I have to remind myself that we can't watch PIN here. There are other news channels, and we could see things that our government doesn't want us to see. The thought is thrilling and frightening at the same time.

"So – what did everyone choose, for the education form?" Amy sounds nervous.

"Vocational!" Says Dan. "More training like the RTS, but from people who actually care about keeping us safe."

Amy smiles, relief showing on her face. "Me too. We need to keep fighting."

"Bex?" Dan gives me a look of concern. "What did you decide?"

I nod. "Vocational." Dan and Amy exchange a glance. "I'm not staying here. I'm going back, and if the OIE wants to make me a better fighter, that's fine with me."

Amy puts her hand on mine, next to me on the sofa. "That's great, Bex. We'll be training together."

"Jake?" Dan nudges him. "You're fighting with us, right?"

Jake looks down at his hands in his lap.

"Jake?" Amy leans forward. "What did you choose?"

He shakes his head, and his voice is quiet. "Academic." He won't meet our eyes.

The room is silent.

Dan sits up and turns to Jake. "Are you serious?"

Jake nods, slowly, eyes down.

"But …" Amy holds a hand out to Jake, pleading.

"They gave me a choice." He still won't look at us. "For the first time since they took me from school, someone gave me a choice."

"Yes, but …"

He looks up at Amy, anger flashing in his eyes.

"I'm not going back. I'm not fighting any more battles for other people. I'm sick of being used, and I'm sick of being left behind. I'm *done*." He throws his words like stones, and Amy sits back in her seat, tears in her eyes.

This is about me. This is about leaving him behind.

"Jake, I'm sorry. I'm sorry we left you at Camp Bishop. I'm sorry about what happened to you. I …"

He looks at me, and I can feel his anger burning into me.

"How can you apologise? How can you sit there and say you're sorry when it was me who had to face Ketty? When it was me with Bracken's gun to my head? Do you have any idea how that feels? Do you have *any clue* what Ketty and Jackson did to us?" He points at Amy, and back at himself.

Amy is shaking her head. "No. Don't put this all on Bex. She knows what Ketty did. Ketty punished her, you know. For looking after Joss, that day on the run. For looking after all of us." Amy points at me. "Jackson beat her up for helping us – for helping you. Did you know that? Did you ever bother to find out?"

Jake looks shocked. He looks at me, wide-eyed. "Is that true? Did you know what Ketty would do?"

I shrug. "Of course not. But I knew what she was capable of." I can feel the bruises. Jackson's fists, landing on my ribs.

"Bex wasn't in control of everything that happened at Camp Bishop, Jake." Dan's voice is calm and reasoned. "There were five of us in the truck, and Charlie made the decision to keep driving."

"And you all went along with it."

Dan shrugs. "Didn't have much choice, at the time."

Jake points at me. "You knew. You knew, and that makes it worse. You left me behind, and you knew what would happen to me." He points at Amy. "To us."

"Leave me out of this, Jake." Amy holds her hands up in front of her.

He folds his hands in his lap. "I'm done with fighting. I'm done with looking down the barrels of other people's guns. The OIE will let me stay here? Great. I'm in. I'll sit some exams, I'll go to university, and I won't look back." He points at us. "If you want to go and risk your lives for someone else's fight, that's up to you. But I'm safe now, and I'm not giving that up." He stands up and walks to the door. "Get yourselves trained, and get yourselves sent to war. Get yourselves shot. Get yourselves killed. Not my problem any more."

He walks out into the corridor and slams the door behind him.

Evidence

Ketty

"Nevill Hall Hospital, High Dependency Ward."

"Corporal Ketty Smith, calling about …"

"Liam Jackson. Yes. Hold the line, please."

I wait while the nurse checks the patient files. My hands are shaking when she comes back to the phone, and I realise I'm holding my breath.

"No change, Corporal. We're still treating the infection."

I force myself to breathe. "Thank you," I say, and hang up the phone.

I sit at my desk, eyes closed.

Fight, Jackson. Between Lee and Conrad and Bracken, I'm losing myself. I need you to remind me who I am.

*****

When Bracken arrives, it's with Major General Franks. I stand up behind my desk and salute as she enters the room.

"At ease, Corporal." She waves a hand at my chair. "Take a seat."

I sit down, hands clasped in front of me on the desk.

"Corporal Smith. I'm here to congratulate you on your strategy for using PIN to unsettle our missing terrorists."

"Sir?"

"Bracken tells me that running daily footage of Ellman's mother was your idea."

I nod. "Yes, Sir."

"And implicating Ellman in the Bournemouth bombing on last night's news? Very clever."

"Thank you, Sir."

"I hear you're planning on putting one of the Makepeace prisoners on trial as an encouragement to the others to cooperate?"

"Yes, Sir. Margaret Watson. She's the RTS deserter from Ellman's school. She joined the terrorist cell instead of coming to Camp Bishop. We thought she'd motivate the other prisoners and give Ellman's friends something to think about."

"I like the way you think, Corporal." She looks at Bracken. "I think you can both expect some career progression to result from this."

Bracken smiles. "Thank you, Sir. Anything we can do to help." He nods at me. "Corporal Smith has been instrumental in shaping our search for the missing recruits, as well as using PIN to reach them."

Franks gives me a friendly smile. "I look forward to seeing the fruits of your labour, Corporal. I'm sure the people of this country will feel safer when we finally have your targets in the cells."

"Yes, Sir. That's what we're aiming for, Sir."

She nods. "In the meantime, I'm sure Recruit Ellman would appreciate seeing more of her mother on TV. Don't you?"

I smile back. "Yes, Sir. I'm sure we can handle that, Sir."

She pulls something from her pocket and hands it to me. "This should help."

It's an access card, for Belmarsh Prison. I stare at it, trying to understand what she's giving me. She points at the card. "That will get you through the front door, and into the interrogation area. No more security checks. The code is on the back." I turn the card over, and there's a four-digit code on a sticky note. "Memorise it. This gives you 24-hour access to the prisoners and the standard interrogation suite. You'll need permission and specialists for Enhanced Interrogation, but Brigadier Lee can give you that."

I nod, still staring at the card. "Thank you, Sir." I try to hide the surprise in my voice.

That's a lot of power, Ketty. Don't screw it up.

Franks smiles. "I know we can count on you, Corporal. Oh – and there's no need to run your prisoner clips for PIN past the brigadier in future. Send them directly to the newsroom. They'll be expecting them." She turns to Bracken. "The Colonel will keep me informed of your progress."

Bracken nods. I stand as Franks leaves, then slump back into my chair.

"I think we have work to do, Ketty," says Bracken, taking his coffee and briefing papers from my desk. I look at the card in my hand, and feel a rush of excitement at the power I've been given.

"Yes, Sir. I think we do."

*****

I schedule a trip to Belmarsh for the morning, and concentrate on the planning for Margaret Watson's trial. We need to make sure everyone's watching – Ellman, Pearce, the OIE – as well as William Richards.

This needs to be the trial of the year.

I need evidence – the kind we can prove. Photos, CCTV, school records. With that as a framework, we can accuse her of anything else that suits us, and the PIN-watching public will eat it up.

We'll need her school reports. Her desertion before the RTS recruiters turned up will make sure she's disgraced before the trial begins. I'll keep Sheena Richards out of the story for now – this will play better if the prisoner is shown to have acted alone.

I can prove she was at Makepeace Farm. The CCTV from the bunker gives me plenty to work with, and there's some dashcam footage from one of the troop carriers in the farmyard. Twinned with the photos of Lee's planted evidence, we can make the case for her membership of a terrorist cell.

And that's a firing squad offence.

But for the trial of the year, why stop there? We can place her at Camp Bishop, which puts her around Leominster on the day of the weapons test. We can hang the whole false flag attack on the Makepeace Farm cell, which gives us automatic firing squad sentences for everyone else we picked up there, or with the stolen armour.

Pick them off, one by one, and use Margaret's trial as the finale.

The feeling of power is growing, and I can't hide a smile. Margaret Watson is entirely in my hands. I don't need Jackson to inflict the bruises – I've got a staff of interrogators to do that for me. I can use her to keep William under control, and I can use her to frighten her friends. I can tell the country that she helped to annihilate the people of Leominster, and it not only guarantees her execution – it also hides the truth.

It removes her, and it protects me.

Perfect.

I pull out an evidence request form, and start to make the case for releasing the CCTV.

*****

Bracken checks my requests, and sends me to Brigadier Lee for final approval. Conrad gives me an unfriendly smile as I walk into Lee's outer office. He lounges back in his chair and watches me.

Feeling threatened, David?

"Corporal Smith. Come to beg me for more inside information?"

"Corporal Conrad. I'm here to see the brigadier."

He looks at the folder in my hands.

"Planning the execution of a schoolgirl? Or giving your missing recruits another chance to escape?"

"What's wrong, David? No stomach for disposing of terrorists? Good thing us country girls are here to do it for you."

He grins, and rolls his eyes. "Go on in. He's waiting."

There's an amused expression on Lee's face as I cross the room to stand in front of his desk. I put the folder down in front of him and stand to attention.

"At ease, Ketty," he says, indicating the folder. "The evidence forms?"

"Yes, Sir."

"Pull up a chair. Let's take a look."

He flicks through the request forms, nodding and making positive comments.

"This looks good. I think we can build a convincing case from the proof you've put together."

"Thank you, Sir."

He looks up. "Do we need to bring Leominster into this?"

"With respect, Sir, I think we do. The prisoner was there, at Camp Bishop – I met her myself. We get public opinion on our side, even though she's technically a minor. No one will want to forgive a terrorist who wiped out a town." Lee smirks. "It's the biggest atrocity yet, and it's fresh in people's minds. If the idea is to show William Richards what we can do, let's go all out and show him that we could pin anything on his daughter. There's no way she's walking out of there if he doesn't play ball." Lee nods. "Plus, it gives us a plausible cover story. We're not just pointing a finger at a vague terrorist threat – we're pointing at this cell, and these people. That makes the truth less likely to come out."

He nods. "OK. Good thinking. I'll approve it."

He picks up a pen, and works his way through the folder, signing every request I've made. I can't help feeling that he's giving me enough rope to hang myself.

Make this work, Ketty. Show him you know what you're doing.

He signs the final form and puts the papers back in the folder.

"You're aiming to turn this into a big event, aren't you?"

"I wouldn't want anyone to miss it, Sir. Particularly the prisoner's friends. I think they should see what happens to terrorists, when we catch them."

He smiles, coldly. "Keep them running scared?"

"That's when they'll make their mistake, Sir."

He watches me for a moment, then nods. "Maybe. And then we need to be ready to catch them."

Won't make that mistake again, Sir.

"Yes, Sir."

He hands the folder back to me.

"This will certainly be an event, Ketty. Feed back to me if there are any problems with the evidence – we should make use of this opportunity."

That's the idea.

I smile. "It's a show trial, Sir. Let's put on a good show."

Superiors

Bex

We all sleep late on our first morning in Edinburgh, catching up for the night we lost on the journey. I went to bed after dinner and slept for twelve hours. By the time I'm up and dressed and headed to the canteen, Charlie has finished her breakfast and the others are helping themselves from the serving counter. I fill a plate with hot food, grab a mug of coffee, and sit down next to Charlie.

"How are you feeling?"

I nod. "Better, thanks."

"Did you sleep OK?" I realise that, in these private rooms, no one can hear me if I wake up screaming. Charlie is asking because she really doesn't know.

I smile. "I did. Thanks." Charlie smiles back. "So," I ask, taking a sip of my coffee. "What have they got planned for you?"

"While you're all training and studying, you mean?" I nod. Charlie thinks for a moment. "I'm not sure. I offered them help in the kitchen, but they seem much more interested in my resistance activities." I raise my eyebrows. "Helping you lot. Breaking out of camp. My police record." She picks up her mug. "We'll see what they decide."

When Jake sits down, it's at the far end of the table. He keeps his head down, and eats in silence. No one pushes him to talk.

*****

Gail and the other Liaison officers arrive as I'm finishing my second cup of coffee.

"Rebecca. Good morning. I hope you slept well."

I nod, and catch Charlie raising her eyebrows at me. "Rebecca?" she mouths, silently.

I roll my eyes. "It's Bex, actually, Gail. Sorry – I should have said something yesterday."

"No problem." She makes a note on her clipboard. "Everything we know about you comes from your government, or from Caroline. If we get something wrong, you need to let me know."

I nod. "I will. Thanks."

"So," she continues. "Today, we've got your orientation. I'll give you the official tour first, and then you can meet with our executive committee."

I look around the table. All the liaisons have their clipboards out, and there are timetables for each of us.

We might be safe here, but we're certainly not in control.

*****

"And this is the laundry – the machines are pretty easy to figure out. This is the store room – towels, detergent, washing up liquid – that's all in here. Help yourselves if you need it, and write down what you take on the sign-out sheet." Gail opens doors and shows me the rooms as we walk past. She's showing me round the residential building, behind the offices and hidden from the road. Our rooms are upstairs, and the conference room and canteen are in the other building. "That's the computer room …" She opens a door into a room with tables lining the walls. Screens and keyboards sit on the tables, a chair in front of each workstation. "You'll work in here from time to time. Not as much as your friend – he'll use this room a lot for his academic education – but you'll all need logins and passwords. I'll get those sorted for you as soon as I can."

We're about to leave, and she catches me looking at the machines.

"You can get to the Internet from here, too."

I look at her in surprise. "That's … available? We can just use it, whenever we want?"

Gail laughs. "You can. But first, we're going to have to give you some ground rules. You've never been online before, have you?" I shake my head. "We'll run through what that means with you – with all of you. There will be some rules. No social media. No blogging or vlogging. We don't want London figuring out where you are because someone posts a selfie. We're keeping your arrival quiet for now, while we figure out what's going on in the government. You understand?"

I laugh. Mum and Dad used to talk about going online, but I have no idea what any of this means. "No selfies. OK."

*****

We've been round the building. Gail has pointed out the gym and the sports hall – no running around outside for us here – and there's a shooting range in the basement. There's a covered walkway between the residential building and the main offices, and as long as we stick to that, no one can see us from outside the site. Gail is worried about reporters and photographers with zoom lenses. If someone snaps a photo of us, London will know where we are within hours.

As we walk, she asks if there is anything I need. Clothes, medicines – anything I couldn't bring with me. I shrug. I'm going to need trainers and gym clothes, and some more jeans and T-shirts won't hurt. She nods, and writes down my list, and the sizes I need.

I think of the book shelves in my room, and the last time I smuggled an adult novel into school.

"Actually – would you be able to get me some books?"

Gail nods. "Anything in particular?" I think about it, and name a few authors. She makes more notes on her clipboard. "I'll see what I can do."

I think of Dan, and the books we both read, discussing them after hours in the common room. It would be great to chat with him again, about something ordinary.

I'm smiling as I walk into my meeting with the Executive Committee of the Opposition In Exile.

*****

"Bex Ellman."

I nod. I'm sitting on a chair in front of a long table. Gail is next to me, and facing me behind the table are twelve strangers – former politicians, heads of companies – people who made it out of the UK before parliament was dissolved. Before the government declared Martial Law.

"Welcome to Scotland. And welcome to your government in exile. I'm Fiona Price – I'm the chair of the OIE Executive Commitee." A woman near the centre of the table smiles as she speaks for the committee, and I can feel all twelve of them watching me. Sizing me up. I'm so used to hiding my face – it feels dangerous to be sitting here in front of so many people. My pulse is racing, and I'm fighting panic. I take a calming breath, and listen to what she's saying.

"You've had an eventful journey, from RTS Camp Bishop." Fiona consults a file of papers in front of her. "You rescued a prisoner, you saved your friends twice, and you've avoided capture – what? Four times? Five?" She looks up and down the line of faces at the table. "We're very impressed with your record, Bex, and we're very pleased to have you here."

There's a moment of quiet. Everyone seems to be waiting. "Thank you," I say, to fill the silence. "Thank you for getting us out of Newcastle."

Fiona nods. She crosses her arms on the table in front of her and leans towards me.

"What we'd like to do today, Bex, is to get a feel for what you can do to help us. We'll give you a place to live, and with the help of the Scottish government, we'll keep you safe." She tips her head to one side and smiles again. "But with your skills, and your record, we're hoping that you can do something for us."

I nod, fighting the impulse to stand up and walk away. Its not enough that we're safe. It's not enough that we've signed up to train and fight. They want more.

She holds up a copy of the poster, my face on the waving flag background.

"We're very grateful for this, Bex. Our volunteers have been putting these up all over the UK, and the response has been fantastic. It's caught the government off-guard, and they've been trying to take the posters down – but we're putting them back up as quickly as we can. We needed a face for the resistance, and Caroline made a good case that it should be you. I'm glad we can work with you."

She doesn't know. No one told her that I didn't want this. She thinks I signed up to be their figurehead.

I can't think of anything to say. These people are in charge of my safety, and my future.

And they're going to teach me to fight. I need to work with them. I need to give them what they want. I need to take their training, and I need to go and rescue Mum.

I force myself to nod. "What is it you want me to do?"

A man sitting further down the table answers.

"We know about your mother, Bex. We know about the broadcasts on PIN." I nod. "We'd like to make a statement to the government. We'd like to make some broadcasts of our own. We can send TV signals into the UK from sea-based broadcast platforms, and we can reach the north of England from here. We could reach ordinary people in their homes."

I stare at him. What is he suggesting?

"We'd like to use you – use your image and your voice – to fight back. To tell the people of the UK that they can resist. To …"

I'm out of my chair and walking to the table before I can stop myself. The man looks up at me in surprise as I stand in front of him. I try to keep my voice calm.

"My mother is in prison in London. She's needs round-the-clock medical care, and she's been arrested and put in a cell." I lean towards him, finger pointed at my chest. "Because of me. Because of what I did. She's being used to keep me under control. *Her* face and *her* voice are being used to make me feel …" I can't put this into words. I close my eyes and shake my head, clenching my fists. "Make me feel as if I'm to blame. For everything. Everything I've done. Everything you're so impressed with."

The man in front of me looks down at his notes. I force myself to keep my fists at my sides. I take a step back and look up and down the table, catching the eyes of everyone on the committee.

"While you're using me as the hero of the resistance, putting my face on posters and putting your volunteers in danger, the government is using my own mother against me. They can do anything to her. If they see my face on a poster, they can take it out on her, and they can put that on TV for me to see."

I take another deep breath, relax my hands, and focus on speaking slowly and clearly.

"If you put me on TV, if you use me as your face and voice, you'll be as bad as they are." There's a murmur from the committee, but I ignore them. "I don't *want* my face out there. I don't *want* my voice out there. And I don't want *anything* I do here to hurt my mother." I point at the poster on the table. "That? I'm too late to object to that. You've already put my face on bus shelters and walls and advertising boards all over the UK. Fine. That's what I've done for you. But the TV? No. No more. I will not put my mother at risk."

I turn back to my chair as Gail stands up.

"Madam Chairman," she says, calmly. "I think it might be time to give Bex a break. Can we reconvene at a later date?"

The woman behind me sounds angry. "I suppose we can postpone this conversation. Bex?" I turn round and meet her gaze. "Thank you for your input. We'll discuss what you've said, and we'll talk to you again." I nod, biting my tongue. "And I am sorry about your mother. We're doing everything we can …"

But I'm already walking out of the room. I don't want to hear what she has to say about Mum.

*****

"Front-line doll. Again." I slam my fist into the table. Charlie puts her hand over mine, but she doesn't say anything.

"It's not all bad, Bex," Amy puts her hand on my shoulder. "They're still going to train us, and get us ready to fight."

"On whose terms? On theirs? What will we be fighting for? Do we get a say?"

Dan leans over the table, pushing his empty plate out of the way. "Come on, Bex. They're trying to help. And they're trying to start a revolution. We're not exactly at the top of their priority list."

I shake my head. "Sure. But they're not taking the time to listen. We're here. They went to all that trouble to get us out of the UK, and they're feeding us and clothing us and giving us somewhere to live, but they can't be bothered to *listen* to us."

Amy squeezes my shoulder.

"I thought it would be different, here. I thought they'd be more …"

"Humane? Kind?" Charlie nods. "That would have been nice. But if you're fighting a military dictatorship, you have

198

to think like a military dictatorship. They know they need to be tough – it's just a shame that they think they need to be tough with you."

We sit in the empty dining room. Jake ate his meal and left, but the rest of us stayed, drinking tea and coffee and talking about our days. The staff who were here for dinner have drifted away, and the kitchen staff have rolled down the serving shutter and left us alone.

Dan breaks the silence. "Anyone know how to get PIN?" He checks his watch. "It's nearly time for the news."

He looks around the table. Everyone shrugs.

We're powerless here. We can't even check on our friends. We can't see the news from home.

I push my plate away. "I'm going to bed. See you all for breakfast."

No one stops me as I walk away.

Elizabeth

Ketty

Bracken is in the office first thing, for a meeting with Franks. I fetch the coffee and the briefing papers, then phone the hospital, but there's no change.

Jackson. Wake up. Tell me what I'm doing here.

I make sure the evidence forms have reached the archive staff, and start drafting a trial announcement for PIN. I need them to play this up – promote it in advance and build up expectations. I need the country to be watching when we put Margaret on the stage. Someone at PIN will write the script for me, but I need to tell them what to say.

Terrorist trials are usually quick and predictable. There's always a guilty verdict, and it's the firing squad, not the trial, that makes the news on PIN. But Lee's right – Margaret's trial needs to be an event. We need to show the evidence. We need to build up the case. We need to bring the audience with us, and have them shouting for blood before we've even passed a verdict. We need to make everyone feel involved, and invested. We need to make William and Bex understand what we can do.

This needs to be good.

*****

The car is waiting for us when Bracken gets out of his meeting. I've called the prison, and by the time we get there Elizabeth is waiting in the interrogation room, handcuffed to the table, with two guards outside the door. My card lets us through the door with no checks, and we're waved through to the interrogation area without an escort. We're free to do whatever we want. Franks has handed me power and confidence, and the feeling is like a lightning bolt in my hands.

Bracken takes the observation room, and I take a seat across the table from the prisoner. She's sporting a black eye and a graze on her cheek, large enough to show up on the TV footage.

I hope you're watching, Bex.

When the recording begins, I give her a broad smile. "Good morning, Elizabeth." She tilts her head and looks at me, but says nothing. "How are you this morning? You look as if you've been in a fight."

"You try taking a shower when your carers are 200 miles away."

I think about my hospital bed. Trying to convince the nurses to let me go back to Camp Bishop.

Careful, Ketty. Don't let her get under your skin.

She looks me in the eye. "How's my daughter?"

My smile widens. "Well, that's the important question, isn't it?"

She laughs. "Still looking for her? Still searching through old ladies' wardrobes and bathrooms? I hope she's not causing you too much trouble."

"Not at all, Elizabeth. In fact, we're very close to tracking her down." I wave my hand at the room. "You might have company soon. A little family reunion?"

She shakes her head. "I doubt it, Corporal. I think Bex has people looking out for her. I think she has a team – I think she has friends. All those people we see on the news." She leans forward, over her cuffed hands. "Do you have friends, Corporal? Are there people who look out for you? Or are you just a cog in this unpleasant machine?"

I let my smile fade. I push away thoughts of Jackson, and pick up the folder in front of me. I pull out a photo of Margaret Watson – handcuffs, jumpsuit – and put it on the table in front of the prisoner.

She sits back, shrugging. "Who's that?"

"Oh, you're right. Your daughter has a team. We think she's the leader of her little terrorist gang. This?" I point at the photo. "This is Margaret Watson. She was at school with your daughter. She's currently enjoying the comforts of the cell two doors from your own."

"So?"

"I don't think you understand. This is a friend of your daughter's. Margaret was arrested at the site of a terrorist camp. We found all sorts of interesting things on the site. Bomb-making equipment, maps – even a rocket launcher. Do you know what else we found?"

"I'm sure you're going to tell me."

I pull out a photo of Sheena Richards and place it on the table.

"We found one of Bex's teachers, from that lovely, expensive school. Probably the inspiration for Bex's desertion from camp. She's locked up down the corridor, too."

I smile. "And then we found one of your daughter's friends from Camp Bishop, guarding a terrorist hideout." I pull a photo of Saunders from the file. He's lying on the floor in the bunker. The image is cropped so you can't see the bullet wound, but it's pretty clear that he's no longer breathing. "Unfortunately, he didn't survive the experience."

She looks at the photo, and quickly looks away. He looks younger than his sixteen years, and the image is brutal.

"What does this have to do with finding my daughter, Corporal?"

"We're certain that Bex was one of the people he was guarding. He was also guarding the people you've seen with her on PIN." I lean towards her. "You see, being friends with your daughter turns out to be a dangerous pastime. I wonder how long it will be before her friends realise that. Before they decide to go their own way. Before her little team evaporates."

Elizabeth looks at me again, steel behind her eyes. She leans forward.

"Corporal. Have you *ever* had a friend? Do you actually know what that means? Do you honestly think that kids who have gone through all this together would *leave each other behind*?" She shakes her head. "I feel sorry for you. You really don't know what's keeping them together, do you?"

"I hardly think that's the point, Elizabeth."

"Oh, but I think it is. I think you're the kind of person who does leave people behind. I think you bail at the first sign of conflict. I think you'd prefer to be alone, and tell yourself that you're tough, rather than take a risk and rely on someone else." She smiles. "I think you'd rather hurt people than help them." She tugs at her handcuffs. "I think you enjoy this. And I think you have no idea what gives my daughter the advantage over you." She leans forward again and lowers her voice. "You see, my daughter's friends know that she won't hurt them. They know that she'll stand by them, and look after them, and encourage them. And she knows that they'll do the same for her. They're a team, Corporal. Not a hierarchy. Not an opportunity for promotion. They're in this together. They're a *tribe*."

She sits back, a smug look on her face. I watch her in silence for a moment.

Don't let her provoke you, Ketty. We'll see who gets out of this in the end.

I force myself to focus on the questions I want to ask.

"And where do you think this *tribe* would be hiding?"

She laughs again. "I have no idea! My daughter doesn't need me any more. She's old enough and smart enough to look after herself, and her friends. I'm just happy that she's still on the run. You people had no right to take her from school in the first place. Good luck to her."

I look down at the table. "You know, that aiding and abetting charge doesn't go away, especially if you make statements like that."

Elizabeth leans forward in her chair, and her eyes meet mine. She's not laughing when she speaks again.

"Corporal. You've got me. I'm locked up, and you can do what you like with me. Too bad. There's nothing I can do to stop you." She puts her hands flat on the table. "But what I can do? I can keep you here. I can keep you talking, and jabbing at me, and making vague threats. You want me alive, so you can put me on TV and use me to threaten my daughter. Fine. Let's chat. Let's put footage of me on the news.

"Because while you're focusing on me, you're not focusing on my daughter. You're not hunting her, and you're not chaining her up in the next cell. There's no *family reunion* while you're in here talking to me.

"Do you know what a mother would do for her daughter? Do you have *any idea*?"

I shrug.

Not my area of expertise, Mrs Ellman.

"You're looking at it."

And there's the sound bite. Aiding and abetting. A confession, ready to go to PIN.

"Thank you, Elizabeth. I think that's all I need for today."

And I'm smiling as I leave the room.

Online

Bex

"Type your username, here," Gail points at my screen with the end of her pen, "and your password, here." She watches me copy the details from the piece of paper in front of me. "And you're in the system."

I'm looking at a desktop, like the front page of the tablets we used at school. The crest of the OIE is in the background, and there are icons and logos down both sides of the screen.

"And click on this one." She points again.

I click, and a white window fills the screen.

"You're online."

"That's it? I'm on the Internet?"

She nods, smiling.

"Now – as we explained. No logging into anything. No creating accounts. No posting information about yourselves, or about us. No posting at all." She looks at me. "Do you understand what that means?"

I shake my head.

"There is information out there." She waves her pen at the screen. "Anything you want to know about – it's out there, somewhere. You just need to learn how to look for it." She leans over and uses the touchscreen to pull down a menu and change a couple of settings, too quickly for me to follow what she's doing. "I think we'll start with safe searching on. No point scaring yourselves on day one. I'll allow PIN, and the Scottish news sites," she types some chains of text into the window, "but let's keep the child locks on for now." She closes the settings and sits back in her chair.

"So what do I do?"

She smiles. "What do you want to know?"

I stare at the screen. Something ordinary. Something everyday.

"There's a book I've been waiting for. Can I find out whether it's been published yet?

She smiles, and points at the screen. "Absolutely. Type the author's name into the box."

I type, and click 'Search', and the screen is filled with text.

"OK – so those are your hits."

"This is all information on the author?"

"Probably. We'll need to check that." She leans forward to look at the screen. "The top one looks good … but the second one is the author's homepage. Click on that."

And there's the author's photo. An introduction to her work. A brief life history. And a list of books. I stare at the screen for a moment. This is incredible. All this information, right in front of me.

I scroll down, and at the bottom of the list is the next book in the series I was reading with Dan, before we left school. I try clicking on the title, and I'm taken to another screen. There's a photo of the cover, and a synopsis of the plot.

"That's it! That's the book."

Gail leans in again. "Published … last month." She smiles. "I should be able to get that for you."

There's a grin on my face as I wave at Dan, sitting across the room with his liaison officer.

*****

We've been playing with the computers all morning. We've looked up our favourite books and authors, our favourite films, our favourite bands. The liaisons left us to it, once we'd got the hang of searching, and we've been calling each other over to see what we've found. Only Jake has been quiet, sitting on his own and looking at sites I don't recognise, and Charlie's at her meeting with the committee.

After lunch, I ask Gail how to get to the PIN website. She types in the address for me, and shows me what they've put online.

"Of course, this is designed for people outside the UK, so they won't cover all the news. They are trying to reach us, though, so there might be some items of interest to catch up with. When did you last watch PIN?"

"Four days ago." I can't hide the surprise in my voice. Since we arrived in Newcastle, we haven't missed a night. Four days feels like an eternity.

She nods, slowly. "OK, Bex. You need to be ready." I look at her, my pulse suddenly loud in my ears. I put a hand on the table to steady myself.

"What have I missed?"

She looks at me, a frown on her face. "It's your mother. They're putting her on TV every night. They're trying to get to you."

I shake my head. "Every night? They're questioning her every day?"

"We don't know. But they're putting new clips up every day. Just – be ready. OK?"

I close my eyes and slow my breathing. "OK."

Gail reaches over and clicks on some links. She pulls up a video, three days old from the date on the file.

It's Mum again, and Ketty. They're talking in the same room, Mum's hands cuffed to the table. Ketty puts something down on the table between them.

"I know the hair is ridiculous, and the glasses are just plain funny, but under that disguise, I think we can both figure out the identity of the missing delivery driver."

It's the ID card. Mum picks it up, and I watch as her shoulders slump. I realise I'm watching the moment when she knows they have evidence against her. That this could mean a firing squad.

I'm fighting for breath. I'm holding onto the edge of the table, but I can't stop watching the screen. The reporter speaks over the rest of the video – some nasty gloating about arresting a terrorist sympathiser. I put my hand up to the touchscreen, and the video stops. Mum, paused in the act of looking at my card. Of seeing the evidence I left behind.

"Turn it off." My voice is hoarse, and not much above a whisper. Gail leans in and closes the window.

"Are you OK?"

I shake my head, still gripping the edge of the table. I focus on stopping the tears, and force myself to look at Gail.

"Is there any more?"

"Of your mother?"

I nod.

"Are you sure you want to see?"

"I'm sure."

"OK." She clicks again, and another video fills the screen.

"Let's try this again. When did you last see your daughter?"

Mum pulls herself up straight and looks Ketty in the eye.

"I don't remember."

"Is that so?"

I can tell that Ketty is smiling. I feel sick, watching her with my mother. Remembering what she could do.

"You're sure about that? Because I'd hate to have to jog your memory."

Mum glares at Ketty. She's ignoring the threat. She's showing Ketty that she's tough. I feel like cheering, and I feel like screaming.

"I don't remember."

I feel like punching the air.

*****

There's more footage of Mum, and there's more footage of prisoners on trial. I work my way through the last three days, and there's no one I recognise. Amy and Dan have joined me for the last few videos, and the other liaison officers have left. When we've seen all the reports we missed, I slump back in my chair.

"Thank you, Gail. That's really helpful."

"Anyone you know?"

"Other than Mum? No. Not that I could see."

"They blamed us for the bomb in Bournemouth." Amy sounds upset.

"Of course they did. We can't exactly explain to everyone that we weren't there. We're easy targets for anything they want to blame on us." Dan looks at Gail. "Can we come back after dinner? Catch up on tonight's news?"

Gail nods. "Sure. I'll come back with you, if you like."

I nod. "Thank you. That would be great." I look at her, my face serious. "They've got our friends in their cells. We want to make sure they're still OK."

"I understand. I'll come and find you in the dining room."

We log out of our computers and leave the room. Jake stays, head down, typing fast. I have no idea what he's searching for.

*****

After dinner, we head back to the computer room with Gail. Jake didn't sit with us tonight – he's found some staff members to talk to, and I'm happy to let him go. Conversation over dinner is much more pleasant when everyone is happy to join in.

Dan, Amy, and Charlie pull chairs over to my computer. I log into the system, and Gail pulls up the PIN web page. She checks the time in the corner of the screen.

"Tonight's videos should be available. Let me take a look."

She clicks through, and pulls up a full-screen image of Ketty and Mum.

But this isn't the same. Mum has a black eye, and there's a graze on her cheek.

I can't stop myself from crying out, my hands over my mouth. Dan puts his hand on my shoulder.

"Do you want me to close it?"

I shake my head, and put my hands on the table.

Dan squeezes my shoulder and nods at Gail, and she lets the video play.

"Corporal. You've got me. I'm locked up, and you can do what you like with me. Too bad. There's nothing I can do to stop you. But what I can do? I can keep you here. I can keep you talking, and jabbing at me, and making vague threats. You want me alive, so you can put me on TV and use me to threaten my daughter. Fine. Let's chat. Let's put footage of me on the news."

Mum, talking back to Ketty. Mum, being brave and strong and showing the government that she's not afraid.

"Because while you're focusing on me, you're not focusing on my daughter. You're not hunting her, and you're not chaining her up in the next cell. There's no family reunion while you're in here talking to me."

There's a smile on my face as I watch my brave, amazing mother stand up to the cruelest person I've ever met.

"Do you know what a mother would do for her daughter? Do have any idea?"

Ketty shrugs.

"You're looking at it."

Dan puts his arm round my shoulder and pulls me into a hug.

"She's amazing, Bex. And she's OK."

I hug him back. And then the newsreader cuts in.

"This confession is breaking news. Elizabeth Ellman declared her intention to continue helping her daughter this morning, under interrogation. Under Martial Law, a confession like this will automatically convict Mrs Ellman of the aiding and abetting charge. It's just a matter of time before she faces her firing squad."

And the video ends. I break away from Dan, my hands shaking. Gail closes the window and gives me a helpless look.

"I'm so sorry, Bex. I wasn't expecting …"

I clasp my hands together in front of me, but the shaking doesn't stop. Charlie stands up and comes to kneel in front of me. She takes my hands in hers.

"They're not going to harm her, Bex. Not while they can still use her against you."

I'm shivering now, my whole body is shaking and I can't see through the tears.

"Charlie's right," Dan puts his hand back on my shoulder. "They're only showing us the stuff they want you to see. I bet the rest of that interview was your Mum telling Ketty where to stuff her questions."

I almost laugh at that. He's right. All these clips of Mum have been so short. I can imagine that there's not much they can use if she's spending most of her time standing up to Ketty.

But it won't help. Standing up to Ketty is what just convicted her on PIN, in front of everyone in the country. She's being built up to be the face of terrorism. Ketty is making sure that my Mum is a focus for all the fear the government wants people to feel. She doesn't have the rest of us, so she's using Mum instead.

I feel sick. I feel completely overwhelmed. If Ketty can manipulate Mum into confessing on camera, what else can she do?

Charlie asks Gail to leave us alone, and my friends take me to my room. Dan and Amy leave us, and Charlie waits while I pull on pyjamas and climb into bed. She holds my hand.

"Do you want me to stay?"

I shrug. I don't want to keep Charlie from sleeping. I don't want to take up her time.

But I don't want to be alone.

She pulls my chair over to the bed, and holds my hand until I fall asleep. When I wake up later, she's gone.

Traitor

Ketty

"Good morning, Corporal Smith!"

Conrad walks into the office as I'm hanging up the phone. No change in Jackson's condition, and now Conrad is smiling at me as if I'm the mouse he's decided to eat for breakfast.

Wake up, Ketty. Don't let him get to you.

I match his smile with my own. "Corporal Conrad. Colonel Bracken isn't in yet. Is there anything I can do for you?"

He stands in front of my desk, grinning at me.

"What is it? What's happened?"

He puts a piece of paper on the desk in front of me. It's a print-out of a message board or an internal news group. Whatever it is, it's above my pay grade. I don't have access to the computer system.

I glance at it, and look back at him. "What's this?"

The victorious grin never leaves his face.

"We've found your recruits," he says.

*****

Bracken is at his desk, and I'm sitting in the chair across from him, staring at the piece of paper from Conrad.

"I don't understand." Bracken shakes his head. "You're saying they're in Scotland?"

"It would seem so, Sir."

"And one of them posted this to an Internet site? In public?"

"That seems to be what happened."

"Have we traced the computer it was posted from?"

I nod. "Edinburgh, Sir."

"So it's genuine." Bracken runs his hands through his hair. "I can't imagine how they got themselves across the border." He looks down at the desk in front of him. "Have we checked up on that?"

"I think the brigadier is checking it out, Sir."

"It shouldn't be possible. We have patrols all along the border. Fences. Checkpoints. No-fly zones. They shouldn't have been able to get across."

"No, Sir."

But they did. And on our watch.

I read the message again.

"You can't catch us here. We're safe. Scotland forever!" And a photo of Jake Taylor, sitting in front of a computer. There are people in the background – one of them could be Bex – all sitting at their own computers, concentrating on the screens.

I take a closer look at the site he's chosen for his message. It's called Connexxion, and he's created an identity for himself. His screen name is 'RebelRefugee', and the image he's using is a photo of a camp-issue rifle.

Of course it is. Taylor's weapon of choice.

I've seen print-outs like this in briefings. I've never been online – I've never seen a live website – but I can see how this site seems to work. Jake posts an image, and then other users respond. There are comments here from other people, and there's a rant from Jake about Bex, and how she's not the hero everyone thinks she is. Other users have asked him who he is, and where he's come from. And he's answered them. There's no detail, but he mentions the RTS, and the bunker.

I sit up in my chair.

He mentions Newcastle.

"Sir, I think he's given us something we can use."

Bracken looks up.

"Newcastle, Sir. He says they were hiding in Newcastle."

"Don't we have the owner of the getaway car in the cells?"

"Yes, Sir."

"He was from Newcastle?"

"Yes, Sir."

"Is it time to ask him some questions?"

I can't hide my grin. "Yes, Sir. If we can't catch the recruits, at least we can round up whoever was helping them."

Bracken reaches for the phone.

*****

Conrad is grinning when we walk into the office. He knows I'm in trouble, and he's enjoying watching me squirm.

"Colonel, Corporal. The brigadier is waiting."

I manage to keep my fists to myself as we cross the office to Lee's door.

Lee is leaning on the front of his desk as we walk in. We waves to the chairs in front of him.

"Take a seat, you two. I gather you've heard the miraculous news?"

We sit down in front of him.

He grins at me.

"Your recruits, Ketty. We finally know where they are!" There's a sing-song sarcasm in his voice, as if this is a good thing.

"Yes, Sir."

"Remind me, Corporal Smith. Which foreign country have they managed to run to? Which enemy government has taken them in as honoured guests?"

Play along. Let him have his fun.

"Scotland, Sir."

"Yes, Ketty. Scotland. And how does this help us to arrest them? How does this help us to get them into the cells?"

I shake my head. "It doesn't, Sir."

Lee looks down at me, his smile fading.

"No, it doesn't." He frowns. "And what about Mrs Ellman? Wasn't she supposed to keep your recruits in line? Wasn't she supposed to stop them doing something like this?"

I'm about to answer, when Bracken cuts in.

"I think she still can."

Lee looks down at him, a sneer on his face. "Oh, please explain."

"Bex and her friends could be very useful to the Scottish government, and to the OIE. We can use Elizabeth Ellman to keep them afraid. Corporal Smith can keep talking to her on camera, and we can keep putting the footage on PIN. It will make them think twice before they do anything to act against us."

Lee stares at Bracken, and then at me.

"Are you planning to keep firing questions at Ellman's mother? Do you really think that will keep their attention, now that they're out of the country?"

I nod, my mouth dry. "Yes, Sir. I do. I think Bex can be persuaded to stay where she is, where she can't launch any more heroic assaults against government targets."

Lee shrugs. "I'm all for putting Mrs Ellman in front of that firing squad as soon as possible. But you think you can still use her?" I nod. "Fine. Keep Bex and her friends under control." He looks me in the eye. "But if they do anything aggressive. If they start making broadcasts or putting out more of these messages? I'm signing her execution papers. Understood?"

She's my hotline to Bex. Don't make her a martyr.

I nod again. "Understood, Sir."

He stands up and walks round the desk to his chair.

"I understand that you've got something else for me?"

Bracken answers. "We have. The messages from Scotland mention a safe house in Newcastle. If we can trace the location, we can find the cell that helped Bex and her friends after the raid on Makepeace Farm."

Lee gives Bracken an appraising look.

"Interesting. How are you proposing to do that?"

Bracken looks at me.

Time to pitch your idea, Ketty.

"I think we need to put the owner of the car through Enhanced Interrogation, Sir. I think he knows where the safe house is."

Lee raises his eyebrows. "The gentleman from Jesmond." He watches me for a moment too long. "Be my guest, Ketty. See what you can get out of him. I'll approve Enhanced Interrogation for this afternoon. I'll have my specialists meet you at Belmarsh."

"Thank you, Sir. If he knows where they were hiding, we'll make sure he tells us."

Lee watches me again, without speaking. I feel like the mouse in front of the cat.

Give me a chance, Sir. I'll get what we need.

He nods, eventually. "I'm sure you will, Ketty."

*****

The Enhanced Interrogation room is larger than the room we've been using. There's no furniture, and the walls and floor are tiled. Bracken and I stand against the wall as the guards bring the prisoner in. They check his handcuffs, and leave him standing in the centre of the room.

He looks at me, and at Bracken, panic in his eyes. I stand still, and stare back at him.

It's not me you need to worry about.

Two men in black jumpsuits walk into the room, closing and locking the door behind them. The prisoner turns as they approach him, and the panic takes over. He's shaking as they move to stand beside him, one at each elbow.

They haven't touched him yet, and already the man is begging us to leave him alone.

One of the men turns to Bracken. "Do you have questions you want to ask?"

Bracken nods, and looks at me.

I smile. I understand this.

Iron fists and steel toe caps.

*****

When we get what we need, we've been with the prisoner for an hour. His nose is broken, and possibly his ankle as well. He'll have bruises everywhere in the morning – he's going to be hurting for days.

And regretting every minute of our conversation.

I'm trying to hide my smile as we walk out. The address we're looking for is in Bracken's notebook, along with names and information on the people who helped our recruits.

One of the interrogation specialists smiles at me as he crosses the waiting room.

"You were good in there," he says. "Not squeamish. I like that in a Corporal." He winks at me, and I give him a cold stare until he walks away, laughing to himself.

Never underestimate me.

Bracken watches him leave, disapproval on his face. I pour us both a coffee, and pretend not to notice when Bracken pulls a hip flask from his pocket and takes a long drink, his hands shaking. When the flask is back in his pocket I stop stirring the drinks and turn back to him.

"Thank you, Ketty," he says, taking the cup, his hands still shaking. "I forget how good you are at … physical persuasion."

"I didn't touch him, Sir." I take a sip of my drink.

Bracken nods. "No. But you didn't hold back on your questions, either." He looks at me, and I'm not sure whether it's fear or respect on his face. "You enjoyed that, didn't you?"

I try very hard to hide my smile. "I suppose so, Sir."

He sighs. "At least we've got our answers." He finishes his drink. "Let's go and find out whether he was telling the truth."

*****

Lee gives us permission to send in the troops from Morpeth. The address we've been given is a health food shop in Wallsend, and the raid is planned for six o'clock tonight. We're hoping the staff will still be on site, and we're hoping to catch the owner. It seems that she was the person who borrowed the car, and judging by the prisoner's description, she could be my mystery driver from the nursing home.

There's nothing to do now but wait. The footage, and any prisoners, will be with us in the morning. I tidy my desk, say goodnight to Bracken, and walk home in the cold.

I change, and head out for a run. The cold air burns in my lungs, and my knee jars with every step, but the pain keeps me awake.

You should be here, Jackson. You'd be proud of me.

Birthday

Bex

There's a loud knocking on my door. I'm waking from a dream, and someone is banging on my door. I crawl out of bed, throw a sweater on over my pyjamas, and stumble across the room. I can hear giggling outside.

I pull the door open.

"Surprise!"

Dan and Amy are standing in the corridor, a cake held on a tray between them.

A cake with seventeen candles.

"Happy birthday, Bex!"

Dan and Amy are grinning at me, and Charlie is smiling. Even Jake is hanging around in the corridor. I rub my eyes, and try to look happy.

"Are you going to let us in?"

I look back at my room, with its unmade bed, and yesterday's clothes all over the floor.

"Or we could go to the common room?" Charlie winks at me.

"Common room sounds great."

We walk along the corridor – me, my friends, and my cake. I'm rubbing the sleep out of my eyes, and pushing my fingers through my hair to tame it. Covering a yawn with my hands.

Charlie turns the lights on, and Dan puts the cake down on one of the tables. Some of the candles have blown out, but Dan pulls a lighter from his pocket and lights them again. I'm facing an inferno of seventeen candles.

My friends break into song, and I wait for them to finish before I blow out all the flames. It takes two puffs, but the cheering is worth it.

"Cake for breakfast!" Dan calls, as Charlie brings a knife from one of the kitchen drawers and Amy carries a pile of plates to the table.

I carry my slice of cake to the sofa, and sit, one leg folded under me while the others sit down.

"So how does it feel, Bex? Seventeen! You're as old as me!" Dan pats his chest proudly.

I roll my eyes, and take a bite of my cake.

"This is delicious!"

Charlie smiles. "I'm glad you like it."

"The benefits of having a chef in the gang!" Dan says, around a mouthful.

Four of us are crowded onto the sofas, and Jake pulls a chair over from the dining area.

"Happy birthday, Bex." Amy puts her plate down and gives me a hug. "You OK?"

I nod. There's nothing I can do about Mum and Ketty, and right now I've got my friends looking after me. I give her a smile.

Dan holds up his slice of cake. "It's almost a sandwich, you know. Cake." He nods, approvingly.

Amy rolls her eyes. "This again? Why does everything have to be …"

There's a noise in the corridor, and we're all on our feet when someone bursts through the door. We've had no warning, but we're ready to fight, and Dan is reaching for the cake knife before we recognise Jake's liaison officer. He marches into the room, followed by one of the soldiers who guard the compound.

He raises a finger and points at Jake.

"You!" He bellows. "Over here. Right now."

Jake reaches down and puts his plate carefully on the floor. Then he turns, giving us all a smug smile before he walks across the room to the two men. His liaison beckons the soldier over.

"Hands out in front of you."

The soldier pulls out a pair of handcuffs and starts to snap them onto Jake's wrists.

And that's when we all start shouting.

The liaison holds his hands up for quiet.

"You'll get your turn. But right now, Mr Taylor here is in a world of trouble. I suggest that the rest of you stay here, and keep out of sight." He looks at the cake on the table. "I'll get some breakfast sent over."

"You can't just take him away." Amy steps towards the two men. "He's our friend. We've fought together, and we've been in trouble together." She points at Jake. "What's he supposed to have done?"

The liaison shakes his head, and the soldier puts his hand on Jake's shoulder. Amy steps closer.

"What did you do, Jake?" Her voice is quiet, and she sounds hurt.

Jake gives her a mocking smile. "Something you lot were too scared to do." He looks over at me, smirking. "Happy birthday, Bex," he says, and laughs.

The soldier takes Jake's shoulder and leads him into the corridor.

The liaison officer looks around at us. "You lot don't leave this building. You stay in your rooms, or the common room. No computers. No training or shooting. Just sit tight." And he follows Jake out of the room.

*****

"What the hell was that?" Dan sits down, his plate forgotten on the floor. We look at each other, but no one has anything to say. I'm shaking my head as I sink back onto the sofa.

Amy wipes tears from her eyes. "What did he do?"

I'm thinking through everything that happened yesterday. The whole day in the computer room, getting used to searching online, and watching PIN. The three of us, sharing our search results. Jake sitting on his own, typing.

And I know what he did.

"He gave us away." The others look at me. "He told people where we are." Dan opens his mouth to ask, and I cut him off. "On the computers, yesterday. He gave away our location."

Dan swears.

Amy leans forward. "Are you sure?"

I shake my head. "I think so." I look up, at Dan. "It makes sense. He didn't talk to us all day. And he was typing, not reading." Dan looks at the floor, shaking his head. "I think he's told the government where we are."

*****

Someone from the kitchen brings us breakfast and a pot of coffee, and we sit on the sofas in silence picking at our bacon sandwiches. We finish the coffee, and the others tell me what they would have bought me for my birthday, if they'd been allowed to go shopping.

We're trying to cheer ourselves up. It should be funny, but no one's laughing.

It's mid-morning before anyone comes to speak to us. We're collecting up the plates and stacking them on the table when Gail walks in.

"Good. You're all still here." She waves us back to the sofas. "Sit down, all of you."

She looks at the birthday cake, and then at me. "Happy birthday, Bex. I'm sorry. I should have remembered."

I shrug.

"Are you going to tell us what happened?" Amy sits on the edge of her seat, waiting for an answer.

Gail waits for us to get comfortable, then she pulls up the chair Jake was using and sits down.

"So it seems that your friend spent yesterday doing exactly what we asked you not to do." I nod, and sit back. I was right. "When we left you to get used to being online, and you all," she points around the group, "ran searches and found out what's out there, he was posting information on public sites. Information about you."

She looks down at her hands.

"He let everyone know that you're in Scotland. He told people about Camp Bishop, and Makepeace Farm, and about your safe house in Newcastle."

Dan sits forward. "He did what?"

Gail waves her hands. "He didn't give the address, or anything specific, but he did say that you were in Newcastle. And that, obviously, puts our operatives in Newcastle at risk." She shakes her head. "As of last night, we haven't heard from Neesh or Caroline, and we're trying to find out whether the other safe houses have been compromised."

I feel sick. I feel dizzy. After everything Neesh and Caroline did for us. After everything we've done already to put them at risk.

"Why would he do that?" Amy is fighting back tears.

Gail looks at me. "There's something else." I see the look in her eyes and I'm starting to panic. "He said some … unfriendly things … about Bex."

Amy gasps, and turns to me.

"In public?" Charlie asks.

"In public." Gail glances at Charlie, then looks back at me. "I'm sorry, Bex. It's better that you hear this from me, than you find it online. There are a lot of people on the sites he used, and they've all seen what he wrote. We've taken the original posts down, but there are plenty of copies out there, and the replies are still up. I can share them with you if you like, but I'd recommend that you steer clear of it, at least for now."

I put my head back and stare at the ceiling. "Let me guess. Everyone thinks I'm a hero, but I'm not. Everyone thinks I save people but actually I leave them to die. I have screaming nightmares because I secretly know what horrible things I've done. And I won't let anyone else be a hero – I want all the glory for myself."

Amy reaches out and takes my hand.

Gail lets out a breath. "I can see this isn't a new disagreement between you."

I shake my head. "Not even close."

"I'm sorry," she says. "Whatever the background is to all that, you didn't need it to go public." She pauses. "And we would have liked to keep your arrival secret for a little longer."

"So what do we do now?" I sit up as Dan speaks.

"Now? Now you stay here. In your rooms, or in the common room. Curtains closed. No access to the computers." She looks around at us. "I'm sorry to do this, but I'm sure you understand. We need to figure out what do to next."

She stands up. "We'll get meals brought over, until we decide how best to keep you all safe. We'll sort this out, but it might take a bit of time. Just, please, be patient. We'll figure everything out as soon as we can."

She walks to the door. "Any questions?"

"Where's Jake now?" Amy asks, her voice a whisper.

"Jake is safe. He's under guard, and we're asking him some questions, but he's not in any danger."

Amy nods, and brushes a tear from her cheek. "Thank you," she says.

"Are you really worried about me, after what Jake said?" I stand up, making sure Gail doesn't leave. "Or are you worried about the face of the resistance. About your image. My face, out there on your posters, and Jake, telling people who I really am?"

"We … we're worried about all of that. We're worried about the effect on the resistance, of course. But we're worried about you, too." I can hear the sincerity in her voice, right up until she's talking about me.

This is about the resistance. They don't want me to go online and retaliate. They don't want me to have a say at all. Front-line doll. Keep your face pretty and your mouth shut.

"Yeah. That's what I thought."

Gail nods, and walks out into the corridor.

"Happy birthday, Bex," I say, watching the door close behind her.

Footage

Ketty

Bracken is waiting when I walk in with the morning coffee and briefing papers.

"Good news and bad news, Ketty," he says from the chair behind my desk.

"Sir?" I put a mug in front of him, put the briefing papers on the edge of the desk, and stand, waiting for him to continue.

"We found the safe house."

I smile. "The address was correct?"

He nods. "Your prisoner gave us the right address."

Iron fists and steel toe caps. Give people an incentive to talk, and don't give them a Plan B.

"So what did they find?"

"Empty flats. That's the bad news."

"And the good news?"

He smiles. "Prisoners."

*****

The footage is grainy, and shot from helmet cameras, but we can see what happens as the soldiers seal off the street outside the shop, then break in through the front doors. Some shouting, some screaming as the staff realise what's happening. Through to the back of the shop and the store room, and then up the stairs to a small flat.

"I thought you said the flats were empty?" This one is furnished and decorated, and full of someone's belongings. We watch as the soldiers sweep ornaments off surfaces, pull drawers out and tip their contents onto the floor, and pull everything out of the kitchen cupboards.

Bracken nods. "Someone lives there," he agrees. "They weren't around last night, though." The soldiers move through the flat, pulling the cushions from the sofa and the mattress from the bed. There's no one hiding, and there's nothing unexpected in the drawers or the cupboards. The soldiers pull back to the stairwell, and head upstairs.

And that's when everything gets interesting.

A solider ahead of the helmet cam points up at a security camera, hidden in a corner of the staircase. Round a turn in the stairs, they come to a landing, and a solid front door. It takes several minutes to break the door down, using an axe and a battering ram.

Inside, there's nothing. The kitchen cupboards are empty. There's a table and two chairs in the corner. The fridge is off, and empty, and there's an empty biscuit tin on top. In the two bedrooms, the beds are stripped bare and there's nothing in the cupboards. In the living room, an ancient sofa sits in front of a coffee table. No TV, no cushions, no more furniture.

But there's a CCTV monitor in the entrance hall, wired to the camera on the stairs. And there are six locks on the reinforced door.

We've found our safe house.

*****

"So who owns the shop?"

Bracken sips his coffee. "Lee has someone tracking them down. 'Morgana Wholefoods'. Hiding in plain sight." He shakes his head.

"And the prisoners?"

"Three of them. Settling into their cells."

"Shop staff?"

"As far as we can tell. They could be terrorists, or OIE agents. We'll find out when we start the interrogations."

I think about the owner of the car, begging the men in black jumpsuits to leave him alone.

I'm sure we will.

*****

Lee calls us up to his office after lunch. He sits behind his desk, his face like thunder. He waves us to the chairs, facing him.

"I thought this raid was going to give us the local cell."

I clear my throat. "Yes, Sir. I was hoping so, Sir."

He leans forward, his eyes burning into me. "You were *hoping*?"

"Yes, Sir. We took them by surprise. We were hoping there would be someone there …"

Lee slaps his hand down onto his desk. "I am not interested in your *hope*, Corporal. Hope doesn't bring me useful prisoners. Do you know what hope does? Hope sends my soldiers searching through empty flats. Hope fills my cells with terrified people who have no idea what we're asking them about." He glares at me until I can feel the floor opening underneath me. "Those people are shop workers, Ketty. That was a legitimate business we took down last night, and the people we're questioning this morning don't know anything about safe houses and terrorist cells. Nothing!" He slaps the desk again, and I flinch back in surprise.

He sits back in his chair and watches us both.

"The good news is that we're watching the shop. We're leaving guards around the building, and if anyone tries to access the flats, we'll be waiting for them." He turns over a piece of paper on his desk. "We've also got a team going through the inhabited flat. Plenty of clues there to help us find whoever was living there. He picks up a photo and holds it out to me. "Look familiar?"

I smile. It's the woman from the nursing home. The woman who drove the getaway car.

"Yes, Sir. I can place her in Stockport, during Bex's escape from Orchard House." I look closely at the photo. "She's definitely involved, Sir."

Lee nods. "Good. That's a start, at least." He thinks for a moment. "Any idea where she is now, Corporal?"

I shake my head. "No, Sir. I've only seen her once." I point at the photo. "Did that come from the flat?"

"It did."

"And was there anything else? Any ID?"

Lee gives me a long, uncomfortable stare. "Do you think we'd be having this conversation if there was?"

Stupid question, Ketty.

"No, Sir."

Lee smirks at Bracken, and I have to resist the urge to roll my eyes.

Come on, Sir. Back me up.

But he doesn't. He gives Lee a quick smile, then looks down at his hands.

Lee stares at me again. "Let's hope the prisoners know more than they're letting on. And let's release some of that footage to PIN for tonight's news. The stuff from the shop should be enough. Can you handle that? And bring it up here for checking?"

"Yes, Sir."

He nods, his eyes on mine.

"Good. Dismissed, Corporal."

*****

Pulling out suitable footage and copying it to a flash drive takes twenty minutes, and I add it to the daily footage of Elizabeth before heading back upstairs to hand it to Conrad.

"Something special for the news tonight, Corporal?"

"As always."

He takes the flash drive and turns it over between his fingers. "It's a shame about the safe house, Ketty. That could have been your saving grace. Something to show for all the work you've done, tracking down the recruits?"

Leave me alone, David. This isn't over yet.

I give him a cold smile. "I don't think I'm done with this. Do you?" He looks amused. "I think there's more here to find. I think we can still track this cell, and find out who was in charge of looking after our runaways."

He smiles back, and shrugs. "I'll pass this on to Lee. I'm sure we'll all enjoy the show tonight."

*****

I'm back at my flat before I realise I haven't phoned the hospital today. I get changed and run, the pain in my knee reminding me not to give up. Not to let the brigadier get to me.

We haven't finished with the prisoners yet. We haven't finished going through the flat.

We'll find something. And when we do, I'll be there to join the dots.

Watch me, Jackson. I'm not giving up on this. I'm going to bring them what they want.

Neesh

Bex

We're confined to our rooms for a second day. Someone from the kitchen brought us food, and we're sitting in the common room, watching rubbish on daytime TV. The 24-hour news channels are fascinating to begin with, but there's nothing exciting going on today. When we've seen the same three news stories repeated over and over, we change the channel.

"Why does anyone watch this stuff?" Dan presses buttons on the remote control, scrolling through the channels. We find a political comment programme, and we watch in amazement as guest after guest criticises the Scottish government and makes personal attacks against the Prime Minister.

"How can they say all this? How can they get away with it?"

Charlie shrugs. "I guess that's life in a free country. Say what you want, and the worst thing that can happen is that someone says the same about you."

No one wants to be stuck in here, but the committee is still figuring out what to do with Jake. How much damage he's done to the resistance. How much damage he's done to me, and my image. My face on those posters. I think about the people risking their lives to put up my picture, and about Jake, tearing me down.

I knew he blamed me for leaving him with Ketty and Bracken. I knew he was upset when the resistance used my photo on their posters. But I didn't know how deep the hatred went.

Someone else I've hurt. Something else I need to let go.

*****

When the kitchen staff bring us dinner, we ask them to send one of the liaison officers over with a computer. We want to watch the news on PIN.

We've just finished eating when Gail arrives, carrying a laptop.

"OK. The committee says you can watch PIN on this, but I need to stay and watch with you."

I shrug. Dan takes his feet off the sofa and sits up.

Gail puts the laptop on one of the tables, and waves us over. "It's better over here. We can all sit round, and you'll be closer to the screen."

We move over to the table, dragging chairs with us across the floor. Gail flinches at the noise, then pulls up a chair of her own. She signs in, types in the PIN page, and scrolls down the list of tonight's stories. We all lean in to see what's there.

"Safe house raid." The others look at me. "Safe house raid," I say, pointing at the screen. Gail clicks on the link.

And we're watching video from the street outside Neesh's shop.

Amy gasps, and puts her hands to her mouth.

It's a camera on someone's helmet, and the film wobbles and jumps as they walk, but I can't look away.

There are soldiers, walking down the street to the door. Someone's blocked the road with black vehicles, and there's a group of soldiers walking towards the shop. They hang back before they reach the shop windows. There are lights on inside, and they're making sure that the raid is a surprise.

I can hear my pulse hammering in my ears as they line up against the neighbouring shop fronts. There's a sick feeling in my stomach.

The lead soldier waves the others forwards, and they run towards the shop, our camera following behind. The doors are locked, but the battering ram breaks through the wooden frames, and they kick the splintered pieces out of the way.

There's a distorted sound of breaking glass, and some screams from inside the shop.

"Nobody move!" The soldiers spread out from the doors, forming a line across the front of the room, cutting off the tills from the shelves. *"Hands in the air!"* There are two – no, three – employees, stacking shelves and mopping floors, visible as the camera swings round. We've never met them – we stayed out of sight in the loading bay and the store room – but these are Neesh's workers. One by one they put their hands in the air, *Morgana Wholefoods* logos visible on their lime green shirts.

Amy grips my hand. Dan leans forward in his chair. Charlie has her hand over her mouth as we watch, the colour draining out of her face.

Two soldiers check between the aisles for anyone who might be hiding, but there's no one else.

"Which one of you is the owner?" The employees exchange worried glances, but no one speaks. The lead soldier waves someone over to the closest employee.

A soldier walks up to him as he stands with his hands in the air. They lift their gun, and point it into his face. *"The owner! Which one is the owner?"* The employee blinks and cowers back. *"No one,"* calls someone else. *"The owner isn't here."* The soldier moves their gun to cover the person speaking.

"Where are they?"

"Off shift. It's just us tonight. The owner's gone home."

"Where's that?" Shouts the lead soldier.

Amy pulls her hand away as my hands curl into fists, the nails digging into my palms.

"Come on, Neesh," whispers Amy beside me. "Don't be home. Don't get caught."

The second employee points upwards. *"First floor."* She points at the door at the back of the shop. *"Stairs are out back."*

The third employee gives her an angry glance, but as soon as he turns back there's a soldier in front of him, bringing the butt of their rifle up. *"Hiding something?"* The angry employee shakes his head, and the soldier brings the butt of their rifle down on his nose.

We all gasp. Amy hides behind her hands. Gail shakes her head, slowly.

The lead soldier leaves four soldiers in the shop, and waves the others towards the back door. The soldier with the camera jogs through the shop, following the others out into the store room.

The store room where we spent our mornings sorting deliveries and stacking boxes.

Amy starts to sob. The camera swings around the room as the soldiers search between the shelves and boxes.

"Clear!"

"Clear!"

The lead soldier waves everyone over to the stairwell. My heart is beating so hard I can feel my pulse moving my arms.

"Come on, Neesh. Come on, Neesh." Amy is whispering through tears.

And then the video ends.

There's a moment of stunned silence before we're all shouting at Gail.

"That's it?"

"That can't be it!"

Gail clicks on the screen. She closes the video, then opens it again. She checks the list for more footage.

"That's it. That's all there is."

And we all stare at the screen.

Dan clears his throat. "We should check the prisoners. The rest of tonight's news."

Gail clicks back to the list of news items, and we work our way through.

There's more footage of Mum, but it's from the same interview as before. The bruises on her face are the same, and there's nothing new in what she says.

Tonight's prisoners are strangers. No one we've seen before. There's some footage of the Morgana employees being led to the back of a prison van, but no footage of Neesh.

"That's a good thing, right?" Says Amy. "If they haven't shown us Neesh, then they haven't found her."

Charlie leans over and gives her a hug. "Let's hope so."

But I remember Gail, yesterday. Telling us that they haven't heard from Neesh, or Caroline.

They're missing. Our protectors. The people who saved us after the bunker.

"Come on, Neesh," I whisper, under my breath. "Be safe."

Loss

Ketty

I'm in before Bracken. I push myself to walk up the stairs and head to the coffee machine and the document drop. The Private hands me today's folder, and then looks up.

"Have you had the message?" He consults a sticky note next to his phone. "Someone's trying to contact you. Nurses? A hospital?" He squints at the note, and shrugs.

Jackson.

I'm running for the office before I know what I'm doing. The Private is shouting after me, and I realise I've left everything – the document case, the folder, the coffee – on his counter. And I don't care.

Through the door. Round the desk. I reach for the phone, fumble it, drop it. I take a deep breath and pick it up, dialling the number with shaking hands.

"Nevill Hall Hospital, High Dependency Ward."

"This is Corporal Ketty Smith. You have a message for me?"

Come on, Jackson.

"Corporal Smith. Just a moment, please." The phone crackles as the nurse presses her hand over the handset.

I stifle a scream of frustration as the nurse makes me wait.

"Corporal?" A new voice on the line.

"Corporal Smith here."

"Corporal Smith. This is the Charge Nurse. We were asked to inform you of any change in the condition of Liam Jackson."

"Yes. Is he …?"

"I'm sorry, Corporal. Liam Jackson passed away earlier this morning."

I can't speak. I can't breathe. I can't stand up. My knee gives way and I fall into my chair. There's no air in the room, and I'm clutching at the neck of my shirt, trying to loosen the collar. I realise the Charge Nurse is still talking. Something about injuries and infection.

"Corporal? Corporal, are you there?"

I force myself to speak. "I'm here. Thank you. Thank you for letting me know." And I hang up, as I do every morning.

*****

Bracken finds me, head in my hands, when he walks through the door. I have no briefing for him, and no coffee. I have no idea how much time has passed since I hung up the phone. In my head, I'm back on the coach. Jackson is at the back door, and I'm jostling Ellman into an empty seat, keeping her away from the recruits.

Three shots. That's all it took. Two shots at Jackson, one at me, and Pearce took us both out.

I'm still here. My knee is a mess, I'm limping, and I'm in pain, but I'm still here.

But Jackson's gone. Dan Pearce and Bex Ellman killed him. They left him lying in the road, and they drove away. They're free, and he's gone. He's been fighting for months, but the damage was too much. Two of Dan's bullets in his lungs and they couldn't save him.

"Ketty?"

I drag myself back to the office, to this morning, and look up at Bracken. I should be crying. I should have red eyes and tear-stained cheeks. I should be angry.

But I'm numb.

"He's gone, Sir," is all I can say.

"He?" Bracken looks confused. "Jackson?"

I nod. "This morning."

It's a moment before he says anything.

"I'm so sorry, Ketty." He stands in front of the desk for a moment, then opens the door to his office. "Come in here. Come in and sit down."

I stand up and walk into his office. He holds the door open for me, and I sit down in front of his desk. Every move I make feels as if it is being made by someone else. There's a barrier between me and the world. I feel as if my ears are stuffed with cotton wool and my skin has forgotten how to feel. As if I'm on my own inside a glass jar. I sit down, and stare at the wall behind the desk.

"Wait here." Bracken leaves, and comes back some time later with coffee for both of us, along with my case, and the briefing folder. He puts the coffee cups on the desk, and pulls today's whisky bottle from the bottom of the filing cabinet. Before I can protest, he pours a generous slug into both coffee cups, and hands one to me. He sits on the edge of his desk, watching me with concern as I take a sip.

It's strong, and it's hot, and it gives me something to focus on. Something to hang onto.

"He was …" I begin, but I don't know what to say. I don't know how to explain who Jackson was to me. How much I'd been looking forward to talking to him again. To taking his mocking and his jokes and pushing back, just as hard. How we competed and how we teamed up. How we could get each other through anything.

Except this.

"I know," Bracken says, gently. And I know he does. He knew us both, and he knows what we did for him. I nod, and take another sip of coffee.

*****

I'm back at my desk. Bracken is covering for me, taking himself to meetings and making excuses while I stare at his paperwork and force myself to think about my job.

You can do this, Ketty. You don't need Jackson.

But I do. I need to talk to him. I need him to poke fun at me, sitting in this dusty office. I need him to make fun of Conrad. I need him to brag about running the assault course. Demand to know what I've been doing to stay tough and fit and better than everyone else. I'm too comfortable here, with my own flat and my Corporal stripes – I need his iron fists and steel toe caps. I need him to show me what I could be, and to mock what this job is doing to me. I've gone from babysitting a camp full of recruits to babysitting Bracken.

Jackson would be laughing at me.

And that's when it hits me that I'll never hear his voice again. I'm sitting at my desk, my head in my hands, and I'm trying to remember the last thing he said to me, on the coach. The last thing I said to him.

"We're good, Ketty. We're good."

And me, shouting his name.

And that's it. No more words between us.

I close my eyes. I can see him on that first night at Camp Bishop, all attitude and danger. His hand slamming my shoulder into the wall, and my fists drawing the battle lines for our relationship. His respectful handshake a day later.

"I've never met anyone like you."

How have I lost him? How did two bullets, and the space of two heartbeats, take him away from me?

I smash my fists into the desktop. It's as if a door has opened, and I can feel again. Anger, and pain. Loss. I stifle a scream, biting my knuckles until I draw blood.

Come on, Ketty. Get yourself together. There'll be time enough to fight this. Focus. Do your job.

*****

Bracken finds me staring at the same report I've been reading all afternoon. There's a pen in my hand, and I've made a few notes, but I've read the same section over and over and nothing makes sense. I have no idea what the words mean.

I'm amazed to find that it's the end of the day.

"Go home, Ketty. Get out of here."

I put the pen down, pick up the report and tuck it into the folder it came from.

"Yes, Sir. Thank you, Sir." My voice is flat.

But I can't move. I can't make myself stand up. I can't face going back to my tiny flat, alone.

"Ketty?"

I close my eyes and shake my head, willing myself to focus. To stand up, to walk out of the office. But I can't.

Bracken puts his hand on my desk.

"Tell me about it." And he walks away into his office, waving for me to follow.

I force myself to stand up and walk in after him. He points me to the chair in front of his desk, and I sit down. He pulls the whisky bottle from the filing cabinet along with two glasses, and puts them down in the middle of his desk.

Like a challenge.

Are you asking my permission, Sir?

I nod, and he pours two large drinks, handing one to me across the desk before sitting down.

"Tell me," he says again, and takes a sip from his glass.

"About Jackson?"

He nods. "Hurts, doesn't it? Losing someone like that?"

"It does."

He watches me. I'm trying to find something to say, but there's nothing I can put into words.

"You two were an unstoppable team," he says, eventually. "It's like you both knew what the other one was thinking."

I laugh, and nod. "We did, Sir." I wave my hand dismissively. "I mean, not really, but we both knew what the other one would do. I could guess what he would do next, and he could second-guess me, too."

He takes another sip. "That's rare. That's what we want to see in a team, but it's almost impossible to train into people. Either you can see it, or you can't." He raises his glass. "You two could see it."

I cradle my whisky, and suddenly I'm talking. I'm talking about working with Jackson. About being Bracken's fists when he needed answers. About the feeling of power and the sense of coordination as Jackson and I moved in on Margaret Watson. On Jake Taylor.

And Bracken is talking, too. About the discipline he was planning to land on Jackson, that first night, and how he realised that I'd handled his behaviour more effectively than a commanding officer could. About watching us running training sessions together. About sending us to question his prisoners.

I start to tell him about the night we dragged Ellman outside the fence, but he holds up his hand.

"I know about that. I know what you two did."

I'm amazed. Bracken's affection for the tiny fighters is what got me busted from the Lead Recruit job. How is he OK with us using our fists on one of them?

"But …"

"You kept it off my desk, and you calmed Ellman down. Win-win." He finishes his drink, pours another, and waves the bottle at me. I shrug, and lean forward to hand him my glass. He pours me another generous measure.

"So why was that OK, but the stunt with Saunders cost me my job?"

"Locking him out in the rain?" He leans on the desk, and puts his glass down in front of him. "That was public, Ketty. That wasn't keeping anything off my desk. It wasn't subtle, and it wasn't helpful."

"You called it cruel, Sir." I shouldn't push this, but the whisky is making me brave.

"And so it was," he says, picking up his drink again.

"But so was …"

"... so was what you did to Ellman, and Taylor, and the prisoner?" I nod. "Absolutely. But those incidents happened out of sight. Behind closed doors and fences. Not outside my front gate, in daylight, in front of the entire camp."

I nod, slowly. "So if we'd been a bit more subtle, we could have got away with ..."

"... with a whole lot more. Yes. As long as you were keeping things off my desk, I was happy to give you two a long leash."

"But ... if we'd known ..."

"You were learning. You were discovering the limits. You'd have figured it out."

If we hadn't been sent out as terrorist bait. If my partner in discipline hadn't been gunned down in the road.

"Invisible rules?" I ask. He nods.

I drain my glass and place it carefully on the desk.

"So what are the invisible rules here, Sir? What do we need to learn to survive in London?"

He stares thoughtfully into his drink and shakes his head. "I'm not sure Ketty. I'm not sure about any of it." He props his head on one hand, his fingers hiding his eyes. "I'm not sure what we're doing here."

I can't think of anything to say.

"I thought we were here to track down the terrorists, Sir. Major General Franks said ..."

"Major General Franks has her own agenda. As does Brigadier Lee." He rests both elbows on the desk and leans forward, eyes on the drink in his hands. "They're putting me on the Terrorism Committee, Ketty."

"That's good, Sir. That's what we're here to do."

He shakes his head. "I'm not sure. There's more going on here than we know about."

I think about what David said, in the bar.

"He won't handle what's coming."

I wait for him to explain, but he stares into his glass.

"Invisible rules?"

He nods. "But it's more than that." He looks up at me. "The people on the Terrorism Committee – they're the same people who ran the weapons test on Leominster. Lee, Holden, some of the support crew."

"The people who ran the false flag attack?" He nods again.

I think this through. Are they chasing terrorists? Tracking them down and bringing them to London for the firing squads? Or are they the ones planning the attacks?

Is the Terrorism Committee tasked with catching criminals, or are they there to keep the attacks coming? To keep people afraid?

I shake my head. This has to be the whisky, clouding my judgement. This is a conspiracy theory.

Wake up, Ketty. Keep it real.

And then Bracken rests his head on his hand again, the colour draining out of his face. "Ketty, I think we might be working for the bad guys."

Grief

Bex

We wake to good news. The committee has decided to let us out of our rooms. We can leave our building, and eat our meals with the rest of the staff. We all hurry to get dressed, and head over to the canteen for breakfast.

It's strange to be eating here without Jake. He's not even at another table, doing his best to ignore us. He's not here at all.

We eat together, the four of us, and after breakfast Gail comes over to explain their decision.

"We know you haven't done anything to deserve this," she looks around the table, "so thank you for your patience. We're holding Jake on site while we figure out what to do next. As for all of you – no more computer access. Your logins have been removed from the system, so the computers won't work for you, even if you try to use them."

Dan protests, but Gail holds up her hands. "As I said, you don't deserve this, but we can't risk any of you getting involved with Jake's comments and the follow-up. There's some nasty stuff on those threads, and we don't want any of you taking it personally."

I nod. "That's fine. There's nothing I need to search for."

Amy shrugs, and Dan looks upset.

"We were going to start your training today, but for now we're going to have to ask you to wait. We'll need some time to sort out what happens to Jake. So – use the gym, use the sports hall. Get yourselves some exercise. Keep yourselves busy. I'll meet you here after dinner with the laptop for your PIN update."

She's about to stand up, when Amy puts her hand on Gail's arm.

"Don't hurt Jake, will you?" Gail looks surprised. "He's done some horrible things, but it's only because he's hurting. Some really bad things happened to him, and he's still angry. Promise you won't hurt him?"

I think about Ketty, whispering in my ear on the assault course.

"Save your effort for where it matters. Leave the losers to lose."

And I shake my head. "Amy's right, Gail. He's not a bad person." I look down at the table. "Give him a chance. Ask him what happened. Ask him what he's angry about. Get him some help. But don't hurt him. He doesn't deserve that."

Gail raises her eyebrows. "I'll bear that in mind."

*****

Dan and I head to the gym after breakfast. It's ages since we've been out for a run, and a running machine is better than nothing. I pull on my new trainers and set the machine for a steady jog. We run for miles, talking occasionally, cheering each other on. It feels good.

I'm on my cool down walk when Gail comes in.

"Bex?"

I switch off the machine, grab my towel and head over to the door.

"Bex. I'm so sorry." I look at her, my mind running through everything she might be sorry for. "It's your father. I'm afraid we've just heard …"

I nod. "He died."

She's touching my elbow. Telling me how sorry she is.

I shrug her hand away. I sit down on the weightlifting bench and put my head in my hands.

Dan's running machine slows and stops, and he's next to me, his hand on my shoulder.

"Thank you, Gail. You can go."

"But Bex …"

"You can leave now." Dan doesn't raise his voice, but his tone is enough to send Gail away. The door closes quietly behind her.

Dan sits down next to me, his hand still on my shoulder. And he waits. He lets me sit.

"This isn't what I expected."

"What do you mean?"

I take a deep breath. "I should be feeling more. I should be feeling sad. But I feel as if I've put down a heavy bag. As if I've been carrying it for years, and suddenly the weight is gone."

"That's OK. If that's how you feel, that's how you feel."

I think about it. About the nursing home. About Dad squeezing my hand.

"I think I said goodbye in the car park, at Orchard House. I think that was when he went away, for me. Everything since – that's just been waiting."

Dan puts his arm round my shoulders. "That's OK, Bex. That's how you've dealt with losing him. You've cried for him already."

I laugh. "And how." Dan laughs, too. He saw my face when we came back from Stockport. I didn't know one person could have that many tears in them.

I sit up, and Dan takes his arm away.

"You OK, Bex?"

I nod.

"Yeah. Yeah, thanks. I think I am."

"There's some birthday cake left." He makes a thinking face. "Aren't you supposed to bring cake to sad people? Cheer them up?"

I laugh. "I thought that was sandwiches, Dan."

And we're both laughing. I reach round his shoulders and give him a hug, and he hugs me back, tightly.

"Cake?"

"Cake."

We head back upstairs.

*****

The day passes in a blur. Charlie and Amy are lovely, bringing me tea and coffee and cake until I can't eat or drink any more. Charlie sits and listens when I talk about my Dad. About how we worked as a team to look after Mum, and all the things I remember doing with him before he got sick.

It's mostly a day of happy memories. Of reliving wonderful days with Dad. I'm sad, but I'm not crying. I'm not struck down by grief. Dan's right – I've done my crying already. I've been waiting for this.

At dinner, the other liaisons come over and tell me how sorry they are. The committee members come to shake my hand, and I'm feeling overwhelmed by the end of the meal. I've forgotten that people can be this kind.

Gail brings the laptop and sets it up while we clear the plates away. We gather round and watch as she pulls up the PIN site. I run my eyes down the list.

There's more film of Ketty talking to Mum. It looks like the same interview – Mum's eye is still bruised and black. When she speaks, she says amazing things about my friends. She calls us a team, and a tribe, and even though I know she's making things worse, I can't hide my smile. I catch my breath for a moment when I wonder whether anyone's told her about Dad. Whether she's OK. It hurts, knowing that there's nothing I can do.

The video ends, and I look back at the list. Prisoners we've never heard of. Sports stories. Human interest.

We're about to give up, when a breaking news story loads onto the screen. Gail clicks on the logo, and I reach for Dan's hand to stop me from falling.

It's Margie. Margie in an orange jumpsuit. Margie in handcuffs.

And they're announcing her trial.

248

Dan groans. He puts his hands on the table, and lowers his head. I think he's going to cry, or shout, or something, but he just stays like that – shirt sleeves rolled up, hair tousled, his forehead resting on the table.

Amy looks at us, and Charlie closes her eyes.

"Who …?" Gail points at the screen.

I force myself to speak. I don't think Dan can hear us.

"Our school friend. Margie." I look up at Gail. "The person we took from Camp Bishop. The person we rescued."

"She's the one they've got in London?"

I nod. "And our teacher. They were both in the wrong place at the wrong time. I couldn't save them."

All the warmth is rushing out of my body. I'm starting to shiver. Everything hits me at once.

Dad's gone. Really gone.

Margie's on trial. And no one ever gets a not-guilty verdict. They're lining our friend up for a firing squad.

They've got more of our friends. And they've got Mum. How many people will they hurt before we're ready to fight back?

And Dan's in pain.

I put my hand on his back, but he doesn't respond. This isn't like Dan. I shake his shoulder, but he doesn't move. Amy sits down next to me, her hand on my arm. I give her a grateful smile, then lean over to whisper in his ear.

"I'm here, Dan. I'm here. You're OK." And I keep talking, but he doesn't answer.

Absence

Ketty

I'm lost. I'm falling and I'm hurting, and there's no one to show me who I am.

Jackson was my anchor. He kept me in line. He challenged me every day to be better, to be more. I need him more than ever.

And I'll never see him again.

Bracken is drowning. The drink gets him through, but what will the Terrorism Committee do to him? If he's right, if we're working for the bad guys, then maybe David was telling the truth. Maybe he can't handle the promotion.

And if Bracken falls, I fall.

I drag myself up the stairs to my flat, Bracken's empty whisky bottle in my bag. I'm covering for him again, but I helped him drink this bottle. It's too easy to be overwhelmed by Bracken's weakness.

Keep it together, Ketty. Stay on top of this. Stay in control.

My knee burns with every step, but I force myself to keep going.

I'm undoing the buttons of my uniform as I reach the door and let myself in. It's cold and dark, and there's nothing I want more than to give up. To drink myself into a coma. To stop this empty, cold feeling in the pit of my stomach. To forget the pain in my knee. To pretend that Jackson will come back.

I can't sleep. I take off my jacket and loosen the neck of my shirt. I untie my boots and leave them in the middle of the floor.

I pull back the curtain from my window, and look out over the rooftops of London. The glass is cold, but I stand and watch the lights against the dark sky.

You should see this, Jackson. You should see this city.
And you should tell me what a fool I'm being.

The darkest hour comes before the dawn. Isn't that what they say?

Then bring on the dawn. Make something go right. Have something go my way.

We've announced Margaret's trial on PIN tonight. Maybe that's my lifeline. My way to wipe the smirk off Brigadier Lee's face, and Conrad's.

To show me where I'm going. To keep me from falling.

And maybe that's enough, for tonight.

Tribe

Bex

Dan is in bed. Gail gave him something to help him sleep, and I stayed while he drifted away. He didn't say anything when we brought him over from the dining room, me under one shoulder and Charlie under the other, Amy and Gail opening the doors for us as we passed.

Dad's gone. Margie's in danger. Dan is in pain. Mum's at the mercy of whatever Ketty decides to do. Jake is lost.

But I'm still here. I'm still standing, and I'm still fighting. I'm letting myself be brave again.

I stand in my room – my own, private room. My space.

And I smile.

This could be worse. I replay everything that brought us here, to people who want to protect us and train us to fight back. We've been saved, again and again. Something has always happened, someone has stepped in, and we've made it through another day. We could have been killed, or caught, so many times – Dan, Amy, Charlie, and me. My tribe, Mum called us. We've carried each other this far, and we'll carry each other again. We'll look out for the people around us, and the people locked up in London.

We'll keep fighting.

Charlie was wrong. The darkest hour isn't behind us – it's now. We're walking through it. Pushing on, ready to meet the dawn when it comes.

When you're in the dark, keep walking. Don't look back, and don't carry the past with you.

I walk to the bathroom and look at my face in the mirror. I feel older. I feel stronger. My old, healed bruises are a badge of pride, a symbol of survival.

I will not waste this opportunity. It has cost so much to get here, to find this place and these people. I will not let this be for nothing. I'll get up in the morning, and I'll fight.

And maybe that's enough, for today.

Note

Alcoholism is not a weakness – these are Ketty's words, not mine, and they come from her unique understanding of her childhood experiences. Addiction in any form is acknowledged to be an illness, not a choice. I do not advocate treating alcoholism as a weakness, any more than I intend to present Ketty as a perfect role model.

**Fighting Back
(Battle Ground #4)
is available now from Amazon.**

Keep reading for a preview!

Chapter 1: Targets

Bex

"Fire!"

I pull the trigger on the rifle and send round after round into the silhouette in front of me. The cluster of bullet holes is tight, centred on the middle of the torso.

"The most important thing is to make the shot. If you don't shoot, you've already missed." The instructor walks up and down behind us, stopping to correct our grip, or check our accuracy. "And if you miss, the soldier you're facing will take the shot. You have to take them out before they can do the same to you."

I remember facing the barrel of Ketty's gun on the coach, and Bracken's as we drove out of camp, and I know she's right. Wait for a moment, doubt yourself for a moment, and you won't live to walk away. Take action, have confidence in your gun, and you stand a chance. I think of Jackson, lying in the road. Ketty, her knee ripped from under her by Dan's bullet. We need to be braver than that. We need to win.

"Cease fire! Let's see how good you are."

I power my gun down and drop it to my side. The instructor powers up the machinery and my paper target moves slowly towards me over the length of the firing range.

"Good, Bex. Very good." She looks over my shoulder as I unclip the silhouette. My bullets have all hit the soldier, a neat circle of holes in the centre of his chest showing the damage I've done.

I try not to think about Saunders, brought down by a single bullet. One day I might have to kill someone, and I need to be thinking about the firing range when I have to make that decision, not my murdered friend. I can't hesitate. I can't allow my memories of the bunker and the gatehouse to distract me. I close my eyes and push the image to the back of my mind.

The instructor checks the magazine in my gun, and counts the bullets left inside. "Next time, concentrate on your speed. See if you can manage this level of accuracy with a higher rate of fire." She puts her hand on my shoulder. "That's good, though. Really good. Keep it up."

I nod, and try to smile. She clips up another silhouette and moves on to check Dan's target.

Amy puts her head round the partition. "How did you do?"

"OK." I hold up my sheet of paper. Amy whistles.

"That's terrifying, Bex! How do you do that?"

Charlie leans out from her booth at the end of the row. "Show me?"

I turn the paper towards her, and she shakes her head. "Glad I'm on your side, Bex."

We can do this. We're getting the training, and we're getting the support we need. We can fight against Ketty and Bracken and the others. We can save Mum and Margie and Dr Richards. We can take our country back. We can take our lives back.

I close my eyes, and focus my anger and frustration. Anger at Ketty for holding my Mum in a cell, and parading her on TV. Anger at Bracken for taking Margie and Dr Richards from me in the farmyard. Anger at the RTS, for taking us from our lives. Anger for Leominster and the bunker and the safe house.

The instructor resets the targets, and the silhouette moves away from me. I watch as it stops at the far end of the shooting range.

"Prepare!"

I power up my gun, and lift it to my shoulder, lining up the sights with the target in front of me. The target is Ketty, and Jackson, and Bracken. The target is the government, and the soldiers they've sent after us. The target is Mum's prison guards.

I place my finger on the trigger and aim for the heart.

"Fire!"

*****

"If I'm driving the getaway car, you're firing out of the window, Bex." Dan shakes his head. "Between us, I think we can get everyone out of danger. I'll cause maximum disruption, and you take down anyone who comes after us. The government won't stand a chance."

He grins, but the smile doesn't quite reach his eyes.

Charlie puts her tray down next to Dan and unloads her plate onto the table. She shakes her head. "I don't want to see the damage you two could do. Not until we need it."

"We need to be ready." It's all I can think of to say.

"I think the government is secretly thrilled that we're all hiding in Scotland." Dan sounds smug. "Less chance of running into us on a dark night. I bet they have nightmares about you." He nods at me. "They certainly should."

"And you, Dan." Charlie smiles. "You two are as bad as each other."

I'd love to laugh about this, but they're not training us for fun. They're training us so we can go home and fight back. My success on the shooting range could make the difference between life and death – not just for me, but for my friends as well. And Charlie's right about Dan – his bullets were as accurate as mine.

I finish my sandwich and check my watch.

"Did Amy go to see Jake?"

"They're letting him have visitors?" Dan sounds incredulous.

Charlie puts a finger to her lips. "Not officially."

I look past Charlie, to the table where our Liaison Officers are eating lunch together. Jake's liaison is there, sitting with Gail and the others. I don't think they've heard us.

"I'll find her. She'll need some lunch before training this afternoon."

Dan nods, and Charlie gives me a smile as I stand up. I take my tray to the cleanup table and grab an extra packet of sandwiches from the serving hatch, pushing them into my fleece pocket as I walk out of the dining room.

*****

Amy isn't in her room, and I wonder whether she's still with Jake. When I track her down, she's in the common room, curled up on the sofa.

The room is dark – no one's opened the curtains this morning – and I can hear her sobbing as I walk through the door.

"Amy?"

She sniffs, and brushes a hand through her hair, looking up at me. "Bex?"

"Mind if I turn the lights on?"

"OK."

We both wince as the room lights up. Her face is red and streaked with tears.

"Mind if I sit down?"

She shakes her head. I sit next to her on the sofa, cross legged, my back to the arm of the chair.

"Sandwich?"

She shakes her head, but takes the packet from me. "Thanks, Bex."

I keep my voice gentle. "Did you see him?"

She nods. "Yeah. The guard let me in for a few minutes, while there was no one else around."

"How is he?"

She looks at me. "He's really angry, Bex. Really angry."

I shrug. "That's not surprising."

"No, but he can't see anyone else's side. He's angry at you, and he's angry at the rest of us for sticking with you. He's furious with the OIE. They said they'd keep him safe, and now he's locked up, and he can't see why. He thinks he should have the same rights as a Scottish Citizen, even though he's on a temporary visa. He can't see what he did wrong."

"Does he know about the raid in Newcastle?"

She nods. "They told him. But he can't understand that it was his fault. He blames the government, and he can't see that giving away the location online is what led the soldiers to the safe house." She shakes her head. "He just wants to be a normal, ordinary person again. He doesn't want all this responsibility, and he doesn't want people telling him what to do. He thinks it should be you they're locking up, not him. He keeps talking about justice, and how it's all so unfair."

She brushes tears away from her cheeks, and her voice drops to a whisper. "And he's really angry with me."

I sit forward and hold out my hand. She takes it in hers.

"I'm so sorry, Amy."

She nods. "He thinks I should be supporting him. He can't understand why his oldest friend is letting this happen."

"It's not as if there's anything you can do, even if you wanted to."

"I know. But he doesn't see it that way. I think he'd rather see me locked up as well, than know that I'm out here with you, training together." She laughs, and squeezes my hand. "He hates the idea that we're still friends."

I smile at her, and clasp her hand more tightly. "So what's going to happen to him?"

She shakes her head. "He doesn't know yet. They won't tell him."

"Are they getting him a tutor? Or someone to talk to?"

"They tried." She sighs. "He refused to listen. He's not cooperating with the OIE at all."

"So he just has to wait."

She looks at me. "They'll figure something out, won't they? They won't leave him in that room. They have to work out a way to help him."

I squeeze her hand again. "I hope so."

She looks at the ceiling and nods. "They have to. They got us out of Newcastle. All of us. They'll find a way to work with him." She puts her hands to her face and pushes away tears. "It'll be OK. He'll come round. He'll see that he doesn't have a choice."

I nod, and try to smile, but I don't share her hope. Jake is gone. We've lost him, and he's only here because the terms of our visas say we have to stay with the OIE – on site or escorted at all times. We're refugees, we're under the protection of the Opposition In Exile, and we don't have the kind of freedom Jake is demanding. We're lucky to be alive, and we're lucky to have people looking out for us.

We'd all like to go back to our lives. No one wants to be in exile, training for the fight when we return, but that's where we are. No amount of wishing or anger will change that. Jake's been through some terrible things, but so have the rest of us. He's just reached the end of his ability to cope.

We need to be there for him. We need to fight for him, as well as for ourselves. And we need to look after each other.

"Come on. We'll be late for training." She nods, and rubs her face with her sleeve. "Go and clean up. I'll wait."

We walk together to her room, and I sit on her bed while she washes her face and pulls on a clean sweater.

"Ready?"

She gives me a hug. "Ready."

*****

It's been a month. Four weeks since they announced Margie's trial, and four weeks since Jake told the world where we're hiding. Mum's been on PIN, every night, and so has Margie. They're building up to her trial as if it's some kind of sick sporting event. They want everyone watching. They want *us* to be watching. They want us to know what they can do.

We've spent the last month learning what *we* can do. Shooting, driving, combat training. The Scottish government has provided us with armour and rifles, like the ones we trained with at Camp Bishop – but this armour is black, to make us look like professional soldiers. We've got the best instructors, and a class of four. Charlie's doing some training with us, to make up our team, and we're learning to work together. To fight, without Jake. Without Neesh and Caroline and everyone else we've come to rely on.

The OIE has plans for us. They know we want to fight, and they're willing to train us. We can't fight yet, but we're all working hard.

When the time comes, we need to be ready.

Chapter 2: Preparation

Ketty

"We've got permission for the trial."

"Sir?"

Bracken waves a sheet of paper at me over the desk. "Margaret Watson can meet her firing squad whenever we're ready." He looks at me. "We need to make this an unmissable event, Ketty. Can we do it?"

I take the paper. A Trial Order, signed by Brigadier Lee.

And just like that, I'm responsible for the trial of the year. I'm responsible for showing the terrorists that they can't win. For showing Ellman and her gang what we can do – to her, and to her friends.

For weeks of interrogations and TV slots. For making Margaret the star of her own execution.

I look up, smiling. "Yes, Sir. I think we can."

*****

The firing range is empty when I check in. The Private on duty hands me a box of bullets and a pair of ear defenders, and I make my way to the furthest booth. I clip a target to the track, and send it to the end of the range.

I pull my gun from the holster on my belt, make sure it's loaded, and line up the sights with the target. I breathe, slowly, and focus on the figure in front of me.

Everything else is gone from my head. I can see the gun, and the silhouette.

And I can feel the power.

The handgun recoils after every shot, but I am in control. I focus on the target, and fire careful shots down the length of the range.

I tear holes in the figure in front of me. I concentrate on my aim, and on the rhythm of my bullets.

I concentrate on being in control. On bringing my opponent down.

When I check out, I leave a pile of shredded targets in the waste paper box. And I can't help smiling as I climb the stairs back to Bracken.

*****

"Quit fussing, Ketty. I don't need mothering."

"No, Sir."

I put the canteen sandwich down on Bracken's desk with a mug of coffee and two painkillers.

"I don't need you fetching my meals. I'm perfectly capable of finding my own lunch."

Out of a bottle, Sir?

I stare at the wall above Bracken's head. "Yes, Sir. I just thought, what with the meeting this afternoon …"

He waves his hand to stop me. "Fine. Fine. Thank you." He pulls the plate towards him, and I notice that the painkillers are the first things he swallows. His eyes are red and bloodshot, and I need to make sure he sobers up before his first Terrorism Committee meeting.

"Are you our runner for this afternoon?"

"I am, Sir."

Assistant to the lowest ranking person in the meeting? Of course I am.

He nods, and unwraps his sandwich.

"Are you going to stand there and watch me, Ketty?" He sounds angry.

I would if I could, Sir. I know where you keep your whisky bottle.

"No, Sir. I'm just wondering whether there's anything I need to know before this afternoon."

265

He sighs, and waves his hand at one of the chairs in front of his desk. "Take a seat."

"Yes, Sir."

I sit and wait while he eats his lunch and washes it down with coffee.

"Honestly, Ketty? I'm not sure what to expect."

"Oh?"

He sits back in his chair, coffee mug in his hands. "It's taken them this long to put me on the committee. I'm not sure what they wanted from me before they gave me a place at the table. And now I'm here?" He shakes his head. "I don't know whether we're chasing terrorists, or telling them what to do. Which places to bomb. Where our security will be lightest. Where we'll turn a blind eye to their activities."

I raise my eyebrows. "Like Leominster, Sir?"

His shoulders slump, and he puts the mug down on the desk, still holding it with both hands. "Like Leominster."

I sit up. "Leominster was a weapons test, Sir. They blamed it on the terrorists, but Holden said they were testing a weapon."

On a town full of innocent people.

"Holden is on the Terrorism Committee, Ketty. Holden, and Lee, and some of the others who planned the Leominster operation. Who's to say they're not running more weapons tests?"

I shrug. "Sir. It's a promotion. It's what you came here to do. Track terrorists, monitor attacks, catch the bad guys."

He nods. "That's true."

"This is how you do that. By being on their committee."

It's how you keep your job, and mine.

"You're right." He gives me a brief smile. "It's what I'm here to do."

"And it beats babysitting recruits at Camp Bishop."

"All right, Ketty," he snaps, anger on his face. "Enough."

He pushes his plate away, drains his coffee cup, and checks his watch.

"Time to go, Sir?"

"Time to go."

*****

"So – any progress with catching your recruits?"

Conrad is perched on the front of the desk I've been given, outside the conference room, attempting to intimidate me. Posh-shabby-gorgeous with a gloating smile on his face. I try not to roll my eyes.

Yes, David. I've got them right here in my pocket.

"You mean apart from putting Elizabeth Ellman and Margaret Watson on PIN every night?"

He smirks, picking up my pen from the desk and playing with it as he talks. "Apart from that."

I raise my eyebrows. "You don't think that will work?"

"I think your recruits are on a jolly holiday in Scotland, and I think you can't get to them. Plus PIN doesn't air in Scotland." He throws the pen in the air and catches it.

"No," I say, as patiently as I can, "but they have ways of reaching international audiences. If Bex Ellman and Dan Pearce can get to a PIN feed, they'll be watching."

"The website? That's hardly the same as watching the news. They get to pick and choose what they look at. You can't force them to watch anything."

Come on, David. Think about it.

"You think we'd have to force them to watch coverage of their own families? Their friends?"

He shrugs. "Maybe the OIE is blocking it. Maybe they don't have access."

"And maybe they're watching every night in case we decide to give one of our prisoners some new bruises."

"Maybe." He puts the pen down. "And I understand using Elizabeth Ellman. Bex must be going crazy, wondering what you're going to do to her next."

267

I smile. "That's the point, Corporal. Keep them wondering. Keep them frightened."

"But Margaret? What's she adding to the equation?"

"School friend of Bex and Dan? Best buddies, right until the RTS recruiters showed up? Come on. Wouldn't you be watching?"

He shrugs again. "I guess."

You're underestimating me again.

I sit back in my chair. "Margaret adds several things. We show Bex and Dan what we can do to them. We don't let them forget who holds the power here. And we make them think twice before they do anything to act against us."

"OK, but you can do that with Elizabeth."

"True. But that's mainly for Bex. What Margaret gives us is Dan."

Conrad raises his eyebrows. "How do you figure that?"

I smile at him, and fold my arms. "Haven't you watched her interrogation footage?"

"Yes, but …"

My smile is growing. "Watch it again. When she's looking at the wanted posters? Take a look at which poster she's most interested in."

He looks at me for a moment. "So you think – Margaret and Dan?"

"I do."

"So we've got Bex's mother and Dan's girlfriend?" I nod, grinning. "And we're putting them both on TV?" He's smiling now – a gorgeous smile that puts butterflies in my stomach.

Focus, Ketty. He's not on your side. Show him what you can do.

"I think that's a useful connection. Don't you?"

He shrugs, smiling. "Can't hurt."

No, it can't.

*****

"How was it, Sir?"

Bracken's hands are shaking as he sits down behind his desk.

"Fine, Ketty. Fine." He won't meet my eyes.

"Is it what you were expecting?"

He shakes his head.

"I can't discuss it with you, Corporal. You need Top Secret clearance for the committee, and while they have seen fit to give that clearance to me, to the best of my knowledge they have not decided to elevate you to those heights."

Watch the sarcasm, Sir. I'm trying to keep us in our jobs.

"No, Sir. Sorry, Sir."

"Was there something else?" He looks up at me, his eyes still bloodshot.

"No, Sir."

I'll leave you to your whisky.

I leave the room, and head out to find two cups of coffee. When I bring them back, Bracken has his head in his hands. I leave his coffee, and two more painkillers, in the middle of his desk, but he doesn't respond.

*****

I have to take two empty bottles from Bracken's office this evening. I try not to leave them for the cleaner to find, and while everyone here seems to know that he's drunk at work, I don't think they need to know how much he's drinking.

My job depends on Bracken. If I can keep him working, then I can stay in London. If he can't do his job, I'll find myself back in the Recruit Training Service, dragging clueless sixteen-year-olds through assault courses and weapons training and cross-country runs.

I'd rather be here. I'd rather be doing a job that matters.

And I don't need to be reminded of Jackson.

It's been a month since I lost my friend. Four weeks where I've caught myself thinking about what I'll say to him, when he wakes up. When I've reached for the phone to call the hospital. When I've pictured him, hooked up to his machines, wrapped in a hospital gown.

But he won't wake up. I'll never see him again.

There was a funeral, but I didn't go. Jackson was energy and attitude and mocking and action. He was the opposite of stillness and peace. I couldn't sit with his family while they said goodbye to him.

I said goodbye when I left the hospital. The person in the bed – that wasn't Jackson. Jackson died on the road outside the coach. They kept him breathing for months, but he never came back. Dan Pearce took away his action and his attitude with two bullets, and left him – left me – wounded and broken.

Bracken and I drank a bottle of whisky and told Jackson stories instead. It was a coward's way out, but it was better than hymns and flowers.

And I know where Jackson would have wanted to be.

The Battle Ground series

The Battle Ground series is set in a dystopian near-future UK, after Brexit and Scottish independence.

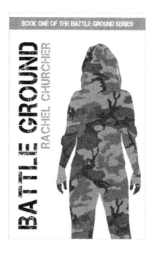

Book 1: Battle Ground

Sixteen-year-old Bex Ellman has been drafted into an army she doesn't support and a cause she doesn't believe in. Her plan is to keep her head down, and keep herself and her friends safe – until she witnesses an atrocity that she can't ignore, and a government conspiracy that threatens lives all over the UK. With her loyalties challenged, Bex must decide who to fight for – and who to leave behind.

Book 2: False Flag

Ketty Smith is an instructor with the Recruit Training Service, turning sixteen-year-old conscripts into government fighters. She's determined to win the job of lead instructor at Camp Bishop, but the arrival of Bex and her friends brings challenges she's not ready to handle. Running from her own traumatic past, Ketty faces a choice: to make a stand, and expose a government conspiracy, or keep herself safe, and hope she's working for the winning side.

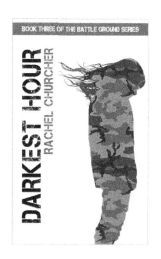

Book 3: Darkest Hour

Bex Ellman and Ketty Smith are fighting on opposite sides in a British civil war. Bex and her friends are in hiding, but when Ketty threatens her family, Bex learns that her safety is more fragile than she thought.

Book 4: Fighting Back

Bex Ellman and her friends are in hiding, sheltered by the resistance. With her family threatened and her friendships challenged, she's looking for a way to fight back. Ketty Smith is in London, supporting a government she no longer trusts. With her support network crumbling, Ketty must decide who she is fighting for – and what she is willing risk to uncover the truth.

Book 5: Victory Day

Bex Ellman and Ketty Smith meet in London. As the war heats up around them, Bex and Ketty must learn to trust each other. With her friends and family in danger, Bex needs Ketty to help rescue them. For Ketty, working with Bex is a matter of survival. When Victory is declared, both will be held accountable for their decisions.

Book 6: Balancing Act

Corporal David Conrad has life figured out. His job gives him power, control, and access to Top Secret operations. His looks have tempted plenty of women into his bed, and he has no intention of committing to a relationship.

When Ketty Smith joins the Home Forces, Conrad sets his sights on the new girl – but pursuing Ketty will be more dangerous than he realises. Is Conrad about to meet his match? And will the temptations of his job distract him from his target?

Balancing Act revisits the events of *Darkest Hour*, *Fighting Back*, and *Victory Day*. **The story is suitable for older teens.**

Book 7: Finding Fire and Other Stories

What happened between Margie and Dan at Make-peace Farm? How did Jackson really feel about Ketty? What happens next to the survivors of the Battle Ground Series?

Step behind the scenes of the series with six new short stories and five new narrators – Margie, Jackson, Maz, Dan, and Charlie – plus bonus blogs and insights from the author.

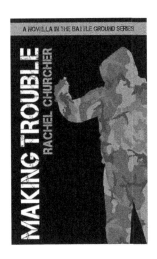

Novella: Making Trouble

Fifteen-year-old Topher Mackenzie has a complicated life. His Mum is in Australia, his Dad is struggling to look after him, and Auntie Charlie is the only person who understands. When his girlfriend is forced to leave the UK after a racist attack, Topher faces a choice: accept the government's lies, or find a way to fight back.

Download FREE from freebook.tallerbooks.com

Acknowledgements

The Battle Ground series represents more than a year of hard work – not just for me, but for the people who have supported me and helped to make it happen.

A huge thank you is due to my amazing proofreaders, who have given up their time to read every book and send me helpful and insightful feedback. Thank you to Alan Platt, Holly Platt Wells, Reba Sigler, Joe Silber, and Reynard Spiess.

Thank you to my *Darkest Hour* beta readers, Jasmine Bruce, Diana Churcher, James Keen, and Karen MacLaughlin, for encouragement and insightful comments.

Thank you to all the people who have given me advice on the road to publication: Tim Dedopulos, Salomé Jones, Rob Manser, John Pettigrew, Danielle Zigner, and Jericho Writers.

Thank you to everyone at NaNoWriMo, for giving me the opportunity and the tools to start writing, and to everyone at YALC for inspiration and advice.

Thank you to my amazing designer, Medina Karic, for deciphering my sketches and notes and turning them into beautiful book covers. If you ever need a designer, find her at www.fiverr.com/milandra.

Thank you to Alan Platt, for learning the hard way how to live with a writer, and for bringing your start-up expertise to the creation of Taller Books.

Thank you to Alex Bate, Janina Ander, and Helen Lynn, for encouraging me to write *Battle Ground* when I suddenly had time on my hands, and for introducing me to Prosecco Fridays. Cheers!

Thank you to Hannah Pollard and the Book Club Galz for sharing so many wonderful YA books with me – and for understanding that the book is *always* better than the film.

Special mention goes to the Peatbog Faeries, whose album *Faerie Stories* is the ultimate cure for writer's block.

The soundtrack to *The Greatest Showman*, and Lady Antebellum's *Need You Now*, are my go-to albums for waking up and feeling energised to write, even on the hardest days.

This book is dedicated to my proofreaders and advance readers. You're amazing. Thank you.

About the Author

Rachel Churcher was born between the last manned moon landing, and the first orbital Space Shuttle mission. She remembers watching the launch of STS-1, and falling in love with space flight, at the age of five. She fell in love with science fiction shortly after that, and in her teens she discovered dystopian fiction. In an effort to find out what she wanted to do with her life, she collected degrees and other qualifications in Geography, Science Fiction Studies, Architectural Technology, Childminding, and Writing for Radio.

She has worked as an editor on national and in-house magazines; as an IT trainer; and as a freelance writer and artist. She has renovated several properties, and has plenty of horror stories to tell about dangerous electrics and nightmare plumbers. She enjoys reading, travelling, stargazing, and eating good food with good friends – but nothing makes her as happy as writing fiction.

Her first published short story appeared in an anthology in 2014, and the Battle Ground series is her first long-form work. Rachel lives in East Anglia, in a house with a large library and a conservatory full of house plants. She would love to live on Mars, but only if she's allowed to bring her books.

Follow **RachelChurcherWriting** on Instagram and GoodReads.

Printed in Great Britain
by Amazon

26917118R00169